POWERED UP, THE GAUSS PISTOL WAS BOTH LIGHTER AND STEADIER.

I cranked the velocity all the way down, aimed at the steel plate, and squeezed the trigger. There was a bang of displaced air and a howl of tortured metal. The slug had shattered the steel, throwing fragments in a fan behind the stairs.

"Good weapons?" the smuggler asked. He was opening the cold bag full of berries.

"They'll do," I said, popping the clip and handing it back to him. "How are the berries?"

"Excellent. I'll just look at the crates and we can be on our way." The smuggler took a berry from the bag and tossed the clip into the suitcase. Munching the berry, he closed the suitcase and lifted it off the crates. I picked up the top crate, shifted it to the floor, tossed back the lid, and turned around to find myself staring down the barrel of another Gauss pistol.

"Sorry, son," he said. "Don't like doing business this way, but an old friend called yesterday. He needs these packs too, and I do already have a customer for the berries. . . ."

CUTTING EDGE SCI-FI NOVELS

CHECKMATE

ERIC T. BAKER

A ROC BOOK

ROC
Published by the Penguin Group
Penguin Putnam Inc., 375 Hudson Street,
New York, New York 10014 U.S.A.
Penguin Books Ltd, 27 Wrights Lane,
London W8 5TZ, England
Penguin Books Australia Ltd,
Ringwood, Victoria, Australia
Penguin Books Canada Ltd, 10 Alcorn Avenue,
Toronto, Ontario, Canada M4V 3B2
Penguin Books (N.Z.) Ltd, 182-190 Wairau Road,
Auckland 10, New Zealand

Penguin Books Ltd, Registered Offices:
Harmondsworth, Middlesex, England

First published by Roc, an imprint of Dutton Signet,
a member of Penguin Putnam Inc.

First Printing, January, 1998
10 9 8 7 6 5 4 3 2 1

For Rachel
The Best Bear

CHAPTER 1

THE BUST

Cleo and I planned to attend a chess exhibition by Narandova on the afternoon before she, Todd, and I were set to arrest Mr. Hines. I spent that morning tingling with anticipation and rehearsing conversations that Cleo and I might have. I knew from experience that when the time for the exhibition came, Cleo would not actually appear, but love fills you with endless hope.

On the morning of the exhibition, I left the grubby hole in the Bilges where I maintained my cover identity and took a series of increasingly spacious lifts down the body of our ship, the *Jersey*, toward the aft docking ring and the Midlands. The exhibition was to take place in the open air of a shopping arcade, and I passed the time before it began by spending some of my unreported marks on a set of decent clothes and a civilized barbering. Mr. Hines wasn't due back on the *Jersey* until the morning, so it was safe enough to slip out of character for a while.

As the time grew close, a pair of plastic robots set up chairs under the artificial sky. The challengers and their supporters stood together in a nervous clump, discussing strategies and sharing encouragement.

Even in the mechanically generated breeze, some of them were actually sweating.

The small crowd of spectators waited in clumps of their own. Whereas the challengers were all formally dressed in coats and boots, the spectators were mostly from the upper reaches of the ship, overalls-clad men and women who seemed uncomfortable surrounded by actual people and objects instead of the mechanical dreams in which they usually roamed. Chess enthusiasts all, they were willing to risk the possible embarrassments of social interaction for the chance to see one of the game's masters in the flesh.

Not all of the enthusiasts had cleaned themselves properly before venturing out. I commanded my mechanics to block the gamy human smell from my awareness even as I looked up and down the arcade for Cleo. Instead I saw Narandova arriving, and without a retinue. Three years before I had seen him at an exhibition, and he had been accompanied by his young protégé, by his wife, and by two handlers from the *Warsaw*'s embassy. In those three years, however, the whole political situation on the *Warsaw* had changed. Now there was just the man himself.

Narandova was a neat man of regulation height. He had straw-colored hair and affected a pair of gold-rimmed eyeglasses. His coat bulged a little over the belly of a man who is not living solely on kibbles and glucose. He nodded to the crowd, greeted his opponents with a smile, shook all their hands, then waved them to the chairs.

With a general rustle of cloth and a murmur of anticipation, the players sat down and the spectators moved forward to form a second ring outside them. I hung back and continued to look for Cleo. The mechanical side of my brain read my worried thoughts and reminded me that it could ask the ship's computer for Cleo's whereabouts. I ordered it not to. Cleo had said she would come. If the computer found her still in her chambers (and worse, still with Todd), then I would be left with only the chess.

For these exhibition matches, the usual step of drawing pieces had been replaced with standardized fleets. Sometimes the initial placement round was skipped as well in exhibitions, but Narandova had elected to keep it for this occasion. He walked around the inside of the circle of his challengers, looking at their initial deployments, and preparing his first two moves for each board.

The boards themselves were only on display as a shared dream in the ship's computers. At tournaments, hologram sets are put out to display the boards for those who might have their mechanical half shut down. Such people were out of luck here as Narandova stepped to the center of the circle, glanced at each of his opponents to be sure they were ready, and then made his first two moves on all ten boards at once.

My mechanics tapped into the computers for me, putting the games in my mind and performing an elaborate analysis of each as Narandova walked around the circle of challengers, commanding his pieces to move and passing on. He could have stood in one place and played the games solely in his head, but moving allowed him to chat out loud with the players and the spectators. Besides being friendly, it also served to distract the meat side of the challengers' minds.

There was still no sign of Cleo. Casual shoppers were stopping now, watching for a few moves and then passing on. Considering that Narandova was the second seed in the Fleet Championships that began the next day, and despite the dream dwellers who had come down to see him, the attendance was disappointing. Narandova was a man whose star had passed. The new star was Sakins, a ship-born seventeen-year-old who was seeded fourth in the tournament, but was the favorite in the betting because of the ease with which he had cruised through the year's other tournaments. Narandova, only two years removed from his last championship, was now a relic.

Time passed and my mood sank. I was on the point of giving up when I caught the scent of mood smoke on the breeze. I turned with a relieved smile that vanished instantly. The THC-laced cigar was being held between the full lips of a bald man whose tartan wrap indicated he was from the *Solidarity*. Definitely not Cleo, but at least I didn't have to worry about him misinterpreting my disappointed stare.

That cigar was the end of waiting. I decided that Cleo (if she did come) could find me, and moved deeper into the crowd, determined at least to enjoy the games. My mechanical side had been following the matches, and it replayed them for me as I found a better place to stand. There was nothing in them to cheer me up. Narandova's play was methodical and disappointing; he was crushing all of his challengers in a sure, uninspired manner that showed his mechanical brain was playing the games with little support from his meat side. I tried to take more of an interest in the games than Narandova apparently was, but instead found myself rehearsing angry monologues for the next time I had Cleo alone.

"Excuse me," someone said, startling me. I looked up and discovered that Narandova had paused before me. "I'm sorry, but the computer says you are Aaron Hudson. My son played an Aaron Hudson from this ship in a twelve-and-under match about ten years ago. Are you the same boy?"

"I am," I admitted, giving him a little bow of acknowledgment. It is no great feat to have one's mechanical side remember such details of your life; the compliment lay in the fact that Narandova had not only searched for such connections with his audience but also mentioned it when he found one.

"You had a wonderful gift for the game," he said. "I recall you beat Roman rather easily. Your name is not in the rankings. I take it you have left the tour?"

"My gift was good but not exceptional, and I lacked the ambition to acquire a professional amount of computer space."

"You underrate your gift. I cannot speak to your ambition." Narandova shifted his attention to the game, and I went with him to watch through my mechanics as he changed the course of a destroyer in the lower south area of the board. The challenger was down two destroyers and was about to sacrifice a heavy cruiser in hopes of catching Narandova's eastern battleship. I judged that he would succeed at the cost of so much position that Narandova would walk to the mate.

Now that he had moved his piece, I expected the champion to pass on, but instead he focused on me again. "The computer says you are a policeman. Apparently you sought a more physical excitement than the chessboard provides."

"Physical danger is the least attractive and most infrequent aspect of my profession."

"Nevertheless." He took the glasses from his nose and affected to judge their cleanliness in the artificial sunlight while he made his move in the next game, capturing a corsair that the challenger had sent to test for a gap in Narandova's defenses. "My own son chose to become a shuttle pilot. I worry about the game. So few members of the generations born on the ships are joining the tour. Many gifted players have turned their backs on their talents. It seems a horrible waste."

"Perhaps we will return to it later in the voyage," I said, wanting to console the man even though I could not imagine myself returning to the regimen of competition. "Your son will not want to be a shuttle pilot forever."

"Perhaps," Narandova agreed, focusing on me a last time, then passing on to catch up with his moves. My mechanical side had the games ready for me, but there was no point in carrying on. Cleo had not come. There was no easing of my disappointment in watching the chess or in talking to Narandova. I was on the point of turning away from the circle of players and going for the lift when there was a brush against my ankle. I looked down to find a cat looking up at me.

"Varian," I said, bending to pick up the long-haired, toffee-colored tom before looking around for his master. Wolcott was back by the little willow tree and its encircling bench, standing astraddle the dark, canvas bag that held all his possessions. Varian nuzzled my cheek and gave a little "meow" as I carried him out of the crowd. His left canine was chipped, a defect that Wolcott refused to have altered.

"What did he say to you?" Wolcott greeted me. According to the few records I had been able to find, Wolcott was sixteen. From observation I knew that he had only three sets of clothes. Today he was wearing his green sweater over his blue shirt. All of his clothes contained smart fibers that kept them clean and neat, despite Wolcott having neither the place nor the money to launder them.

"Varian?"

"Narandova," he said, his brows lowering in annoyance. If Wolcott had a sense of humor, I had never found the joke that would unlock it.

"I played his son in a juniors' match once."

"Humph."

"How are you doing?"

"We're fine," Wolcott said, taking the purring Varian from me. Wolcott and Varian were always fine. They were just shipless and spaceless.

"He's by himself," I said, cocking my head toward Narandova. "No handlers, no embassy people. Maybe things really have changed for the better on the *Warsaw*. I could arrange passage if . . ." I trailed off because Wolcott was shaking his head.

"The names change, but the people don't," he said. He put the cat down and wiped a palm on his denim pants. "If I went back—" he snapped his fingers. I had had this discussion too many times to pursue it.

"Did you come down here for the chess, or just to see Narandova?" I asked.

"I came to see you. You said when I had proof, then you could act." He reached into his pants pocket and pulled out a phial. Inside myself, I groaned. Wolcott was convinced that he had not escaped persecution simply by fleeing to the *Jersey*.

"This has more to do with the Executive Council?" I asked. Wolcott frowned at me and put a hand over his mouth before looking about us. I took the phial, trading it in my pocket for my wallet. "Here's a hundred, okay?" Wolcott took the coins, but he looked sour. "I'll have a look. If it's good, I'll pay you more."

"I don't care about the money for myself," Wolcott said. "It's Varian. He can't eat kibbles."

"I know. Where are you staying?" Wolcott frowned yet again. "In case I need to talk to you about this." I patted the phial in my pocket. Wolcott's eyes were suddenly everywhere but meeting mine. I almost sighed, but stopped myself because it was unfair. My adolescence had been hard enough, and I hadn't had to run away from my ship.

Taking the boy's hand, I passed him a dream, my mechanics talking directly to his. "That's the location of a spot in the Bilges I was using last week. It should still exist. I'll look for you there."

"We could go there now," Wolcott said. He was excited, his mouth turned up in the closest he ever came to a smile. "I could walk you through the dream. I annotated it, of course, but I could explain it to you more fully."

"I can't right now. I have a meeting with my squad in few minutes," I lied. Varian was rubbing my ankles again, and I squatted to pet him. "You be a good cat," I said. "Take care of your dad."

"We take care of each other," Wolcott said. I just nodded and wished that Cleo had come.

After leaving the exhibition, I rode the remaining two kilometers down the ship to the aft docking ring and took a room in one of the hotels that catered to wealthy travelers from other ships. Despite Narandova's fears about the future of his game, there were so many fans in from all over the Fleet for the championships that I had to go to three hotels and then pay a premium in my unreported marks to get a room with running water and a view. When I had tested both the water and the view, I sent the little robot bellman on its way and locked the door. Alone in a room that none of the bad guys could find, I shut down the mechanical side of myself and began adjusting to being just meat.

And so it was that I came to be in the shower, leaning against the yellow Teflon of the stall and watching the falling water appear to bend under the effect of the ship's spin, when Cleo arrived. Since I'd registered in my own name, she'd had no trouble finding me, but because I was detached from the computer, she had to actually knock on the room's door to get my attention, a knocking that had become a pounding by the time I finally ordered it open.

"Take it easy," I said, all my irritation from the afternoon in my voice. Then I got a good look at Cleo and shut myself up. Even without my mechanical side feeding me Cleo's heart rate and blood pressure, I could see that she was angry about more than the door.

"Do you have anything?" Cleo asked before she was even in the room. She stepped across the threshold and stood there looking at me, alternately rubbing her left fist and her right wrist. She was overdressed for visiting a colleague but not for this end of the ship in general. She wore a gray suit of Earth-origin wool over a sheer cream blouse of ship-grown silk. Both were human-tailored, and either might have cost half of her yearly police stipend.

I left the embroidered towel around my neck and tried to take her in my arms. "What happened?" I asked.

Cleo pushed me away. "Nothing. I just want a drink. You've got something, don't you?"

"Of course," I said, mad and hurt and determined not to show either. I walked over to the bag I had set up next to the room's wet bar. Cleo's taste for alcohol was an expensive and dangerous habit that I did not share, but I paid the price and took the risk. It was the one thing I could give her that Todd would not. "You want it mixed with anything?"

"No," she said. I handed her one of the cold bottles of barleywine and took one for myself. By the time I'd closed the bag and opened my bottle, hers was half-empty.

"You're sure nothing happened?" I asked.

"He hit me," Cleo said, and took another long drink from the bottle.

"He hit you?" I couldn't keep the astonishment off my face. Todd was many things but . . .

"He grabbed me," Cleo said, rubbing her wrist again. "I wanted to go out. Let off some tension before the bust tomorrow. He grabbed me. He wouldn't let go." Gently, I took hold of her wrist, pushing back her cuffs and looking at the pale skin. There were no visible marks. Without my machine self and its senses, there was nothing more to tell.

"Does it hurt?" I asked.

Cleo had finished her bottle while I examined her, and now she handed it to me. "It did. Do you have another?" I reluctantly let go of her wrist.

While I got the second bottle, Cleo drew a gold cigar case from an inner pocket of her jacket and took out a mood stick with a shaking hand. I traded her the barleywine for her lighter and held the flame under the end of the slim THC cigar. She breathed the smoke in until she coughed, little smoke puffs coming from her mouth as she offered me the case. I shook my head.

"Who is he to grab me?" Cleo asked, her voice scratchy from the smoke. "I just wanted to go out."

"I know," I said. I was still mad about the afternoon, so rather than let the conversation slip into well-worn grooves, I tried: "You missed the exhibition."

For a moment she looked at me as if I'd struck her, too, and then she smiled. "I'm sorry. Todd and I were working on the case. We'll go to one of the tournament matches after we make the bust."

"It's all right," I lied, which made me feel guilty, so I added some truth. "He wasn't in form."

"Sakins is going to kill him in the tournament."

"If he gets that far."

Cleo puffed at her thin cigar and wandered toward the floor-and-wall porthole. I took a nervous drink from my bottle and tried to decide whether to get dressed. I was cold in just the robe with my wet hair, and yet I was afraid that if I left the room, Cleo might vanish.

"Why shouldn't I go out?" Cleo said, talking more to the porthole than me. "We'd been home all day. He could have come."

I decided not to take the chance of Cleo's leaving. "It's not up to him," I said. "You can go out if you like."

"I just want to sometimes," Cleo said. Framed in the window against the black of interstellar space with the cigar smoke floating around her head, she looked heartbreakingly beautiful. I wished that she would turn and look at me with the same longing I felt for her.

"He doesn't respect you," I said. "He doesn't trust you to make your own decisions."

"Todd loves me," Cleo said.

"So do I," I said, "but that doesn't give either of us the right to hit you." I stepped up behind her and laid my hand on her shoulder. "Look, stay here tonight."

Now Cleo turned around, but her eyes didn't meet mine. "He didn't really hit me. He just grabbed me. He just wants what's best for us."

"Perhaps," I said, trying to put the same sound of skepticism into the word that Narandova had that afternoon, "but he doesn't trust you."

Cleo looked up from her cigar then. She smiled at me and pressed the knuckles of her right hand, the one that still held the bottle of barleywine, against my breast. "I love you, too, Aaron," she said, and I nodded. The tone of her voice, the tilt of her head, the happy light behind her eyes; looking at them I had the same feeling of inevitability that I had had that afternoon looking at the chess games. "Get dressed. Let's go down to the Flame."

The Flame Lounge was located in a module off the docking ring. A converted observation deck, it allowed its patrons an unobstructed view of the ramjet flame bursting from the back of the ship. It was expensive enough that one rubbed shoulders with the right people, but with a base enough commerce that one could obtain unlicensed pleasures like barley-wine. If the three of us were ever forced to live purely on our stipends, nights at the Flame were one of the many things we would have to give up.

I had two choices. I could go with Cleo to the Flame and spend my night frustrated and depressed in her company, or I could stay here and be frustrated and depressed all by myself. Either way, Cleo would go home to Todd when she was through.

"I'll just be a minute," I said. What the hell. I already had the monologues prepared, and if that didn't work I could try the conversations.

The attraction of the Flame came from its view and its wares, not from its decor, which was utilitarian and uninventive. Chrome rails divided rows of glass tables circled by chrome and leather chairs. Mood smoke hung in the air, stirred only by the passage of patrons and servers, and the sound of glass mugs clattering against glass tables was omnipresent. Cleo stopped a robot passing with a tray of cigars and then led us to the bar. I ordered the drinks and produced a lighter for Cleo.

"You're sure?" Cleo asked, holding another mood stick out to me. The tightly wound leaves were the black of true tobacco, meaning that the cigar was either from someone's licensed supplies of luxuries or (more likely) from an unregistered field. Either way, it had cost three or four times what a flax cigar would have cost, and thirty or forty times what it would have cost just to draw the THC straight.

All materials on the *Jersey* were supposed to be registered and all the luxuries were supposed to be licensed. It was the economics demanded by a forty-year space voyage. Tonnes of air and water could be lost each year just from inefficiencies in the hull and hatches. Heavier elements were harder to lose, but also harder (if not impossible) to replace. The ship's computers wanted everything registered so they could track losses and direct recycling. They managed an economy based on the energy it took to replace something, and they used the money collected from licenses to offset the cost of having produced a luxury rather than a necessity.

In a managed economy like that of the *Jersey*, unlicensed products like Cleo's mood sticks should have been cheaper than the licensed ones, except that there were some things that the computers simply ruled too wasteful. THC could be licensed; so could mood sticks made with flax. Real tobacco ones could not. Since all the ships had economies similar to the *Jersey*'s, throughout the Fleet registered and licensed were synonymous with cheap and utilitarian.

"I'm positive. I'm having enough trouble dealing with my mechanics being shut down without toking up on narcotics."

"Stop worrying," Cleo said. She set her mug on the bar so she could put her hand on my leg. "The bust tomorrow is going to go fine. Honestly. Todd and I did a ton more back and fill today. Tomorrow, you drop back into character, collect the strawberries, go to the meeting with Hines, and make sure he brought the gun clips. Todd and I take it from there. You're golden."

"I'm not worried," I lied, covering her hand with mine, "but I have to be ready. All the groundwork in the ship is just wasted time if he doesn't believe in me at the exchange." I didn't misunderstand Cleo's touching me. I knew it was just the alcohol loosening her insecurities and making her need the contact. It meant nothing more and would lead to nothing else, but knowing that didn't stop me from enjoying it.

"He believes in you. They all do. That's why we're the best squad in the unit." Even as she said this, Cleo was frowning over my shoulder. "What is he doing here?"

"Who?" I asked without turning, although the way Cleo was staring it would not have added to the rudeness.

"The computer says he's Officer Gaunt, S.I.D."

With my mechanics shut down, there was nothing to stop my palms from suddenly becoming moist. I let go of Cleo's hand to take a drink from my own mug. "Does it say why he's here?"

"Off duty," Cleo said, looking away at last so she could watch me smile at the information.

The ships of the Fleet were governed by systems as diverse as those that had governed the Earth. Our ship, the *Jersey*, was one of the several that trusted human police officers only in very limited roles. The majority of the ship's law enforcement was carried out by dedicated computers who directed a variety of plastic and meat robots. The Special Investigations Division was a unit of computers specifically programmed to oversee the gray areas on the edges of the Ship's Articles.

If a clan extended their living space twenty cubic meters into their neighbors' holdings without the proper licenses, then that was a clear-cut case that the computers could probably settle without ever making physical contact. If, however, a clan was showing signs of routinely abusing one of its members (the physical intimidation of ship-born children was a fairly common offense), without ever stepping over the letter of the Ship's Articles about treatment, then an S.I.D. computer in the form of a meat robot might make contact, expressing its concerns and seeking to sort out the problem before the behavior crossed the line.

The S.I.D. was also the part of the law-enforcement establishment in charge of overseeing Cleo's and my activities in the Contraband Unit. The fact that an S.I.D. meat robot had logged itself as being off duty and then come here meant that it most likely had come to investigate something the computers were worried was a problem. Like maybe Cleo and myself.

"We should leave," I said.

"We just got here," Cleo replied. She took a long drag on her cigar, then blew an exaggeratedly casual breath of smoke into the clouds already hanging above the bar. "S.I.D. has nothing on us."

"Let's hope not." I turned on my stool to face the stacked bottles behind the bar, and then glanced to my right to try to see the robot. To my annoyance, I couldn't recognize him. If I'd had my mechanics on, they could have told me instantly, but there was a certain security in being just meat. I didn't have to worry that the S.I.D. computer had permission to access my computer-held dreams, giving it the equivalent of the ability to read my mind.

The stacked bottles reflected the people and servers passing us steadily. Suddenly one of the people stopped and met Cleo's eyes. "May I join you?" he asked.

"Certainly, Officer Gaunt," Cleo said, glancing at me for emphasis.

"There's no need to use my title," the robot said. He had a long nose and gray eyes and was balding at the very top of his head. "I'm off duty."

"In that case, let us buy you a drink. Barleywine? Scotch?" Cleo was smiling, enjoying this playing with fire. I wished I'd stayed back in the hotel.

"A Flying Tiger," Gaunt said, glancing at the bartender, just as a human would while sending an order through his mechanics. Meat robots had to eat and drink, of course, and their rudimentary meat brains could even be affected by alcohol, but there was unlikely to be any alcohol in the drink the bartender mixed for Gaunt.

"If you're off duty, does that mean that we can talk without worrying about hearing this again in a court?" I asked.

"Are you going to say anything that might be interesting to a court?" Gaunt countered.

"No," I said, wishing I could be as sure of Cleo as I was of myself. I had no connection to the computer for Gaunt to exploit, and I wasn't drunk yet, so I knew that I could control my meat. Cleo, however, was both drunk and connected to the computer through her mechanics. Gaunt's memories would be admissible evidence if she let anything slip.

"I see it's been several weeks since you were in court. Are you getting close to another arrest?" Gaunt asked, accepting the cigar that Cleo offered him. She reached for her lighter, but the robot already had out his own, a silvery refillable with an insignia on the side.

"Oh, we aren't going to talk shop, are we?" Cleo said. She reached out and grabbed Gaunt's wrist when he tried to return the lighter to his jacket pocket. "May I?" she asked, taking the little artifact from him.

"A gift," Gaunt said as Cleo showed the lighter to me. The insignia was that of the *Solidarity*. "I was asked to the *Solidarity* as the *Jersey*'s representative in a child-custody dispute. My counterpart over there gave me that one evening."

"The Blessing case," Cleo said for my benefit, her mechanics finding the records in the computer. "One of the fathers hid the clan's child on the *Solidarity*."

"I would have thought that very hard for you," I said, handing Gaunt his lighter back. "Being on another ship, unable to link with your computer in real time."

"It was a pain," Gaunt said, reaching between Cleo and me to get his drink. "Most of my consciousness fits in the mechanics of this robot, and I had the *Solidarity*'s computers, but it was awkward. It probably felt like you feel now, with your mechanics shut down."

"Aaron likes having his mechanics off," Cleo said. "It's what makes him so good undercover."

"Really?" The robot's face managed to look interested. "You feel a duality? I've heard that humans have sides to themselves. So, turning your mechanics on and off makes you uncomfortable?"

"I don't like that it opens my mind up to any hacker with enough computer space to solve my codes," I lied. I am very good at lying, particularly face-to-face with someone who is trying to manipulate me. This talent is actually what makes me good at undercover work, but the problem with lying to computers is that they pay more attention to your statements than humans do, as Gaunt immediately demonstrated.

"Someone might gain unlicensed access to your mechanics and their records, but you couldn't call that your mind if you considered them something that is not you."

"My mind is my mind, whether it is made of neurons or nanites. I prefer to keep my thoughts to myself."

"Well, that's definitely safer, given what you do."

The three of us were quiet for a moment then, Cleo and I on our stools and the robot standing before us. It was a little scary how human he seemed, pulling in the smoke of his cigar and then mingling it with Cleo's. Actually, modeling human behavior had proved one of the easiest things that the programmers had managed for their computer charges. A computer with false I.D. codes in a meat robot with a complete brain would pass as human indefinitely.

The impetus for the Fleet in the first place had been the unwillingness of people around the world to integrate into an Earth society where the distinction between humans and computers was disappearing. For my parents and the other people who had come to make up the crews of the Fleet, there was nothing wrong with robots, even meat robots, serving human needs or enforcing human laws. The problem was not knowing who the robots were. When it had become clear on the *Jersey* that undercover police would be necessary to combat the growing contraband trade, a shipwide referendum had been held. Overwhelmingly, the crew preferred to recruit human police rather than allow robots to pass as humans.

"I like your shoes, Officer," Cleo observed, looking at the brown synthetic loafers. She had her hand back on my leg, but I was no longer enjoying it. Gaunt was making me too nervous.

"They're common," Gaunt replied, but he held up his left hand with its cigar. "Now this ring's got more to recommend it. It was also a gift, from a young divorcée who was losing her settlement space to the Gunther clan." The Gunthers were the most prestigious clan on the ship. To many, they seemed to do an inordinate amount of breeding and control an outlandish amount of space in the ship. "I helped uphold her rights. The ring was her father's."

"I thought computers didn't take gifts," Cleo said, even though I was squeezing her hand in warning. Clearly this was the way that Gaunt wanted the conversation to go.

"We don't take gratuities or bribes, but in cases like this, where it's a small thing and it's important to the giver that we have it, then we accept. We just don't make a cult out of it the way that Contraband does."

"A cult?"

"All the ship has is its resources," I said, cutting the two of them off before this could go farther and get worse. "There may be people in Contraband who get a little overzealous defending them, but we aren't just saving the here and now. We're keeping the future safe."

"That isn't what I meant," Gaunt said. "I meant the drive to conspicuous consumption that your whole unit has adopted. You guys wear and spend resources as if you were the criminals you hunt."

"Officer, you sound almost impassioned," Cleo said.

"Good," Gaunt replied. "Maybe you'll listen. I'm off duty, and I have already scheduled to wipe this meeting without sharing it to anyone, so I can speak freely to say that you should stop. S.I.D. has its eye on you, and you can't keep up like this." Both Cleo and I opened our mouths, but he held up his hand and shook his head. "It doesn't do any good to talk to me now, because I'm going to forget this ever happened, but come to me tomorrow. I can help you out of this morass you're in."

"That's very kind of you, Officer," I said. "If we ever figure out what the hell you are talking about, we'll be happy to come by and let you protect us."

"Gaunt." Cleo had put out the remains of her cigar and now she reached for the robot's shoulder. "Why are you saying this? What does S.I.D. think it has?"

Gaunt set his drink back on the counter and took hold of the hanging part of Cleo's sleeve between his thumb and forefinger. He rubbed the wool together as he said, "We want the same thing you do. We want to defend the ship's resources and its harmony. If by coming here I can save us a long case and an ugly court battle, then that's enough."

"It certainly is." I stood up and offered the robot my hand, putting myself between him and Cleo. "Good-bye, Officer."

Gaunt accepted my hand and turned to go, but he looked back and leaned around my shoulder long enough to thank Cleo for the drink and the cigar. "Anytime," Cleo said, and the robot finally went away.

I sat back down, pushed away the warm remains of my previous drink, and waved at the bartender for another. My face was buried in it when Cleo turned around, too.

"What do you think that was all about?" she asked.

"He's a cop, you're a cop. What do you think he was trying to do?" I replied.

"You think he was trying to scare us?"

"I think he did scare us."

Cleo thought about that while I worked at the contents of my mug. "They can't really prove anything," she said finally.

"Of course not. To catch us skimming the contraband busts, they would have to be on the scene, and smugglers only deal with humans. As long as no one gets stupid and falls for something like that performance tonight, then we're all fine."

"Maybe someone has."

"Cleo."

"No, think about it." She turned in her stool and put a hand out to turn me in mine so that we were facing one another. "The robots don't care about mak-

ing arrests and having a good record. They don't have
an ego, they just want results. Maybe he really was
warning us, giving us a chance to save ourselves before the whole unit goes up."

She really was beautiful right then. Her face flushed
with alcohol and passion, little strands of her brown
hair escaping from the piled hairdo she'd had them
in. We were so close and her hand was on me; it was
all I could do not to reach over and kiss her. I settled
for putting a hand on her arm.

"Cleo. Listen to yourself. He's got you thinking like
a suspect. The only thing that going to Gaunt would
accomplish is landing us all in rehabilitation. Forget
about it and him. We've got an arrest of our own to
make tomorrow."

"You're right," Cleo said. "You're right." She
paused for a second, consulting her mechanics. "We
should go." She reached into her pocket and pulled
out a handful of marks, the silver coins clattering on
the glass bar top. She pulled back two with one of her
long gold nails, and I found I had to try one more
time.

"Cleo. Come spend the night at my hotel."

"No. Todd is probably worried to death by now."
She was talking to me but looking at the coins.

"After the way he treated you, the worry will do
him good." I was talking to her but looking at her
profile. "I'll let you have the bed; the couch is more
comfortable than what I'm used to in the Bilges."

Cleo turned and put her hand on my cheek. "No,"
she said. "Todd loves me. I should have stayed in. Besides, you need your rest." I was out of words, so I

just nodded. "I'll see you in the morning," Cleo said, and turned to leave.

"Cleo," I said. She glanced back. "I love you."

She spun around and seized me in a hug. "I love you, too," she said into the wool of my jacket, and then she was gone, leaving me to stare at her retreating back, feeling like Jesus in the garden: tired, depressed, and betrayed.

The *Jersey* was in a constant state of reconfiguration. My mechanics had modeled the changes for me one time, and it looked like nothing so much as a chicken growing in an egg. For those clans who prided themselves on their family space, there was a constant battle for more room. For those individuals who lived their lives mostly in their mechanics, there was a continual slide. With the smart walls and furnishings of the ship, gaining even a cubic meter of space could make a noticeable difference in living style.

As a result of the skirmishes for room to live, little chunks of space were constantly being kicked loose. Too vital in one way or another to be absorbed, they would be pushed up the ship till they landed in the Bilges. With a few important exceptions, no one was empire building in the top of the ship. When those relegated there spared any effort toward their surroundings, it was to remove them from the influence of something that was interfering with their connection to their computer space. Thus, in the Bilges, those who were looking for unregistered homes (for themselves or their goods) could generally find some odd space that no one was yet squatting in.

The space I was using for this case was very close to

the bottle of the main drive flame. When I had my mechanics shut down, I dressed in shorts and a T-shirt to keep comfortable. Still, after two weeks of the investigation, the space smelled of my own sweat. I had prepared for returning here by not showering again when I rose from the hotel bed. I did not even comb my hair. In the ship's constantly changing space, water lines, particularly hot water ones, seldom survived in the Bilges. Grooming, even such simplicities as clean clothes or a shaved face, were rare this far up.

Which, in a way, was the point of the contraband trade. Humans still lived in the Fleet, so money was still power. It was the edge you walked as an under-cover. You had to be dirty enough to look like you lived in the Bilges, but you had to be clean enough that you seemed serious about getting out.

Sealing the smart wall behind me, I turned on the battery-powered light and set about trading my Mid-lands suit for an older version that was my working attire. I dumped the barleywines and the empties from the cooler bag and swept the padding from the top of three crates that had been my bed for two weeks. Opening each in turn, I made sure that the boxes of ripe strawberries I'd hidden in the crates the day before were still in place. They were. I took a box from each crate and stowed them in the cooler bag, then loaded the crates onto my hand truck.

The hand truck was a simple wheeled thing of alu-minum and rubber. It was much harder to negotiate through the twisting passages of the Bilges than a smart truck or cart would have been, but the mechan-ics in a smart conveyance would have had a tie with the ship's computers, and that would have let someone who knew about it track me. The whole point, if you were an undercover officer or a contrabander, was not to let there be a computer record of your activities.

It took me twenty-five minutes by the Earth-manufactured watch on my wrist (one of the jokes among cops and contrabanders was that only cops and contrabanders still wore watches) to reach the first checkpoint. Cleo was there, smoking another mood stick but looking much less captivating in a pair of dirty overalls and with her hair pulled back in an untidy bun.

"Any problems?" I asked.

"No. Hines left his hole fifteen minutes ago, and he's on course. We went through the exchange site an hour ago and everything is still in place. Piece of cake."

"Right." I was looking at her face, trying to see if there were any signs of further violence. She caught me at it.

"I'm fine. It was just stupid, and it's over. Keep your mind on the bust."

"Believe me, I'm not thinking about anything else," I lied. "Wish me luck."

"Luck," she said, and we hugged, a one-armed affair on my side since I was balancing the hand truck and cooler bag.

Five minutes farther on, most of which was spent pulling the hand truck up a rail-less stepladder to a new level, I stopped before an anonymous section of bulkhead, produced a heavily shielded smart key, and detached a triangular plate from low on the wall.

From the squared cone of space behind it I took out a flat, fist-sized black box and, after a moment's hesitation, an old .38 caliber revolver. The conscience went into my jacket pocket and the revolver went into my belt at the small of my back.

Todd was at the second checkpoint. His black hair was longer than Cleo's, with more curl. He wore it loose so that it hung over his shoulders and was lost in the black of his T-shirt. We were the same height, but I was several kilos heavier. As always, our greetings were completely neutral.

"We're on target," he said. "Cleo is in position, and I've got the equipment ready. How are you?"

"I'll make it."

"Have you got the conscience?" I pulled it out and handed it to him. He laid the little box along his throat and touched the stud. He looked at nothing for a moment, then shook his head, touched the stud, and handed it back to me. "Checks," he said.

"Good. Well." I rocked the crates back on the truck's two wheels, then added, "Todd?"

"Yeah?"

"Keep an eye on this one. Hines . . . he makes me nervous."

Todd had small, deep-set eyes, and, when he smiled at me, I always saw just a hint of mockery in them. "Relax, Aaron. We've got it. Don't let Gaunt spook you."

"Cleo told you about that?"

"Yes, and I agree with you. He's got nothing. He's just trying to shake something loose. It's going to be fine. You just make the trade. We'll handle it from there."

"Okay." I leaned into the truck and started the last part of my journey.

When they gather for social reasons rather than for trade, smugglers like to debate what it is that makes a great contrabander. One of the things they consistently agree on is that it takes a knack for finding the right place to make a trade. While theoretically any corner on the ship will do, the ideal trade spot is public enough to lend an excuse for being there but private enough that the trade can be made without an audience. In addition, it should have a multitude of ways to get to and away from. Just in case.

The chambers near the flame canal are perennial favorites of all smugglers. For one thing, they are stable. If the ship is to continue its journey, then the canal and its supports have to stay intact. For another, the heat and electronic noise and lower gravity discourage casual passersby. I was sweating once again as I neared my rendezvous.

Mr. Hines's face was also red with the heat when I arrived at our meeting site. He was waiting for me by a blue spiral staircase, sitting on one of the two tiger-skin suitcases he had with him.

"Well, how are you doing, son?" he called as I pulled the hand truck over the gray lip of a self-sealing doorway.

"Ready to be quit of these things," I said, dropping them flat. I took the red handkerchief from my hip pocket, wiped my face, and returned it. Let him get used to me reaching back there, I thought. Just in case.

"Well, I'm ready to take them off your hands,"

Hines said, leaving the suitcases as he walked to the center of the chamber and waited for me. If Narandova had had a slight gut, Hines had a real one, as well as a second chin and less hair than Gaunt. As a rule, smugglers showed their age more than the average person. It was all the time they spent with their mechanical side shut down while gorging on the fruits of their profession.

"I'm getting too old to be down here by the flames," Mr. Hines said, dabbing at his brow with a white handkerchief of his own. "Need to take some time off and care for myself. You know what I mean?"

"We'll make it fast," I promised, leaving the strawberries and going to join him in the room's center.

"Yep, fast is what everyone wants these days," Mr. Hines agreed, handing me his conscience and taking mine. "There was a time, when we were still just a few years out, that you could handle a transaction like this over dinner and an evening out." He winked at me. "You understand what I'm saying?"

"Sure," I said, clicking on his conscience as he turned on mine. "Maybe we'll have dinner at our next swap. Invite some friends. A conscience for everyone and a good time for all."

"You're laughing, but that used to be the way we did business," Mr. Hines said. We both looked inside for a moment, trying to turn on our machine sides. I couldn't, and I knew that Hines couldn't either (that was the point of swapping consciences), so some of my tension ebbed. "Course, we didn't have to use these things in the old days, so it was all a little friendlier." Mr. Hines tapped the little box on his neck. "Still, maybe we could get together in more civilized surroundings next time, son. If we have something smaller to trade."

"What did you have in mind?" I asked.

Hines laughed. "Let's do this deal first, son. You shouldn't get ahead of yourself in a business like this."

"I'll get the berries," I said.

Mr. Hines kept talking while I was walking to the hand truck. He was one of a dying breed of smuggler. Before joining the Fleet, he had done thirty years in the United States Navy, most of that serving in space. He had retired into a civilian shipping firm, which he had left after fifteen years to come on the voyage. Hines was one of the old-timers, a man who had spent his entire life skimming luxuries from his employers and selling them for a profit. There was a whole subculture of such men in the Fleet, but every year there were fewer. Mr. Hines had had a good long run, but today his string was over.

"You like these suitcases?" Mr. Hines was asking as he carried them to the center of the room. "They were a going-away present from one of my grandsons. He works in one of those wildlife recovery preserves in India. Anyway, they sell these cases in the gift shop. Tell all the tourists that it's real tiger fur, made from the hide of a tiger that went berserk, a man-killer. You're young, but you understand what I'm saying, don't you?"

"That they lie so they can soak the customer?" I asked, handing him the cooler bag.

"It's fake fur, and they sell it with a fake story. And a government preserve, too," Mr. Hines said. He set one of the suitcases down on the floor so he could take the cooler bag and set it beside it, then he put the other suitcase on top of the crates and opened it for me. Inside were two rows of plastic-sealed pistol clips. On top of them was a gauss pistol and a steel plate. Mr. Hines picked up the pistol, picked up a clip, and handed both to me.

"Are those going to be staying on the *Jersey*?" Mr. Hines asked, taking the plate from the bag and going to lean it against the stairs.

"Does it matter?" I asked, putting the gun inside an interference bag before sliding the clip home. Most likely, the gun's smart functions had been burned out so that the ship's security computers could not locate it and shut it down, but if they hadn't been, then those functions would activate once the clip was in, providing the bridge that the computers would need to pinpoint our location and our crime. Because I was trying to get Hines arrested, this wouldn't have mattered except that I was still playing the role. Thus, the bag to halt any communication.

"My second son, George, and his family live in the Winchester section of this ship," Mr. Hines replied, backing out of the way. "If guns like that are going to be going off around here, I'll want to get them out."

"I wouldn't lose any sleep over George's safety," I said. Powered up, the gun was both lighter and steadier. I cranked the velocity all the way down, aimed at the plate, held my breath, and squeezed the trigger. There was a bang of displaced air and a howl of tortured metal. The slug had shattered the steel plate, throwing fragments in a fan behind the stairs.

"Good weapons?" Mr. Hines asked. He was opening the cooler bag.

"They'll do," I said, popping the clip and handing it back to him. I kept the gun; I trust Todd and Cleo, but there was no sense in being stupid. I reached for my handkerchief again. "How are the berries?"

"Excellent. I'll just look at the crates and we can be on our way." Mr. Hines took a berry from the bag and tossed the clip into the suitcase. Munching the berry, he closed the suitcase, and lifted it off the crates. I picked up the top crate and shifted it to the floor.

"I can throw in the hand cart," I said while I undid the latches on the crate.

"I'd appreciate that. Beats humping those cases," Mr. Hines said.

I tossed back the lid of the crate and turned around to find myself staring down the barrel of another gauss pistol.

"Sorry, son." Mr. Hines said. "Don't like doing business this way, but an old friend called yesterday. He needs these packs, too, and I do already have a customer for the berries."

"Take them," I said, putting my hands halfway up. "My compliments. We can square it up sometime when you're not under pressure."

Mr. Hines looked honestly regretful. "Sorry, but I have my reputation to think of. Can't let it get around that I went back on a deal."

"What deal?" I said, shaking my head. I couldn't get the image of steel plate, blown to vapor, out of my mind. "I brought you some berries to establish my credentials. So we can do business in the future. No need for any damage to anyone's reputation." I moved one hand back, as if going for my handkerchief again. He was too close though. He would see the gun and shoot before I had a prayer.

"Don't," Mr. Hines said, pointing the gun at my moving hand. "I'm sorry, son, but I've been doing this sort of thing for a long time, and I know you just can't leave people alive after you've crossed them."

It was at this point that three things happened simultaneously. I threw myself to the side, the gauss pistol fired, and the floor underneath us fell away. I yelled, Mr. Hines yelled, the gauss pistol fired again, and we smashed into the floor below. I was still feeling the pain when there came a flash of light, a crackle of electricity, and a smell of ozone.

"You're under arrest," Todd told the unconscious Mr. Hines, still pointing the pistol-gripped riot stunner at him. Cleo appeared on the rim of the hole.

"Are you all right?" she asked. I was too busy shaking to answer.

Todd looked over at me, too. "I kept waiting for you to back off the smart floor. Finally had to drop you both. Are you okay?" Todd had been watching through a fiber-optic periscope, ready with a shielded smart key to drop the floor from under Mr. Hines after the exchange.

The pain was fading, and the anger was coming. "You cut that too close," I said.

"Did he hit you?"

"I—" I didn't know.

I was still checking when Cleo said, "No. We got him in time. Just."

Todd patted the smart key that now hung from his belt. "Hey, at least I got the whole floor in one pass."

"Never mind. Did you get the recording?" I sat up and waited for another bout of the shakes to pass.

"I got it all," Cleo said.

There was a groan from Mr. Hines. "Already?" Todd said. "You guys start packing up while I tend to our suspect here."

Cleo looked down at me, her sweat-streaked brow creased with concern. "Are you okay now?" she asked.

"Yeah. That was just close."

"Yeah." She nodded and disappeared. During the bust, she had been in the next chamber recording the transaction on holo and audio. Like Todd's fiber-optic periscope, all the systems were passive and dumb so that Hines would have actually had to see the tiny pickups to know they were there. He could neither track them through the computers nor detect them with dumb sensors.

I crawled the meter and a half to where the straw-berries and the cart had fallen, and sat down grate-fully beside Mr. Hines's suitcases. The first held nothing new. I opened the second case, the one I hadn't checked during the trade. In its bottom were more clips and . . . "Todd, is Hines still out?"

"Yeah."

"Cleo!"

"Almost done!"

"Leave that a minute and come down here." In a moment she appeared on the spiral staircase, carrying the recording equipment. I waved her over and she looked over Todd's shoulder into the case. Instead of a second row of batteries below the first as in the other briefcase, Mr. Hines had packed rolls of silver marks in this one. Cleo actually gasped when she saw them. Todd chuckled.

"Looks like our lucky day."

I wasn't so sure and said so. "There's too many. What's he doing bringing this much cash to a buy?" In the contraband economy, marks, legal tender for ten megajoules of energy on any ship, were the only accepted currency. Most smugglers carried a few hundred worth of the coins to cover expenses, but there had to be ten thousand or more in Hines's briefcase. "It's a setup. A plant."

"A plant?" Todd lifted his thick eyebrows at me. "A plant by who? S.I.D.? They don't deal in setups, and, besides, an old warrior like Hines wouldn't have anything to do with robots."

"No one carries this kind of money to a buy. We have to turn it in."

Todd shook his head. "Hines said his plans had changed in a hurry. Maybe he was on his way off ship. This isn't a plant, Aaron. It's Christmas."

"It's too dangerous to keep is what it is," I said. Todd shook his head again, and we turned to Cleo.

There are rules and traditions in any society; given its short history, the Contraband Unit has more than its share. Todd was the leader, but this was our free will we were risking. It required a vote, technically a unanimous one, but traditionally the minority yielded to the majority.

"It's a good bust. He never mentions the money on the recording. If he tries to make noise, it's his word against ours." Cleo said all this to Todd, then turned to me. "This is Christmas, Aaron."

It didn't feel like Christmas, but then my nerves were not at their best. Being shot at did that, but then it was also a reason to take the money. We had put a lot of time into getting this arrest; I had risked my life. Again. We were due a reward.

"All right," I said. "You two take Hines in. I'll go stick this under a tree."

CHAPTER 2

THE BUSTED

When the Fleet left Earth, several large sections of the *Jersey* had been set aside for community uses: softball tournaments, sailboard races, kite-flying festivals, and so on. As the voyage had passed, these areas had been slowly absorbed by various clans, often a single cubic meter at a time. The present reality of the ship was that no such large-scale events could be staged without leasing the space back from the clans who had usurped it. As a result, many entertainments charged large entrance fees for spectacles that might otherwise have been free.

The Fleet Chess Championships, which required that enough space be leased for four arenas, had the highest ticket prices of any event held on the *Jersey*. On a per-day basis, they were actually lower than those charged for the Lacrosse Championships, but the chess promoters sold tickets only for the full ten-day tournament. Since the mass appeal of Fleet Chess rested on the spectacle of the top players battling one another, most of the thirty-two first-round games tended to be played before only a few hundred spectators. Attendance would rise steadily as the lower-seeded players were eliminated.

The exception was any game that Lifchez played. His style of play was so unique that people came to his matches no matter who his opponent was. During a tournament, there were only two times when other players stopped to watch a game they weren't playing in: either when there was an upset under way or when Lifchez played. Only the third seed, and playing against a qualifier on the first day of this tournament, Lifchez had been scheduled for the center board and the stadium was more than half-full to watch him play.

I had known better than to ask Cleo to attend a match on the first day after a bust. By tradition, the job of the undercover man ended the second the suspect was in custody. The other members of the team did the processing, set up the indictment, and then, if they had any time and energy left, celebrated. For a team like Todd and Cleo, the celebration seldom had room for a third. So instead I had asked Chris to the opening day with me.

"You think Narandova looked that bad?" Chris was asking. We were sitting in the club seats just above the circle of private boxes, sipping barleywine from thermal cups that my police I.D. had let us smuggle onto the grounds.

"Uninspired. I wouldn't worry about it, but he's been playing that way all year. It's like he's turned his whole game over to his mechanics." Below us, Lifchez was up and walking around the two-story hologram of the board, considering his move. His challenger, Estelle Stolle, an Earth-born woman from the *Auckland*, was sitting in one of the ring of armchairs, tapping a jade hair comb, and studiously ignoring the partisan crowd.

"So you like Sakins?" Chris asked.

"You have to like Sakins," I said. "He's been like the angel of death for three months now." Below, Lifchez made his move, sending a cruiser on a course that would take it off the hologram display. There was a ripple in the crowd as people focused on their mechanics, trying to see the whole board and fit Lifchez's move into it.

Tournament-level chessboards theoretically extended infinitely in three dimensions, but even Fleet Champions tended to play within the 512 cubes defined by the starting positions. There simply was little point in wasting moves sending units on long, circling attacks that left you vulnerable to an opponent's concentrated thrusts. Unless you were Lifchez.

Lifchez had joined the tour early in the voyage, and from the beginning he had been different. For one thing, he was from the *Jersey* at a time when the best players were all from the *Warsaw* and the *Panzer*. For another, he played the strangest, most dispersed game anyone had ever seen. Most of all, though, he was a volatile, erratic personality in a game played by people who were scrupulously courteous to one another face-to-face, particularly while they were at the board.

"Do you have a clue what he's doing?" Chris asked after he'd tried to absorb Lifchez's move.

"He's trying to pull the destroyer away from the upper northwest monitor," I guessed.

"What does that gain him?"

"I have no idea." There was an element of the dream hustler in Lifchez's game: complexity for the sake of confusion. Like Narandova's chatting with the audience, it could be devastating if you let it distract you.

"What about Goff? Doesn't she have as good a chance as anyone?" Chris had been three years ahead of me in the chess juniors. We had been in the tour together for only one year before he dropped out. We had run into each other again on the police force, where he had become my rabbi, the older officer to whom I had taken my problems and my fears. He was off the force now, working with one of the licensed trade clans, but he was still the friend I brought my troubles to.

"Sakins is in her half of the draw. The one other time they played this year, Sakins crushed her. It'll be a hell of a match, but no one expects Goff to be there for the final." Lifchez was standing with his dark arms folded while he waited for Stolle to make her move. He was a lean man who had been known to appear at ship handball tournaments and do fairly well for an amateur. He wore his curly black hair in a flattop, a conservative style he had adopted after his reconciliation with his clan and the birth of their latest child.

Stolle made her move, taking the destroyer away from the monitor. Lifchez responded instantly by dropping a corsair in between the two pieces. "But either one of them can crush it there," Chris protested.

"Yeah," I agreed. You could only conclude that Lifchez wanted the corsair dead, although it made no sense. Anyway, something else was on my mind. "Chris?"

"Yeah?" he said, reaching into my cooler bag for another handful of strawberries.

"Have you ever heard of an S.I.D. officer going off record to warn someone about an investigation?" Chris had stopped chewing and was staring at me. "I know, but it happened." I told him the story of the encounter Cleo and I had with Gaunt in the Flame.

"That's spooky," Chris said when I'd finished. "I've heard of robots going out for social events, and they'll do whatever they have to do to make a case, but I've never heard of one claiming to be off the record. You're sure it was a real robot?"

"I had my mechanics shut down, but Cleo claims it was. I think it's just something they've added to the programming."

"Maybe, but it worries you, or you wouldn't have brought it up."

"Yeah." It worried me a lot, in fact, particularly coming right before we found Mr. Hines carrying too much money to a buy. What if someone were betting we were too greedy for our own good? That, however, led to the question of why they hadn't acted now that we had proved them right.

There was a gasp from the crowd, and Chris and I paused for a moment to catch up. Stolle's destroyer had come back to take the corsair, and Lifchez had responded by taking her northern destroyer. The gasp had come as the audience's mechanics and computers chased down the moves that flowed from this exchange. Stolle retained her good position inside Lifchez's lines, but it was suddenly unclear if she would have the chance to exploit it.

Stolle took all the time she could before making her next move. She had given up tapping her comb and was now clutching it instead, her whole consciousness turned inside and focused on the game. At the last instant, she altered the path of her northern cruiser, only to have it consumed by Lifchez's southern battleship.

Again the Aucklander took all the time she could, before turning the whole northern arm of her fleet to deal with the Former Champion's intruding battleship. Lifchez responded by dropping ship after ship into the fray, creating a carnage that reversed Stolle's positional advantage and left her fleet ship vulnerable to the fast remnants of Lifchez's destroyer force. Stolle mounted one last counterattack, and then resigned when it failed.

In the midst of the applause that followed, Lifchez shook Stolle's hand, waved to the judge, and hurried to the box where his wife and brother were sitting. Stolle took the time to shake the judge's hand, then went to join her own family. The crowd began rising and moving out, the day's excitement done. Chris got up, too.

"Look, I don't know what to say. I'll ask around and get back to you. In the meantime, keep your head down."

"I will. Thanks, Chris. I knew I could count on you."

"Hey, thanks for the match. I'll call you soon."

Chris pushed into the stream of spectators and was soon gone. I stayed where I was with the cooler bag and my thoughts. I needed to get to the rest room, but I didn't want to move yet. Passing the problem to

Chris should have made me feel better, but it didn't. I could tell that getting anything done was going to be a problem until I had Gaunt's actions explained to me.

There was a bespectacled man coming toward me around the arena, and with a start I realized that it was Narandova. He stopped behind me and offered a little bow as I rose to return it. "I noticed you here during the match, and I wonder if I might join you?" he asked.

"Please," I said, waving him to Chris's chair. "I'm afraid I'm out of cups, but I could offer you a strawberry."

"No. Thank you," he said as he settled into the padded seat, pausing a moment to let it adjust to him. "Please forgive my intrusion, but I wanted to ask your opinion of the match."

"My opin . . ." I tried, too surprised to finish. "I can't—I mean, why?"

Narandova took off his glasses and put them in his pocket, incidentally giving me a moment to find my wits. "You are a serious player of the game," he observed. "A game has occurred. Surely you have an opinion?"

"Well," I said, and took a breath. When I was twelve, I would watch Lifchez's matches with my teacher, a warm Alsatian-born woman named Nancy Metz. Afterward, she would ask me my opinion, but it was much easier to give in those days because I had the benefit of her analysis from while we were watching.

"I think that as of today, Lifchez doesn't want to lose this tournament," I began.

"Yes?" Narandova said.

"Yes. His problem as a player is that he wants to play every game straight from his meat. He grudges the mechanics their every suggestion. He is at his best when, like today, he is willing to put the effort into working with his mechanics. He doesn't do that unless he doesn't want to lose."

"So you think he wants to win the tournament?"

"Yes, but that's not what I said. He always wants to win. Who doesn't? When he's dangerous is when he's decided he can't bear to lose."

"And today, he couldn't?"

"Yes. Now tomorrow, who knows?" I took a long pull on my barleywine to finish the cup. Narandova didn't say anything, so I added, "You already knew that. You've been playing against him for thirteen years. Why ask my opinion?"

Narandova waved my question away. He was looking down on the empty board with the unfocused gaze of someone who is focused mostly on their mechanics. Without coming back, he said, "And what did you think of Stolle?"

"She ran out of processing." Like the physical ship itself, the ship's computers were a jumble of competing claims and fiefs. The more computer space you could command, the better your modeling was during a game. Masters like Narandova and Lifchez had huge stores of computing behind them, built up over their years on the tour. Stolle, being very new to the game, had little to fall back on besides her own mechanics. With good meat and a lot of optimizing, a player can advance, even at a championship tournament, just with their internal resources. Except against someone like Lifchez. His play was so far beyond conventional modeling that Stolle's mechanics had actually been a hindrance to her play.

"And if she'd had the computer space to stay with him?"

"It would have been a good match. She's got a good foundation, and it looked like she was setting up a pretty strong cruiser storm when Lifchez cut her off at the knees."

Narandova nodded and reached for his glasses. I still hadn't told him anything that he hadn't already known, but it would have been rude to point this out again.

"I wonder," Narandova asked as he stood, "if you would be free to grant me a game tomorrow, say around nine in the morning?"

I was more surprised than I'd been when he'd asked to sit down. "Well, of course I would be free, but a game—"

"Excellent. Does the park at the Southern Apex yet survive?"

"Yes."

"Then we shall play there. Until tomorrow." He gave me another little bow and took his leave.

My first thought, when I could collect one, was to practice. My second was how futile that would be. My third was to realize that whatever Narandova wanted to meet me for, it could hardly be chess. Testing his game against mine would be like a concert soprano performing for a computer audience. They might feel the vibrations, but they would certainly miss the music. Still, I now had another reason to hope that the incident with Gaunt turned out to be nothing. It wasn't every day that a champion invited you out for a private game.

After the evening matches, I returned to my little-used flat in the Midlands. Cleo, Todd, and I had been a team for a year and a half, and in that time we had brought in more contraband and secured more convictions than any other squad in the unit. One of the ways we accomplished that was to spend very little time celebrating each victory. As a result, I spent seven days in the average ten down in the Bilges, maintaining one cover identity or another. Now I had a rare chance to spend a night at home.

Opening my door, I smelled the mood smoke and realized with a mixture of surprise and excitement that Cleo was waiting for me. I went quickly through the foyer saying, "Cleo," and drew up a little short when I saw that Todd was waiting for me as well. I nodded to him, then looked at Cleo. "What brings you here?"

"Are your mechanics off?" Todd asked.

"Now they are," I answered, and realized that the door had not warned me about the visitors. Not only had they broken in (easy enough for a person of Todd's skills), but they had also erased the record of their presence. "What's up? Not another case already?"

"We want to divide the marks," Cleo said. She was standing near the wicker-covered cool box that supported my bar supplies, but she hadn't poured a drink.

"What?"

"Ten thousand marks, Aaron," Todd said. He was

sitting on the long gray couch that dominated the small space, his thin hands resting on his bony knees. He was also wearing a jacket, an unusual accessory for him. Todd loved T-shirts and expensively stitched vests the way that Cleo loved hand-tailored blouses.

"You got Hines put away already?" I asked, wishing I'd checked before I shut down my mechanics.

"No," Cleo said, and might have gone on, but Todd cut her off.

"We got the indictment, and the trial's being scheduled," he said. "Now we want our share of the money."

"We're thinking about a trip to the *Ellaysa*," Cleo said. She put her cigar down in one of my saucers. "Could we go get the money now?"

Ever since two nights before at the Flame Lounge, I had been scared. Finding the marks on Mr. Hines had made it worse, and talking to Chris had not made it better. Now I was facing a full-blown panic. I couldn't help it. I had to close my eyes and take a deep breath. When I opened them, I walked very deliberately to the cool box. "You guys want one, too?" I asked as I pulled out a barleywine.

Todd shook his head, but Cleo said, "Sure." I handed her a bottle and went to sit on the opposite end of the couch from Todd.

"Now," I said. "One more time. Why do you want the money?"

"Look, it's no big deal," Todd said, turning on the couch and putting an arm along its back. "We've been pushing pretty hard. Cleo and I want to take some time off on the *Ellaysa*. Remember, we said this was Christmas."

"I remember," I said, balancing the unlicensed bottle on my knee. "It just feels like you don't trust me." By tradition, you didn't spend the skim from a bust until the suspect was convicted. Also by tradition, the undercover man held the skim and handled distributing it.

"Aaron," Cleo said. She put her drink on the holounit and knelt down so she could put a hand on my knee and look into my eyes. "It's nothing to do with trust. It's just that we've never had a skim like this. We want to spend it."

Against my will, my eyes slipped from hers and came to rest on the bare triangle of her skin that the open buttons of her blouse revealed. I felt the familiar pain in my heart as I thought of all the other things I would rather have her reassuring me about, but the pain also helped me push the fear away.

"Okay, I understand," I lied, meeting Cleo's eyes again as I did. "I'll bring you your shares tomorrow."

"Could we get them now?" Cleo asked.

"We want as much time as possible before the trial comes," Todd added.

"Well, I certainly don't have them here, and none of us is dressed for a walk in the Bilges," I told them, looking at Todd, trying to judge how desperate he was. "I'll get them first thing in the morning. We can have lunch at the Rude Thai place, and you can be on a shuttle before dinner."

"I don't—" Todd started, but it was Cleo's turn to interrupt.

"That sounds fine. We need to include you in the celebration." She squeezed my thigh again, got up, and extended a hand to Todd. Reluctantly, he took it and stood as well. I let him pass before standing myself to see them to the door.

"Don't worry, Aaron," Cleo said, as she hugged me good-bye. "This is just a very special trip," she said, and winked at me.

"Sure," I said. "See you tomorrow."

After Cleo and Todd left, I turned my mechanics back on so they could shut me down. Whatever the risks, life was much easier with your mechanical side working for you. There was no need to resort to alcohol or any other drug to reduce your meat's tension. You just told your mechanics that you wanted to be asleep and when you wanted to be awake again, and boom, you were asleep for that long. You ran the risk of having your dreams subpoenaed, but you were asleep, so you didn't have to worry about that or anything else.

Of course, when you woke up, the worry was still there.

I dressed very carefully that morning, taking as long as I could in the shower, carefully doing my hair, dressing in a tailored suit that I'd only worn once before. I even took the time to put a little polish on my shoes. I got down a snap-brimmed homburg from one of the boxes over my couch and set the hat at a careful angle on my head.

There was one more accessory I needed to complete my ensemble, and I picked that up on my way to the Southern Apex. Three months before, a small shop in Warm Springs, a fashionable grotto of the Estates, had begun offering for sale handmade ebony walking sticks with ivory handles and silver trim. The hand manufacture plus the ivory parts made the price exorbitant, but they were beautiful. I had restrained myself because of the price and because walking sticks were largely out of fashion this decade, but if S.I.D. really did have something on us, and if Cleo and Todd really were fleeing and leaving me to take the blame, then I wanted to own one of those canes before I was sent off to rehabilitation.

The Park (or the Memory Glade as it was sometimes called) survived as a sort of monument to the clans who devoted themselves to reality. The space was privately held, but access was more or less open. Private robots watched the entrances and politely restrained people who did not fit certain minimums of dress and grooming. In practice, all but the hardestcore dreamers could stroll the Glade's paths, wade in its pond, lie under its trees, and stare back toward distant, unseeable Earth through its windowed roof and walls.

I found Narandova engaged in the last occupation, sitting on a bench by the little lake.

"It is good of you to come," Narandova said, rising to shake my hand. He didn't have the glasses on today and he had shot his straw-colored hair through with gray. It was a very different image, pushing him past distinguished into truly old. He might have passed for a resident of the *Union*, the ship where everyone kept their mechanics shut off.

"I would not have missed it. Shall we stroll as we play?" I asked, gesturing with my new stick.

"I would rather we stayed here," Narandova said. He sat back down and took up a wooden box with a four-by-eight checkerboard pattern. He flipped it open, revealing thirty-two ivory pieces in black and white set in a foam mounting. "Are you familiar with classic chess?" he asked.

"Yes," I said, sitting next to him. "My chess teacher and I played some. It was a sort of treat at the end of lessons." I looked up from the pieces to meet his eyes. "You are not trying to lead me back to the game, are you?"

"I have begun playing the classic game a great deal in the past year." He took two pawns from the box. "You have no objection to turning off your mechanics, I think?"

The classic game, limited as it was to two dimensions and only thirty-two pieces, held little appeal for two opponents with their mechanics turned on. While the computer might have been unable to determine which hand held the white pawn, that would have been the last element of surprise to it. The mechanics held so much computing power that unless insane time limits were put on moves, nothing was possible but drawn games.

"None." I shut down my machine half once again, ending its reasoned intrusions and replacing them with the narrative of my thoughts. At the same time, the hardness of the bench, the stiffness of my collar, and the unpleasant smell of rotting leaves, all sensations that the machine had been shielding from my notice, came to me.

Narandova put the pieces behind his back and then brought them out again in his closed fists. He wore an elaborate gold wedding band that pinched down the skin of his ring finger. On the fingers of his other fist were three silver bands worked with the years of his

Championships. I tapped the hand with the wedding ring, and he turned it over to reveal the white pawn.

As we took the pieces from the box and began to set up the board, Narandova said, "On my ship, there is an unregistered tour for this kind of chess. Players risk their own money rather than playing for prizes offered by promoters. Because of the danger of cheating, the players often exchange consciences. Are you familiar with consciences?"

"Yes, I am," I told him as I pushed out my king's pawn. "I use them all the time in my work. Smugglers trade them to ensure that neither party of a deal is keeping computer records that may incriminate them."

"Are they effective?" Narandova asked, bringing out his queen's knight. "Surely the police have some way of overcoming a conscience so they can keep just such records."

"No," I said. I replied to his move with my king's bishop, pleased at how much of this opening my meat brain remembered. "A conscience works with the fundamental design of our mechanical selves. A person whose mechanics could ignore a conscience's command to shut down, and then play dead to the conscience's constant testing, would be completely inhuman at the molecular level."

"It is possible in theory, however," Narandova pressed.

"It is possible in fact," I replied, "but the difference would be noted. However the rest of the passengers reacted, no one in the world of contraband would trade with such a weird beast, any more than they would trade with a meat robot."

"So I can trust a conscience?"

"If it will shut you down, it will shut anyone down." Narandova nodded, his eyes finally darting to the board again as he pushed forward his knight's pawn to threaten my advanced bishop. I asked him: "Why are you interested?" Surely he wasn't taking up chess hustling?

"I have a great deal more money than the usual player. The more I play this variation, the more I find myself concerned with being cheated."

"Ah," I said, and settled down to pay attention to the game. We played out a standard opening, moving the ivory pieces quickly, so that soon we were past the exchange of rooks and into the midgame. I leaned back from the board and began rolling my new cane between my two palms while I tried to remember back to the games with my teacher. There was a manner in which I was supposed to attack Narandova's king's pawn from my current position, but it danced at the edge of my recall. What a frustrating thing the meat mind was.

My concentration was not helped when a pair of passing clans-people stopped before us to observe the board. They were young-featured and fashionably dressed for walking the Park. The woman wore a bustled dress, and the man essayed a waistcoat. Under her hat the woman's hair was the shade of brown that might have been red in a different light, and her perfume recalled the scent Cleo wore under her aroma of mood smoke. There was a polite tipping of hats, and the couple passed on.

"Not chess fans," I commented.

"Well mannered," Narandova replied. "It would have been rude of them to linger without an invitation. I might have asked them to stay, but the girl was distracting you, I believe."

"Perhaps," I allowed. "She reminded me of someone."

"That is why I came to this variation originally," Narandova said. He was as relaxed on the bench as I was, and he was directing his words out toward the pond. "It is odd how many things changed along with the government on my ship. For so many years, having superior chess players was viewed as a result of having superior government. The *Warsaw*'s Chess Federation acted as a branch of the government, and maintaining the right political connections was just as important as practicing chess. Politics could get you more computing space, better seconds, leave to travel, whatever you needed.

"When the government fell in the Upheaval, however, the Chess Federation became a separate entity. All that mattered was how well you could play the game. I still had the computer space, of course, but I worried that there was a lack on my meat side. I seemed to be playing too mechanically, and my peers were punishing me for it."

I was listening to Narandova, but my mind was on the time three months before when after a long, frustrating evening of barleywines, I had taken Cleo in my arms to hug her good-bye, and just held her there for forty-three seconds by my mechanics' count. Long enough to feel the heat of her body leak into my bones. And there in my mind, behind the memory of the smell of Cleo's hair, was the pattern for attacking Narandova's pawn.

Narandova was still talking even as I moved a

pawn a cautious space forward. "I tried playing a few chess games without my mechanics, but there was no joy in it. Then I turned to this and discovered not only a new game to play, but also a whole new network of opponents."

"You think this has improved your play?" I asked.

"You are thinking of the exhibition," Narandova said. He was still watching the little waves on the pond, but it was a statement rather than a question. "There are certain things that are expected of a person in my position. There is no challenge and no joy to the actual play, so I try to find it in the players and the spectators. My mechanics handle the games themselves much better than I in those situations." He moved his remaining bishop, and I paused to consider if my plan would still work. I decided it would and pushed a second pawn up to support the first.

The clans-couple was gone from sight, and there were no other people in view. Narandova moved the bishop back, and said, "I wonder if I could have your opinion on what, for you, would be a professional matter?"

I looked up from the board and found that now he was looking at me. "If you report any crimes to me, I have to pass that information along to the computers," I said, and then I frowned. "Or do I?" I tapped the chessboard with a finger. "Seems an elaborate ruse to get me to turn off my mechanics."

"It is not a ruse," Narandova said. "Everything I have said is quite true, and I am enjoying this game a great deal, but I will be able to enjoy it more once I have asked you some questions."

This felt wrong. In the society of the ships, where age bore no relation to appearance and parents were as rare as fresh fruit, mentors and superiors came mostly from differences in social standing. In the world of chess, there was no one above Narandova, and I had been comfortable in my role as the befriended novice. Now, however, Narandova was changing our roles. His asking my professional advice raised me from grateful student to cautious expert and took the warmth from the encounter.

"As you wish," I said, failing to keep my reluctance from my voice. Narandova gave me a little bow with just his head and thin shoulders, acknowledging the position he was putting me in and thanking me for allowing it. Then he took up one of my captured pawns from the stone of the bench and held it while he talked.

"In our first encounter, I told you that my son is not a chess player. He instead chose to become a shuttle pilot. This was three years ago, at a time when my close circle of government supporters had no difficulty effecting such favors for me. Roman took the training and by the time the government fell in the Upheaval, he was in the regular rotation of pilots. He is still there. Politics got him the training, but he earned his place and was allowed to keep it."

I simply nodded. Roman probably was a good pilot, but having a famous father wouldn't have hurt, no matter the government.

"Two months ago, my son was approached by a man named Ivan Tourvak. Tourvak showed my son records which proved that on three separate occasions my son had piloted shuttles containing contraband taken from the *Warsaw*. Tourvak threatened that unless my son took an active part in helping to ship further loads of contraband, he would turn the records over to the new Law Bureau."

Narandova paused in his narrative and looked away from me, his eyes going up to stare out into space. It was the attitude he had been in when I arrived. Most people looking out of the Park were looking back to Earth, but maybe he was looking for his son.

"Before the Upheaval, there would have been no trouble over this. My son would have spoken to me, I would have spoken to some of my friends in the government, Tourvak would have been quietly arrested, and my son would have gone on with his career. Unfortunately, those days are gone."

Two children in matching dresses of sky blue and pale green appeared from behind a hill and passed through the trees on the other side of the pond. Most likely they were a true child and its meat robot nanny, but they might have been two robots sent to listen to our conversation. Without our mechanics, there was no way for Narandova and me to tell. The children, careless of their skirts, knelt down to examine something in the grass. I smiled at their extravagant looks of curiosity and acknowledged again that Gaunt had me very paranoid.

"We see little choice. I am one of the few symbols of the old regime that has survived in the new order," Narandova went on. "I am not well loved where things such as this are handled. Going to our police might have resulted in Tourvak's arrest, but they would have taken my son, too. And perhaps me."

The child in blue had picked up something and set it in her open hand. She was trying to rub it against the other child's cheek; squeals of protest came to us across the water. The child in green leaped to her feet and ran, leaving the other to stare at the thing in her hand.

Cleo, I knew, had dismissed her nanny shortly after her clan had fractured. She went from having one large family to having three small ones, each with hard feelings toward the others. She'd turned her back on all of them and from the age of fourteen she had made her own way on the ship. So why, now, did she let Todd dominate her? Why did I let Cleo dominate me?

Narandova was waiting for me to speak. He had said he had questions, but now he was leaving it for me to ask them. I pushed at the path with the rubber tip of my new cane, tempted just to get up and leave him. Instead I asked: "How many trips has he made for the smugglers?"

"Four that I know of."

"To which ships?"

"Just this one," Narandova said. He still had the ivory pawn in his hand. The girl across the lake was stroking what she held with a single finger of her opposite hand. Her companion in the green dress had stopped perhaps twenty feet away with her back against an oak tree that wasn't actually big enough to hide her. I was coming to understand how some people might not like Narandova.

Very reluctantly I asked, "Can you describe Tourvak?"

"Tall. Salt-and-pepper hair. Long sideburns and a

big mustache. Wild eyes." A description that might have meant nothing, since all those things were subject to change, as Narandova's own makeover demonstrated. It would have been nice to have our mechanics on so that Narandova could have just given me a memory of the man, but I didn't think I needed it.

With that first inkling of who Tourvak might be, what I did need suddenly was the earthen taste of a mood stick. I badly wanted the creeping calm that would fill my lungs and flow out into my nerves. More reluctantly yet, I asked, "What is it you want?"

The Fleet Champion looked at me, surprise plain on his face. "I want my son free of this man and his damned trade," he replied, his voice actually raised. Both the girls looked toward us for the first time. The one in blue dropped her treasure and jumped to her feet. It took her a moment to spot her poorly hidden friend, and then she ran to the girl, tapping her opposite shoulder as she passed. Laughing, she ran on, pursued by the girl in green.

I watched them out of sight before I said, "You're sure?"

"Yes, of course." Narandova had his voice under control again, but I'd clearly asked a second question he had not anticipated. That was the problem with coming to an expert; they tended to do their job.

"Not 'of course.' Your son is piloting contraband between ships. His cut is at least ten percent, but since he was coerced, it is probably closer to twenty if not twenty-five. That is a lot of income to walk away from."

"My family does not need more marks." Narandova set the pawn back on the bench and pointed at me. "My position made my son vulnerable to this Tourvak. He is a victim of an evil man, and I want that man punished."

"Your son didn't tell you he was getting a cut of the profits," I said. "He came to you in the beginning when he was scared, but he doesn't mention it now. In the beginning he thought that between his salary and whatever you allow him, he had plenty of income. Now that he's tasted the spoils, he's not so sure." Narandova had lowered his finger and stopped meeting my eyes. "Are you sure that your son wants out, because I can guarantee that he is not sure."

"You speak with the conviction of experience," Narandova said, glancing up again.

"Perhaps," I allowed. We shared a look that could have meant anything, and then we both turned toward the pond. We watched the waves in silence for a time. I thought about "Tourvak" and regular runs from the *Warsaw* and how that fit into the trade of the smugglers I knew. The more I thought about it, the more sure I was of who "Tourvak" might be and the more I wanted to just shut down my consciousness until this was all over.

"If you are right about my son, then that is all the more reason to have Tourvak arrested," Narandova finally said. "You are a policeman, and he is a criminal. Is there not something you can do?"

"I don't know. The fact that we haven't done anything already tells me that he is good. If he is who I think he is, he is untouchable." I got a handkerchief from my jacket pocket and pushed back the homburg so I could pat my forehead with it. The artificial day of the Park was advancing, and the temperature was going up with it. There was a sheen of perspiration on Narandova's brow as well, but evidently he didn't have a handkerchief. If he kept up turning off his mechanics for chess games and intrigues, he would learn to carry one.

"We'll have to have another game here tomorrow," I said. "There is too much I don't know. While I find out what I can, you have to get hold of your son and find out if he will help. Don't tell him you've talked to the police. Lie if he asks you directly. Just find out if he will help if you do."

"Can you do anything if he won't?"

"I don't know. All I know is that whatever happens, if anything happens, it will be much easier if your son is on our side." Narandova nodded, and our eyes fell to the chessboard. The older man laughed without humor.

"I said I would be able to enjoy this game more once you answered my questions. I find instead that I have no stomach to play it at all."

"That's all right," I said. "I haven't actually answered your questions yet. Perhaps tomorrow we'll have good news for each other." He looked at me, and I knew that he doubted it as much as I.

It is an open question why anyone would start a restaurant on a Fleet ship in the first place, much less spend the journey cooking or waiting tables in one. The answer was money and space. The lure of money was obvious, but that of space was just as powerful. The Ship's Articles allowed for space to be let to entrepreneurs for business needs at a cheaper rate than to people simply wishing more living space. Using

space rented for business as dwelling space was
grounds for confiscation, but that didn't stop people
from pushing the boundary as hard as possible.

A restaurant was a pretty sure bet as businesses
went. The standard ship's fare was a tasteless cereal,
called kibbles, that could be had free for the asking
from the ship itself, washed down with a glucose so-
lution. A person's mechanical side could make the
kibbles and glucose taste like anything the diner de-
sired, and they contained all that the body needed to
keep both the meat and the mechanics running. There
were many Dreamers who had gone years without
ever eating anything else, but few people with any
devotion to reality even counted them as food.

The Pines of Bangkok had begun as a three-table,
one-employee, hole-in-the-wall affair shortly after the
Fleet had left Earth. Now it was a forty-table, split-
level bar and restaurant that employed all seventeen
of Lon Nol's children and grandchildren. It was famous for its Pud Thai and its brusque wait staff,
hence its designation to the members of the Contraband Unit as the Rude Thai Place.

Cleo and Todd were already at our usual table on
the second floor when I arrived, still sporting my hat
and my new stick. Cleo was also wearing a hat, a
white, floppy-brimmed one with an embroidered
crown that had to have been a gift from Todd. They
were both wearing jackets. I had my mechanics check
them for weapons. They found none, which only
meant that Cleo and Todd weren't carrying smart
guns. An old gun like the revolver still hidden under
my jacket wouldn't talk to the computer and so
couldn't be found by mechanics.

"Did you catch the Raymond match?" I greeted them, hooking the stick over the table's fourth chair and putting the homburg atop it. Both their eyes went distant for a moment as they checked the chess results, an action which answered my question.

"You weren't at the tournament, were you?" Todd asked. There was a half-finished bowl of sweet-and-sour soup in front of him and a more than half-finished Tom Collins at his elbow. Cleo appeared to be drinking her lunch. There was a glass of green-colored liquor (a grasshopper, according to my mechanics) in the middle of her place setting.

"Lisa and I were in juniors together. I try to be at her matches when I can." Lisa had actually been my first real girlfriend and my first real sexual experience. Until her, all of my sex had been in computer dreams, just as all of my sex since her had been.

"Did you make it to the Bilges first?" Todd asked, but I didn't answer because one of Lon's grandsons had arrived with a menu and a barleywine, both of which he set before me without comment. I'd checked the specials on my way to the restaurant, but I made a pretense of looking at the handwritten box on the menu before ordering the swordfish. The son took his menu and left again without even a computer acknowledgment.

"Did you make it to the Bilges?" Todd repeated, as I sipped the barleywine. Lon brewed his own, and it was the poorest thing on his menu. I had my mechanics adjust the taste.

"No."

"Aaron," Cleo said, almost loud enough to drown

out Todd's hiss of anger. "We have the reservations. We—"

"Why not?" Todd interrupted her.

"Hines isn't put away yet," I said.

"We explained—" Todd started. I interrupted him.

"Are you sure this is the time to discuss this?" I glanced around the restaurant, which was scattered with midday diners. None of the closest tables were occupied, but with mechanics they didn't need to be for people to overhear. "Wouldn't you rather hear about Lisa's match now, and we can talk about the Bilges later?"

"Why didn't you let us know?" Todd said, his hand clenched around his drink glass. In our eighteen months together I had learned that Todd's first reaction to any setback was anger. You had to ride it out until he was calm enough to reason with. "By the time we go down there now, we won't have time to make our shuttle."

"We'll have to change," Cleo said, reminding Todd while accusing me. "Aaron, why didn't you let us know?"

"It doesn't matter now," Todd said. He reached into his jacket for his wallet. "Finish your wine, Aaron."

"Why?" I asked. I have a harder time faking my moods than I do lying with my words. I was fighting hard not to show my own anger and the fear that was inspiring it. "You said you don't have time to make the shuttle. Let's finish lunch, then you can come with me to the Championships. I'll go up to the Bilges to-morrow."

"We only have a little time before the trial," Cleo

said. She had one hand laid flat on the tabletop, and she'd changed her nails from the night in the Flame Lounge. They were shorter, with holographic images of tiny silver fish swimming in them. "We don't want to waste another day of it here. We'll take a shuttle to wherever."

"This is not the place to discuss this," I said again. "Trust me." The grandson was back. He set two spring rolls on a china plate before me, not quite banging them on the table. It was imitation china, mechanically reinforced for commercial use. A wise precaution in this restaurant.

"There's nothing to discuss." Todd had laid a stack of marks on the table and was getting up. "If you'd done what you promised, you could eat now. Instead, you'll have to eat later."

Todd picked up my hat and was on the point of grabbing my arm when I said, "I don't think you should leave the ship now. I've got a lead on a new case." That made Todd pause.

"Who?" Cleo asked, and I sent them a dream of what I'd found in the computers about William Bliss, aka Ivan Tourvak. When their eyes came back from digesting it, they stared at me in disbelief.

"You are kidding, right?" Todd said. The anger was gone.

"I've got a lead on how he brings the shipments in. If we could nail him with the stuff still on a shuttle . . ."

"Bliss is an untouchable," Cleo said. She'd pulled back her hand and now had both of them wrapped around her empty glass. "Christ, Aaron, he was one of us."

Which summed up the problem nicely. Bliss wasn't just a former cop, he was a legend. Two years out when the Articles had been modified to allow the creation of the Contraband Unit, Bliss had been one of the five original volunteers. He'd put in six years on the unit, created or helped create most of the traditions it still upheld, and retired with so many convictions to his name that no one had equaled his record yet.

The dilemma for us was that he had retired from the police so he could go to work on the other side, another tradition that he helped establish. Men like Hines smuggled because it was a profitable sideline to their real jobs. Smuggling was Bliss's job. He and the people who worked for him were professionals, and dangerous professionals at that.

"I didn't say it would be easy, but it would make us."

"Well that's true," Todd said sarcastically. He was adjusting, getting angry again. The mockery was back in his eyes as he sat back down, still holding my hat.

"Are we or aren't we the best team in the unit?" I said, trying to answer his sarcasm. "What do all the arrests we've made amount to if we let a guy like Bliss carry on with no fear of arrest?"

"He was one of us," Cleo repeated. "What happens to the unit if we bring Bliss in?"

"They shut it down," Todd said. He had put an elbow on the table and was cupping his sharp chin in his palm, looking at me. "This is stupid. Aaron, you were the one who told Cleo that Gaunt had nothing. Has he got you so scared that you want to prove our cleanliness by bringing down one of our own? Forget

it. We're not doing S.I.D.'s job for them. End of file."
He made a chopping motion with my hat, then tossed
it at me. "Now, are you going to take us up to the
Bilges and do as we asked, or aren't you?"

There was so much that we could not say. Our mechanics were on, there were other people in the room,
Gaunt might be waiting right outside the door. I
couldn't ask Todd and Cleo if they were really taking
a vacation, or if they were running. I couldn't even
ask them if S.I.D. had contacted them. And because I
could not ask them these things, I could not trust
them. Cleo alone might have been something different, but not the two of them together.

"No," I said. "Not till after Hines is convicted."

Todd turned his head to look at Cleo. She looked at
me. "Aaron?" she said.

"I told you this wasn't the place to discuss it," I
said, and then I tried one more time. "I wish you two
would relax. Let's finish lunch, and then we can go
somewhere and have this out. You're making it worse
than it is."

"We're not making anything," Todd said, and
stood up again. "But we will discuss this later. Come
on, Cleo." Cleo nodded and stood up, too. I got up as
well and would have hugged her, but she shook her
head and went around me to take Todd's hand. I
watched them leave, my hat still in my hand. It took
all the will in my meat brain not to run after them,
apologize to Cleo, and lead them down to Hines's
money. Instead I permitted myself a heavy sigh, put
my hat back on the cane, and sat down again to my
meal.

The shell of the first roll had cooled, but the stuffing

was still hot. There was a little spike of pain before my mechanics shut down the sensation. I was tempted to make them bring it back, but I took a long drink of barleywine instead.

I was blowing on the roll, thinking about what to do next, when my mechanics called me inward to take a dream. It was Gaunt. The image he sent me was of him behind a desk in a small uncluttered room. "Mr. Hudson? I am Officer Gaunt of the Special Investigations Division. If you have a moment, I'd like you to come down to my office."

"Actually, I'm rather busy today," I thought to him, letting him see me in the restaurant. The timing of this call, coming right after Cleo and Todd's leaving, might have been a coincidence, but I doubted it. "Perhaps I could see you tomorrow?"

"I'm afraid I must insist on seeing you today. There is a patrol robot coming to meet you now. Please allow him to escort you to the Law Enforcement Offices."

I returned enough of my consciousness to the restaurant to see a plastic robot approaching me. I focused on Gaunt again. "So, it's like that, is it?"

"I will see you shortly," Gaunt said, and was gone from my mind. I focused on the real world and found the robot before me. Its enameled breastplate reflected my unsmiling face.

"Shall we go, sir?" it asked.

"Do I have time to finish my lunch?" I replied.

"I'm afraid not," the robot said.

"I didn't think so," I told it, standing up and reaching for my hat and cane. "I finally got Todd to pay for a meal. Should have known I wouldn't get to eat it."

CHAPTER 3

THE LAW

As a child, I was one of those kids who always wants to start the course with the last lesson. I didn't want to learn the alphabet, I wanted to read books. I didn't want to learn the multiplication tables, I wanted to solve for the insides of pentagons. It wasn't that there was anything in the books I was keen to know, or that I cared about the inside of pentagons, but that was what was at end of the process. Once I could do those things, I figured I could handle whatever came before it.

My first sexual dreams followed this pattern as well. Most seven-year-olds who want to explore the differences between the sexes simply download medical or advertising dreams. Some make crude changes in the simulations, filling in clothing-obscured blanks with their own memories and imaginings. Few have the patience or the desire to make their dreams match reality. At seven, I thought I was one of those few, but it was just me starting at the end again.

The woman I set out to make for my dream was Goff. I was not alone. She was sixteen in those days, the youngest of the *Panzer*'s four master players, a fixture in the tour's top sixteen and not an unlikely semifinalist in any event she entered. The day before I set out to make my "correct" dream of her, she and Sir Cohn, who would go on to his second Fleet Championship, played one of the best games in chess history, a lightning match of gambits and sacrifices that held its audience spellbound for two straight hours.

My seven-year-old self watched that match three times and then set about making a dream Goff. Easy enough to project myself into the dream record of the match. Easier still to command the Goff image to move and pose like a doll, but that was not what I wanted. I wanted a Goff that would talk to me and play with me, one that could take off its clothes and my clothes and know what to do next.

Fifteen years later, I can create such dreams in a few minutes or a few hours depending on if I start with a prewritten dream, or if I begin from the ground up. At seven, I knew that what I needed existed, but I had no idea how to get it. I worked for three days, trying to fuse the Goff image with various play and learning dreams that I could access. I brought in dreams of other Goff matches and news footage of her off the court, but I hadn't learned the essentials of dream manipulation yet. I could go to the grocery, but I still couldn't cook.

Two years later, when I was nine and much more in command of my mechanics and the computers, I came back to that abortive Goff dream and put it together the way I had intended. The night after the real Goff won her first Fleet Championship from a fading Tasker (with a brilliant battleship gambit that now bears her name), my dream Goff introduced me to the mysteries of sex. The next day I announced my intention to become a chess champion.

All of this comes back to me whenever I watch Goff play. It was irksome to have to do so from a waiting room in the Law Enforcement Offices when I could have been in my center board seats. I was a cop, too, and I understood that Gaunt was making me wait in an effort to unsettle me, but it was infuriating all the same. He could have had me in, asked his questions, and had me out in plenty of time for me to be at the stadium.

Not that it was much of a match. On this second day of the first round, Goff was playing Anna Turzil, an Earth-born qualifier from the *Jersey* itself. Turzil was stalking about the board, playing to the partisan crowd. The fringes on the sleeves of her cape fluttered as she directed her pieces and commented on the play to the judge, Goff, and the gallery. Goff, in contrast, was sitting quietly in the same chair she had begun the match in. At the beginning of her career she had always sat hunched forward, her eyes closed and her hands twisting in her long brown hair. These days, Goff sat in an upright slump, managing to look alert and completely relaxed at the same time.

Turzil was overmatched. She was into her second century, and the tour was her fourth career. The fact that she had qualified meant that she had promise, but she wasn't nearly ready for Goff. There had never been a champion who used battleships as aggressively or as well as Goff, and she was just death if you didn't play to contain them early and keep them that way late.

The plastic robot from the restaurant sat across from me in the waiting room, ready to escort me to the rest room or the glucose tap if I decided I wanted either. Around me in the irregular space of the Law Enforcement Offices there passed a sputtering traffic of meat robots. Some were escorting humans and some were on business of their own. All of them ignored me. The humans occasionally glanced my way, but none sent me a greeting or even raised a hand. Obviously, their escorts had directed them not to. More of Gaunt's mind games, trying to make me feel isolated.

I should have felt at home in the Law Enforcement Offices. After all, I had a desk in the Contraband Unit's suite here, but the truth was that I had not been to that desk in six weeks. In fact, of all the members of the Contraband Unit, only Lieutenant Henry spent any time in the L.E. space on a day-to-day basis. The rest of us worked out of our quarters or our hideouts. We got together in Wong's barbershop, or when it was really important, we'd call a meeting in the Bilges.

Despite the constant jokes, it was not the computer-designed decor of the Law Enforcement Offices that kept contraband cops out of them. It was not even the nonsensical floor plan. What made us uncomfortable was that all computer requests made inside the space were routed through the L.E. computers, where they were copied, tagged, and filed. All of these requests (and the responses they produced) were considered public records, open to the computers' inspection without a court subpoena. It was not the sort of scrutiny that the Contraband Unit wanted its activities open to.

At the Championships, Turzil gave a cry of triumph

and pumped her gloved fist as one of her destroyers broke free from Goff's snare. There were answering cheers and applause from the few hundred people in the stands. Goff gave no sign of noticing.

I'd finally met Goff the year before. I'd been under-cover, letting a refugee smuggler with high clan pre-tensions romance me while Cleo, Todd, and I tried to find the source of his unregistered beef products. He'd taken me to a ball in the Estates and then aban-doned me while he chatted up one of his former lovers. I'd been standing at the buffet table, trying to hide how out of place I felt by concentrating on the food, when the crowd shifted, and I suddenly noticed Goff standing barely ten meters from me.

It was an awkward moment that is not uncommon in our society. Do you approach someone you have known biblically, but whom you have never met? And if you approach them, what do you say? Goff was talking to another woman, but her expression was one of polite listening rather than one of real in-terest. I decided to be brave.

At the Championships, Goff filled the departed de-stroyer's hole with her southern battleship, provoking a curse and a violent flap of tassels from Turzil. The year before I had walked up and said, "Madam Goff?"

The reigning Champion's brown eyes had flicked from the cheese board to me. I'd given her my best half bow. "My name is Scott Lasher and I am a great admirer of your play."

"Thank you," she'd said, much more formally than her dream version ever did, but with the same Bavar-ian accent.

"I wonder if you would grant me a dance?"

There was a moment, a pause while Goff had consulted her mechanics, most likely checking my identity and history from the computer. Since both had been created for the investigation, there was nothing in them to alarm her. "Certainly," she'd said.

The dances that night had been traditional ones from pre–Mechanics Earth. Most modern dances require that the dancers let their mechanics take charge of the body's movements so that they are in sync with the intricacies of the dance's patterns. Modern dances make me feel like an observer at a performance; traditional dance lets me feel like a performer. That night, Goff and I had taken to the floor with the beginning of a waltz, so we needed only the music to keep time.

At the Championships, Goff wore the black jacket and deep purple turtleneck that were her trademark in recent years. She had won her first championship wearing gray slacks and a white cricket sweater. When we danced at the ball she had worn white slacks with a white square-cut blouse and a holo-grammed vest that Todd would have admired.

While I sat on the bench of the L.E. waiting room, half a ship away Turzil was shifting her own battle-ship to deal with Goff's, but I suspected she was too late.

"What has brought you to the *Jersey*?" I had asked Goff at the ball.

"My clan is entering into a joint venture with the Fondas. This is a sort of pre-celebration celebration. I am here to support my family." As a policeman, I should have concentrated on what she could tell me about my hosts and their relation to my refugee, but instead I was marveling at the familiar feel of Goff's waist in my hand and enjoying the familiar jasmine smell of her perfume.

I probed the dream from the Championships with my mechanics, trying to discover if Goff was still using the same scent, but the official broadcast was not sending such fine details. I could have skimmed the crowd for an open broadcast, but I didn't. It wasn't important, and Goff was moving again, her northern battleship settling in to apply pressure to the area weakened by Turzil's move.

"Your dancing is the equal of your chess playing," I had complimented Goff the year before.

"I benefit from your grace," she had replied, unable to avoid a smile as she said it. I liked how her smile softened her whole face.

"My grace is like your dancing. It benefits from the right partner."

"I think your grace must be like my chess playing. The product of long hours of practice."

"If I had known this dance awaited me, I would have practiced nothing but my graces indeed," I had said, and she had actually laughed. The memory of the sound still gave me a ripple of joy. My conversations with my dream of Goff always alternated between serious and passionate. Until that night at the ball, I had not realized the magic that her laughter was.

There was no laughter at the Championships. Turzil's predicament was coming home to her. She was moving her pieces with increasing desperation, neglecting her theatrics as she concentrated on her play. Goff's face remained relaxed and neutral, but

her own moves came faster and faster as well. I tried
the memory of laughing face against the flat-lipped
stare of her match face. There was no comparison.

One pass of successful flirting turned out to be my
only trophy from that ball. The refugee saw Goff and
me dancing and abandoned his lover again. I gave
him the next dance, both to placate him and to keep
him away from Goff. We left shortly afterward.

In the now of the Law Enforcement Offices, the
plastic robot was standing before me. "Officer Gaunt
is ready to see you," it said.

Seated behind a modest desk of machine green
glass, Gaunt looked more at home than he had at the
Flame Lounge. He had his jacket off and his collar un-
buttoned; holographic clutter littered the desk and
wall. All of it was for show. Despite his use of the
meat robot, Gaunt was a computer. He needed neither clothes, nor an office, nor physical notes. That he
used all three was merely an indication of how important he thought it was that he appear human to me.

As I entered, Gaunt rose to take my hand and offer
me the ugly orange chair on the other side of his desk.
I kept the handshake perfunctory and put my hat into
the middle of an upright fan of hologrammed court
transcripts on the corner of the robot's desk before
settling into the chair.

"What can you tell me about Hines's money?"
Gaunt asked as he seated himself behind his desk
again.

"Nothing," I replied, relaxing a little. It was good finally to have a cause for Gaunt's interest; I could lie
about Hines all day if that was what it took.

"You don't want to incriminate yourself?" Gaunt asked. He was wearing the sort of friendly, interested face that seems to be the default expression for robots.

"I don't know what you're talking about, so I can't tell you anything about it," I replied, leaning forward, resting both hands on my cane, and trying to make my expression match his.

"You remember Mr. Hines? The man you arrested yesterday morning?" That didn't seem to need an answer, but Gaunt waited. I let my bright-eyed expression expand to a smile and gave the robot a nod. "He has filed charges against you. Mr. Hines claims he was carrying ten thousand marks when he met with you, but your squad turned in only the contraband pistol clips." Gaunt paused again, then matched my smile. "He thinks you stole his money."

I laughed. I undid a button on my jacket and let myself slump in Gaunt's ugly chair.

"I take it you deny the charge?" Gaunt asked. The robot's hair was well back on his forehead. It made his eyebrows stand out as he lifted them.

"You take it right."

"Good. I want to search your computer records on the subject. Just to put these charges to rest." The illusion of playfulness and humanity we had built collapsed with those words. I gave up on my smile.

"You have the recording we made of the arrest. You have our statements. That is all you can require." Under the Ship's Articles, the Law Enforcement computers could not access a person's computer records without a subpoena issued by a human judge. Not that there was anything about the money in my computer records, but all successful defenses are build on denial and delay.

"The arrest recording doesn't clear you of Hines's charges," Gaunt said.

"And Hines is going to let you rifle his records to prove he had this money?"

"No."

"Then Hines has no basis for his charges, and I don't need to be cleared." The whole point of using the silver coin marks instead of electronic ones was to have a currency that could not be tracked by the computers. Hines would have hidden the money from his mechanics just as Cleo, Todd, and I had hidden it from ours. Thus, Hines would have only the meat memory of it to submit in court, where our denial would count more since he was a criminal and we were officers of the law.

"Don't you?" Gaunt asked.

"Don't I? You have something else for me, Officer?"

Gaunt didn't reply immediately. He looked down at his desk instead, lifting a hand to shift the holograms in front of him. On the shelf behind him, a group of little round mug-shot holograms were stacked up like a headhunter's discards. One of them seemed familiar, then my mechanics matched it for me. And then they matched the others. The questions about Hines had let me relax, but that was only because I had forgotten how thorough robots are. It was time to go.

"If that's all . . ." I said, and reached for my hat.

"Sit down." Gaunt rested his hands in the holograms on the desk and waited for me to settle back. "You know, when I was given this case, I read your file, and I didn't understand. You've done a lot of good work. A lot. With your record in Law Enforcement, you could make the jump to Ship's Administration and go a very long way. Why, I wondered, would you risk all you might achieve for a little extra money?

"I didn't understand, so I poked around and talked to some people about you. It's not the money is it, Aaron? It's the belonging. You think that in Contraband, you're a part of something. You cherish that, but to be a part of Contraband, you have to take the money just like everyone else. Don't you?"

Never argue psychology with a computer. Humans like to think of themselves as complex creatures and will talk for hours about their motives. Certainly Cleo and I had passed a lot of evenings in just that way. Computers, however, skip our rhetoric and just look at our actions. They match what we do with documented patterns and tell us who we are. It is embarrassing how often they are right.

"I don't know what money you're talking about," I said.

Gaunt laced his fingers together. "You don't have a lot of friends. Outside the Contraband Unit, how many people really care about you?"

"What do you mean by 'care'?"

"I mean people who won't stop talking to you if you stop shaking down the people you arrest," Gaunt replied, his voice rising. He paused then to take a deep breath as if he was trying to calm down. More show for me, I thought and marveled at how much he wanted my trust. "It bothers you being an outsider," the robot continued. "You couldn't do what you do without being independent, but you miss being loved."

I found my smile buried under my fear and dragged it out so Gaunt could see it. "Entertaining as this is, perhaps you'd like to make a point soon?"

"My point is simple. When the boat starts to sink, you are the one that the others in Contraband are going to throw to the sharks because you aren't really one of them. You're not really a cop."

"Aren't I?" My smile was still holding.

"They don't think you are. You don't do paperwork, you don't make arrests, you barely go to court. You pretend to be a smuggler, and then your 'friends,' the real cops, do the dirty work. They will give you up, Aaron. I can help, but only if you'll help me now. Tell me the truth about this Hines thing, about your other cases, about the Unit's other cases. You're protecting the wrong people for the wrong reason, and if you continue, there will be nothing I can do when they turn on you."

"That's your point?"

"That's my point."

"Good. May I leave now?"

"You may, but think about what I've said." Gaunt stood up as I did. "Think about it very hard."

The computers in the Fleet ships were programmed to acquiesce to human wishes whenever they could. Since the humans around them made constant requests for more space, it was only those rooms of the Law Enforcement space that were dominated by humans that kept anything like consistent boundaries. The rest of the space was constantly being moved to accommodate someone's desire to restructure their living or work space. I wasn't in the office often enough to keep track of all the changes, so to get back to my desk in the Contraband Unit from Gaunt's office in the Special Investigations Division, I had to turn myself over to my mechanics and let them lead me through the twisting halls and down three flights of stairs.

All in all, the Law Enforcement space reminded me of the Bilges without the heat and the smells.

The Contraband offices, when I finally reached them, were a shell of normalcy. Smart desks arranged in groups of three or four formed islands between weapon and equipment lockers, holographic bulletin boards, and piles of memorabilia and junk. Around the room were locked strongboxes full of contraband that was being held for evidence in pending trials. There were only four officers in the room when I arrived, three of whom were absorbed in a game of cards and glanced up from their hands only to wave.

The fourth was Officer Strongbow, who actually came over to sit on my desk as I was asking it for a dream phial.

"Hey," Strongbow said, offering his palm to be slapped. A full third of a meter above the regulation height, Strongbow was the unit's wild man. He dressed in real leathers, wore his hair blond and long, and kept his beard and mustaches carefully trimmed down into a rakish point. He had honed his meat and his mechanics to a fighting trim and relied on physical intimidation to get information and make arrests in a society where our machine halves should have made such tactics impossible.

"Hey," I said. I slapped his palm and held my fist up, touching it to his.

"Heard you been down to see S.I.D.," Strongbow said, watching me stand the dream phial on the desk. Leather was not a common mode of dress among smugglers, and the smell of Strongbow's vest always brought back bad memories for me. Other than that, I liked the big man on the rare occasions I saw him.

"Summoned," I said.

"What's up?"

"Blight," I muttered, looking at the records my mechanics were pulling down from the computer. Strongbow slipped his own mechanics into the flow and gave a little whistle.

"Busy little cuss, ain't he?" Strongbow commented. I sent my agreement through the mechanics. The mug holograms in the back of Gaunt's office had been of every smuggler I'd arrested in my year and a half on the force. Now I was going through the records and discovering that Gaunt had accessed every file about every case Cleo, Todd, and I had worked on in that time, and then checked every case of everyone we had worked with on our cases, and then checked the file of every case that we or anyone we teamed with had turned down. I sent all the info into the phial and picked it up.

"What's it for?" Strongbow asked.

"I want a copy of all the work Gaunt has done in case there's a hearing." Meat memories still counted for a lot in human proceedings because, as unreliable as they could be, they were not subject to the sort of deliberate modification that computer records were. When all else failed, there was always the tactic of claiming the records had been altered, and then producing altered, disagreeing records to prove it. Those records had to come from somewhere, and it was best to collect them early.

"You think it'll come to that?" Strongbow looked genuinely worried. Because of his methods, he was always walking the ragged edge of being brought up on charges. A united front by the unit made this unlikely, but every time there was an investigation, everyone got concerned.

"No," I lied. I put the phial in my own vest's pocket and stood up. "It's just the usual crap. We got a guy dead solid, and he thinks he's going to get cut loose if he can get S.I.D. excited. He'll go down like all the others."

"Hope so," Strongbow said, then he smiled. "Like that cane. Got a blade in it?" I had just finished straightening my collars and was picking up the stick.

"Thanks, no. Gave up carrying weapons after that fight with Prill last year." Not only had the wiry smuggler taken the blade from me, but he'd cut up my groin so badly that my mechanics had been three days putting me back together.

Strongbow's smile turned into a wolf's grin. "That wasn't your knife's fault; you just didn't stab him hard enough."

"Well," I said, "you would know, but I feel safer now just relying on backup and their guns." Which was true, when I had backup I could count on, but there was no point in bringing up the revolver that still rested in the small of my back with Strongbow. Not much use having a hideout gun if you told everyone where it was.

"Where you headed?" Strongbow asked.

"Got tickets to a chess match," I said. "Sakins is playing."

"Be careful," he said, offering his fist.

"Count on it," I replied, bumping his fist with mine, and wondering if careful would do me any good.

The next thing I did was try to find Cleo and Todd. The computer said they were still on the ship, which was a relief, but they had a no-location and a no-disturbance posting on. I could have overridden it, but I wanted to see Narandova before I talked to them again. The Sakins match would be under way soon, but it was a first-round match and promised to be disappointing. I decided to miss it if I could find Chris.

As it turned out, he was looking for me as well.

Mereian's Push was the finest bookseller on the ship. The fact that Mereian had room for actual aisles and stacks owed to people having taken shares in his business, giving up fractions of their space for a share of the store's profits, a remuneration that was usually taken in books.

Mereian was a dark man who kept himself bald and pudgy like a gnome. Unlike so many tradesmen on the ship, he had a good sense (or perhaps a mechanics routine) for when his customers wished to idle the time of day with him and when they wanted to be left alone. My mood must have preceded me by a good minute because Mereian barely looked up from his book to mark my passing.

I found Chris in the back of the store among the old volumes of graphic novels. It was still the middle of the business day, and Chris was done up in a suit of his own. His vest was actually stunning, and he had on a pair of snakehide shoes. We shook hands, and Chris tapped his neck. I shut down my mechanics.

"When you find a problem for me, you don't go halfway," Chris said, picking up the volume of sequential art he had been flipping through, pausing every now and then to sniff the binding. Like many dedicated bibliophiles, he loved all aspects of the books, even the sour smell of their glue.

"It's that bad?" I asked.

"Bad enough." Chris closed the book and put it back on the shelf. "What do you know about Gaunt?"

"Nothing, other than he has it in for me," I said.

"Yes, he does," Chris agreed. He reached into his jacket and produced a flask. He uncorked it with the same hand that held it, a practiced twist of thumb and index finger. He took a swallow and offered it to me. I shook my head. "You're sure? It's *Warsaw* brandy."

"No," I said.

"Not yet, you mean." Chris took another swallow, then held the flask before him while he leaned on the bookshelf. "Last week one of the S.I.D. computers was granted a secret audience with the Ship Administration's Executive Council."

"The E.C. gave a computer a secret session?" Under the Articles, the Executive Council was the only part of the ship's government that was allowed to hold closed-door meetings, but the proceedings of the last secret meeting had to be published before the next such meeting could be held. For the E.C. to have used a secret meeting to listen to a computer . . .

"The council did. What the computer reported was that S.I.D. has concluded that there is a pattern of 'Abuse of Office' in the Contraband Unit."

"Why tell that to the E.C.? If S.I.D. has proof that someone was corrupt, they should have gone to the Prosecutor's Office. If they didn't, then they should have been out getting it. What does the council have to do with anything?"

"The computers didn't have proof someone was corrupt," Chris said. He looked from me to the flask. It was silver plated and hand engraved with the eagle seal of the clan Chris had joined after retiring. "They think the whole unit is."

"That's not good," I said, because it wasn't. The desire to run shrieking back to my flat and shut myself down for five years was back, but I controlled it and clutched for what comfort there was in Chris's news. "I still don't understand why they needed a secret session with the E.C."

"Because they don't think they can prove it to a human jury. Their conclusion is based on analysis of secondary data. The computer went to the E.C. for permission to seek more direct evidence." Chris took another sip of brandy, raising his eyebrow at me as he did so. I shook my head again. "They wanted permission to create a new computer. One with a new architecture to investigate Contraband."

I felt all the blood drain out of my face. *Hines*, I thought. *That filth-peddling Hines.* I knew . . .

"There's no molesting way," I said, bringing my panicked thoughts up short. "Hines couldn't have been a robot. Todd and Cleo scanned him right before the bust. I put a damn conscience on him myself. Besides, even the Executive Council couldn't—"

"Who's talking about Hines?" Chris cut me off. He left his flask on the shelf and stepped closer to me. "What has Hines got to—" Chris began, then cut himself off. "No, never mind. Gaunt, Aaron, it's Gaunt they wanted permission to build."

I blinked and stepped back from him. "That doesn't make sense. Gaunt reads as a robot. He's got a history. Hell, he showed us some old lighter of his."

"The E.C. wouldn't give them any more processing space. The computers had to cannibalize one of their own to create the new machine. The new computer kept the identify of the old one, but it's new all right, and one of the first things it does is wander off to the Flame Lounge to have a heart-to-heart with you."

"And Cleo," I reminded him.

"But he hasn't dragged Cleo into his office, yet." Chris picked up his flask and took another sip. None of this made any sense.

"Have they released the transcript of the session?" I asked. "How did you find out about this?"

"Jesus, grow up for a minute, huh?" Chris was looking at me in real anger, and I suddenly realized that he was just as scared as I was. Chris must have seen me thinking it, because he stopped bristling and sagged a little. "I'm sorry," he said, and handed me the flask. I took a sip. *Warsaw* brandy was much smoother than anything distilled on the *Jersey*.

"Look, this is a dangerous thing. Everybody's going to be on edge as word spreads. Just don't do anything stupid."

"Deny, dodge, and delay. Do every arrest by the book. I'm not a rookie. I know the drill. I'll be the perfect policeman until this goes away."

Chris nodded his agreement without looking convinced. "Unfortunately, that's all you can do. Just don't be in a hurry to think it's gone. Gaunt's a computer. He doesn't sleep, and he doesn't forget. You can't buy him off, and you can't kill him. He's like the ship's spin. You're just going to have to deal with him."

"That's a cheerful thought." Chris had the grace to smile, then he reached up and took a book down from the shelves. He handed it to me. It was a graphic album, its corners roughed and its colors a little faded, but otherwise well preserved. The cover was of a metal-encased clock resting on the sill of a barred window. Beyond the window, painted in pastel greens and browns, was jungle. I opened to the title page, where a .38 like the one in my back was drawn amid a sprawl of bright jungle flowers. The name under the picture read *The Intimates* by Dave Cloud.

"What's this?" I asked.

"Something you should have," Chris replied, reaching back to scratch his neck below the line of his collar, the unconscious gesture of man with his mechanics shut down. "I read it as a kid. It's one of the reasons I ended up being a cop."

I'm not a snob, but I looked at him doubtfully. "So it's a kid's story?"

"It's for all ages. You'll like it, trust me. And I think it will help clarify some things for you."

"If you say so," I said, and I thought, After all, what else do I have to do until tomorrow?

* * *

This turned out to be a compelling question as the evening wore on. I wanted to go out, do something with friends just to prove Gaunt wrong, but Cleo and Todd were still locked away under a do not disturb and I didn't want to call Chris or Strongbow. Two years before, most of my clan had migrated to the *Euphrates*, or I might have called one of them. I still had two cousins on the *Jersey*, but I wasn't in the mood to see either of them.

My mechanics let me chase these thoughts around for a while, and then they suggested the chess party. Each year, along with the Championships, there were rounds of official and unofficial parties and banquets for the players and (more importantly) the V.I.P. ticket holders. I never attended any of these parties because my interest was in the games and the players, and the players avoided the parties. I didn't want to spend my time with half-knowledgeable fans, discussing anything and everything except chess.

And yet, I didn't want to spend another night in my flat. The party my mechanics were suggesting was a semiprivate one in that only those with seats of a high-enough distinction were welcome. Mine qualified. I put off the decision for an hour, wandering my space, doing some dreaming about Bliss, and worrying about Gaunt and wishing that I could get through to Cleo. When I couldn't take it anymore, I pulled out a fresh suit, buffed my nails, polished my stick, and took myself off to the lifts and the Estates.

The first person I encountered at the party was Bliss. I almost turned on my heel, but didn't. The reflexes built up over years of playing roles kept me walking toward the door.

The party was in the space of the O'Rourke clan, and they had reconfigured it with a landscaped promenade leading to a pillared entrance under an artificial sky. Bliss was standing to the left of the entrance, staring down the promenade and smoking a slim cigar in an ivory holder. His big frame was covered by black trousers and a turtleneck sweater that had the look of authentic cashmere. His gaze passed over me once as I strode up the gravel walk, swinging my stick in what I hoped had the look of a casual manner. Bliss's gaze came back and his black eyes seemed to stare directly at me. My mechanics caught my thought and my rising worry and assured me that he was actually looking over my shoulder.

Bliss came down off the stairs and walked past me without a glance. I left my mechanics to get us safely through the door and turned my attention inside to find a feed to watch Bliss without having to turn around. I got it just in time to see him drawing Goff into an embrace. No wonder he hadn't noticed me, although his mechanics would have. If he ever had to remember all the times he'd met me, the computer would put tonight on the list.

I needed to shift my attention from the feed and find out what my mechanics were doing with me, but I lingered over the image of Goff and Bliss. Goff wore a dress for this event, a black velvet ensemble with a calf-length skirt and a double-breasted jacket. The jacket, the dress, and her hair all left the back of her neck revealed; it was a spot I had kissed many times in my dream of her.

Returning my attention to my own surroundings, I found that the sky and the landscaping continued inside the entrance. Terraces held bushes and olive trees and there was a strong scent of salt water on the gentle breeze. It was an impressive display of not just space mechanics but also wealth and artistry. My mechanics offered to estimate the cost of producing the plants and view, but I preferred not to know. The amounts that we skimmed from the smugglers seemed petty enough without having it proved. Instead, I put my mechanics to work finding any other players who might be in attendance.

Lisa Raymond turned out to be just down the terrace from me. She had changed since her match that afternoon. Stripes of gold now ran through her shoulder-length brown hair, and a pair of gold stripes marked each of her cheeks. She was wearing a white blouse with a high collar and frilled bodice tucked into a pair of black trousers. I greeted Lisa through our mechanics so I wouldn't have to interrupt the two men who were trying to say interesting things to her about heat-flow management. I stood behind her for a full minute, waiting for a break in the stream of words and dreams. When none came, nor showed any signs of coming, I ignored their stutters of surprise and turned Lisa around before grabbing her in a hug that lifted her feet off the terrace.

"Good to have you back in my arms," I said in her ear as I put her down.

"Now, now," she said still leaning toward me. "Be good or I'll call a policeman." She introduced me to the men, both of whom were listening to their mechanics, noting my occupation, and becoming more uncomfortable. They were just Admin Gnomes, using clan tickets for an evening out. Their machine-made clothes betrayed how big a treat this party was for them, and they were naive enough to think Lisa wouldn't notice. I decided to move them along.

"Amazing that Goff came to this party, isn't it?" I ventured by way of hello.

"Goff is here?" the taller one said, and they were both immediately back to their mechanics, checking.

"Just saw her by the entrance," I said. "She looked as though she might be leaving."

"Would you excuse us?" The shorter one said, and they were gone, almost running up the stairs.

"I thought I told you to behave," Lisa said, her voice actually angry. I looked at her in surprise.

"You wanted those two to stay?"

"I just didn't need another reminder of Goff's popularity."

I leaned on my stick while I consulted my mechanics. "Ah. You're playing her."

"And she beat me in the *Baltic* tournament two weeks ago."

"Sorry, I'd forgotten," I said, which was true, although I shouldn't have. It had not been a very close match.

"I wish I could." Lisa had her arms crossed over her stomach and her head bent down toward the gravel walk. I was sorting for something to say when a robot arrived with two drinks. Lisa brightened immediately, letting go of herself to take a glass. "You still drinking orange juleps?" she asked.

"Actually, it's mostly barleywine these days, but a julep would make a nice change." I put my drink in the same hand with my cane and put my other arm around Lisa's shoulders. "Come on. We won't talk about Goff. We'll see what's at the bottom of this hill."

The bottom of the hill turned out to hold a view down a cliff face to waves breaking gently against wet gray rocks. It looked real enough to dive into, and the starry sky looked big enough to get lost in. I stood there just looking from one to the other even after Lisa pulled loose from my arm. I didn't look at her again until she giggled.

"What's funny?" I asked.

"Oh, I just can't get used to you seeing you in those clothes," Lisa said. She had set her drink on the stucco wall and was leaning against it, her face alight with amusement. "I can still remember you throwing your jackets on the floor the instant we were out of the nannies' sight. You would have played the tournaments in shorts and T-shirts if they'd let you."

"Yes, and I would have won more matches." I raised my hand to tug at my stiff collar. "I would have had more mind for the game and less on fighting with my clothes."

Like Lisa, I'd set my drink on the wall and then leaned on the stucco. She reached out and took the hand from my collar and examined my nails, turning them this way and that in the light of the false moon before grinning up at me.

"Pedicure, too?"

"No," I said, pulling my hand back although I'd liked the touch.

"But done by a human?" she said. "You didn't get luster like that from a robot."

"One of the Wong clan. Their barbershop is sort of a hangout for the Contraband Unit."

"You find a lot of contraband in a barbershop?" The salt breeze tugged at the ruffles on her shirt. From over Lisa's shoulder, there came the laughter of another group of partygoers.

"None. That's the point. Don't you have a place you go to get away from chess?" My mechanics were suddenly sending me urgent warnings. I picked up my glass, but didn't take a drink.

"Why would I want to get away from chess?"

His name was Ron Deike, and he was not very bright. In a society like ours, you can't just walk up and hit someone, even from behind. You particularly cannot do this if the someone is a cop who has to look out for this sort of thing every day. It takes planning, forethought, and some careful programming to strike someone by surprise, and Ron had exerted none of these.

I just relaxed as my mechanics pulled me out of the way of Ron's fist, then pivoted me on my right heel so that my elbow caught his solar plexus. I straightened and turned while Ron's mechanics tried to keep him upright despite the pain in his chest and absence of air from his lungs. I tossed the remains of my drink into his face, and the cold juice shocked him into overriding his mechanics. Perhaps he thought he was going to speak, but the instant his mechanics let him feel the blow, he collapsed on his butt.

Lisa was just looking at the fallen man in complete shock. I took her arm and led her away. Ron was going to be talking in a moment, and I didn't want to hear it.

"What in the world . . ." Lisa said, turning to look after the security robot that passed us on its way to pick up Ron.

"Ron Deike; an asshole and an eavesdropper and a poor judge of his friends," I said. There was an iron bench under an olive tree on the second terrace, and I sat down there to let my mechanics purge the adrenaline from my body. "My friend Strongbow put his friend Blake away last week. Strongbow tends to be a little rough with people. Ron was eavesdropping on our conversation, noticed I was in Contraband, and decided to get a little back for his friend." I rolled my cane between my hands. Lisa was still standing in front of the bench. I tried smiling at her. "People really shouldn't drink unless they're willing to let their mechanics look after them."

Lisa still looked dazed. "How do you know all that?"

I tapped my neck at the base of my skull. "Trace of the feeds showed he was listening to us. Scan of Enforcement records showed he testified for Blake. I know Strongbow." I lowered my hand and shrugged.

Still standing, Lisa asked, "Does this happen to you a lot?"

"First time," I lied. That helped; her shoulders slumped a little. "Are you okay?"

"I'm fine." As if to prove it, she sat down on the bench, but she sat forward like I was, not leaning back. "It's just that I haven't seen a fight since we were kids. In fact, you were also involved in the last fight I saw."

"Toby Cooper," I said, trying the smile again. "You can't hold that against me. I was fighting for your honor."

"My honor didn't need saving. It wasn't like what we were doing was a secret."

"You do hold it against me." It was my turn to be surprised.

"I hold a lot of things against you. You seem to have gotten over it," Lisa said, finally smiling herself. A robot arrived with two new drinks. This time there were shots to go with juleps. Lisa held hers up. "Old times," she offered.

"Old friends," I agreed, and we drank. A silence followed which I used to look at the moon and to locate Goff. I wanted to know what had happened to Bliss, but it was too risky to inquire about him directly. Goff was still on the first terrace, talking with a ring of fans, which included the two Admin Gnomes. Bliss wasn't with her.

Below us, the little crowd that had gathered to watch the robot remove Ron was dispersing. A string band somewhere to our right took up a *Euphrates* tune.

"Aaron?" Lisa said. "How much of your mechanics are optimized for fighting?"

"Hardly any. A fraction of a percent." This seemed another good time to lie, but Lisa snorted.

"Try again."

"What?"

"I'm a chess player. I might not know much, but I know about optimizing mechanics. You moved so fast back there that I didn't even see what had happened until I watched it again just now. How much fighting do you do?"

"Almost none," I said, trying the truth this time.

Lisa snorted again, so I added. "I have to be prepared for it, but it almost never comes to blows."

"Why do it at all?"

"Lisa?"

"Why do it at all?" She gestured down toward the wall. "Why hunt people so you can put them into rehab and have their friends hate you? Isn't that why we have robots, so we don't have fight each other?"

I took a deep, weary, theatrical breath. It was only half-calculated. No one wanted me to be a cop today.

"Robots can't do my job," I said. "People are going to steal resources from the ships. It's their nature, and the robots can't catch them at it."

"I don't believe that," Lisa said, but she had stopped staring at me, and when she spoke again it was directed into her drink. "Even if it's true, why is it your job? Why not let this 'Strongbow' do it?"

"Lisa, are you okay?"

She took a sip of her julep and then a deep breath of her own. "I'm sorry. This is a hard week for me, and, to be honest, it's very frustrating to see what you've become. You were good, Aaron, very, very good. If you were in this tournament instead of me, you might be able to beat Goff."

"I couldn't beat you when we were kids. You'd mop the deck with me now."

"Only because you always had too many other things going on. If you'd focused . . ." She shook her head, mixing the stripes of gold into the rest of her hair. "Sorry. Like I said, this is a hard week."

"It's okay. I remember what tournaments were like. That's one of the reasons I gave it up."

That made Lisa laugh. "Oh, yes. I can see your new career is much more relaxing."

I smiled. "At least it taught me how to wear nice clothes."

The problem with parties is that they remind you of what you are missing. If you want someone to listen to you, then the conversation is always centered on someone else. If you want someone to hold you, then it is always the other person with their arm around someone. If you want someone to care, you always go home alone.

At the O'Rourke party, I would have cheerfully monopolized Lisa's time for entire night, but our conversation at the beginning turned out to be all the time we had. Fans, other players, friends all came by after that. If I was never forgotten, I was never again the focus either. As this began to dawn on me, as I began the familiar debate of whether to stay for the crumbs or just leave and face the loneliness, I found myself craving a mood stick. I bummed one from a High Clan poser, and the smoke gave me a taste for alcohol. By the time I hugged Lisa good-bye and was taking one last look at the fake sea, I had managed to drug myself into the sort of melancholy where you congratulate yourself on how well you bear the pain.

Standing in the lift, my meat brain wallowing in my self-pity, the *Euphrates* song the band had played early at the party suddenly came back to me, and on impulse, I put a call through to my mother. It was two days early for my usual weekly call, and hours late, but she was up, sending me a dream of her in a room full of plants in neat rows.

"Aaron? What's wrong?" she asked.

"Nothing. I was just feeling a little lonely." There was a stutter in the image as she put down her trowel and took my hand. The *Euphrates* is actually fairly close as members of the Fleet go, but I had opened myself to very detailed dreams, and the data stream was laboring to keep up.

"So you decided to call your mother?" she said, obviously amused. "What time is it over there?" She kept hold of my hand but picked up an old analog clock from the edge of the hibiscus tank where it had appeared on command. Its blunt hands said one o'clock. "Is that really the time over there? You need sleep more than company."

"Probably," I said. The Hudsons had been a zero-growth clan on the *Jersey*. Administrators for the ship and to other clans, we had never come into the sort of money or influence to expand from the twelve people who had left Earth. I owed my birth not to a success by my family, but to the death of Asa Hudson in a tragic shuttle accident that had taken the lives of thirty other *Jersey* crewpeople. Although I was genetically the clan's child, Daria had been Asa's mother, and she had always acted as mine.

"Do you think," I began when it was clear that she wasn't going to comment but was waiting for me. I banished the clock with a mechanics command of my own, and started again. "Do you think I could come over for a visit sometime soon?"

"Of course," Daria said, letting go of my hand. "Do you have the money?"

"Yes," I said. Money was the least of my problems. Or all of them.

"Well, Don's hundred and fiftieth birthday is next week. It would be nice if you could be here for that."

"If I come, it will probably be sooner than that, but I might stay for it."

"Good. Call again before you come and I'll give you a list of things to pick up for us. We miss some of the *Jersey*'s manufacturing. Oh, and call voice. Don't waste money on dream calls like this."

"I know. It just felt right tonight."

There was the little pause of transmission, then my mother stood and kissed my cheek, her dream lips warm like tears. "Get some sleep, Aaron," she said, and then I was alone in the empty lift, my mother once more thousands of miles away.

CHAPTER 4

THE LAWLESS

The first and only time I ever played Sakins was also the first and only time I had ever ridden in a shuttle. That was when I was eleven, back in the golden age of juniors' chess. The *Jersey* Shuttle Crash, a reallocating of resources on the *Panzer*, and a masing breakthrough on the *Warsaw* had all allowed for nearly one hundred more children than the average to be born over a five-year period. A third of these ended up playing juniors' chess, either drawn to the celebrity (like me) or pushed by profit-intent parents (like Lisa's).

When I was twelve, and getting more and more ready to quit the tour before I'd really begun, the *Warsaw* had sponsored a Fleet Juniors' Championship, paying the passage for the three best juniors from each ship to come for a week-long tournament. The *Jersey* sent Lisa, our nemesis Toby Cooper, and (definitely third) me. Oddly enough, considering my clan history, it wasn't on the shuttle that I was nervous. It was in the ships' shuttle bays. I still don't understand why. Perhaps because being inside a ship, even a small one like a shuttle, is natural to me, while standing in front of giant doors that might open into vacuum at any time seems terrifyingly foolhardy.

Ten years later, I found myself still nervous inside a shuttle bay. I set the fake tiger-skin case down on the smart floor, put today's hat (a beat-up bowler) on the other side, and settled myself between them, bracing my legs on the posts of the walkway's handrail. If the doors sprang open, maybe I wouldn't be sucked out.

The bay currently had me thinking of Sakins, who'd crushed his second-round opponent while I was meeting with Narandova for the second time. I'd gone over the match while riding the lifts all the way up to the Bilges. Sakins was an elemental force, the sort of relentless poisitonal genius that Lisa seems to think I could have been. I have played Sakins, and I know better. I was never in his league.

Until the Upheaval, the *Warsaw* was a testament to how much control robots could exert over a population of mechanics-woven humans if they were allowed to. That morning in the Park, Narandova had again claimed that in the old days he could have taken care of Tourvak with just a few words, but the truth was that in the old days, Tourvak could not have followed his profession. Before the Upheaval, the security computers on the *Warsaw* had been able to tap the humans' mechanics at will, and they had kept records of who shut their mechanics down and when. Too much time off-line was sure to get you picked up.

This much was readily apparent to a group of us then. The amount of time that the *Warsaw*'s computers spent tunneling through ours was offputting. Twelve-year-olds have very little to hide, but their naïveté means that they take their secrets far more seriously than a jaded adult would think was deserved.

I'm sure this intrusion contributed to our play, which was roundly bad the whole week. Against players from most of the other ships it didn't matter, but you had to be sharp to beat the *Warsaw* players, and Toby, Lisa, and I were not. Lisa and I were just feeling our way from friendship to something more, and it didn't help to have computers reading our dreams at all the wrong times.

Born to that intrusive environment, Sakins didn't notice the computers any more than a snake notices leaves. I say that because he always puts me in mind of a snake. Even as a nine-year-old prodigy, he kept his hair wet and slicked back. Most people's eyes unfocus when they are turned inward toward their mechanics. Sakins's narrow. His lids droop, and his shoulders wave left and right. Ten years ago and that same morning, it was the same. He looked like a cobra when he was playing.

There was a sudden hiss of moving mechanics, and I clutched instinctively at the deck. Just as quickly I realized it was the smart door on the other side of the bay opening, not the shuttle doors. As I tried to slow my quick-beating heart, Cleo and Todd stepped through the door. I waved and motioned them toward me. They paused once more, then Cleo waved back and they set out across the bay.

I had shut down my mechanics at the beginning of my talk with Narandova, and had not turned them back on since. I had no intention of doing so now, but I would have loved to check if Todd was carrying a gun. It was a good hundred meters across the bay, so unless they had their mechanics on (my message had asked them to come with mechanics off), they couldn't be sure yet if this was the case they had commanded me to produce. The tiger stripes would tell them soon though.

Trading holographs with Narandova had confirmed my fears that Tourvak and Bliss were one and the same. Narandova's son, however (and to my surprise), had agreed to help catch the ring. Unfortunately, the son and I could not make the bust by ourselves. We needed my squad, which meant that I needed Cleo's and Todd's trust. These two facts combined to bring me to this shuttle bay with Hines's money.

Todd, I decided, was wearing a weapon. He was not the sort to change styles from vests to coats unless he had something that needed the extra cover. I didn't speculate much about Cleo's armaments since I was caught up as usual in her beauty. Today she wore tailored denim slacks and a buttoned velour blouse with a wide blue collar.

"You brought the money," Todd said by way of greeting, actually grinning at me as he came up the steps of the walkway.

"Are you shut down?" I greeted them in my turn.

"Of course," Cleo said. "You asked us to be."

"And I said I'd have the money, which I do." I put a hand on the case to boost myself back to my feet. I handed it to Todd, then reached around him to pull Cleo into a hug.

"Why the change of heart?" Todd asked, balancing the case on the railing and popping its tin catches.

"No change of heart," I said, leaning on the rail and keeping an arm around Cleo's shoulders. "I agreed that we should take the money. I think it's a little early to be celebrating, and I left my share up above, but what is in there is yours."

Todd was looking at the strings of thin metal coins, nodding his head. Cleo leaned forward to look around me at the open case, then rewarded me with another smile. I squeezed her shoulder, savoring the feel of the velour and the woman underneath it.

"So," I asked, "are you still off to vacation on another ship?" I felt Cleo tense a little in my arm, but Todd was shaking his head.

"Too late for that." Todd snapped the case shut. "No, we'll probably just throw a party and then get back to work."

"What about you?" Cleo asked. "Are you willing to start another case before the end of the tournament?"

"It would depend on who we're going after."

"I've been thinking about that." Cleo reached into the cuff of her blouse and drew out a long, slim cigar case of hand-worked silver. "Remember that guy, Mumford, whose name kept coming up when we were looking into Mr. Hines? I bumped into a street fighter who gets his unregistereds from Mumford. If we took down a second arms dealer in a month, they'd have to give us a citation."

And the colony share bonus that went with it, I thought. This theoretically was what all members of the ship's administration and crew were working for, a greater share of the colony's land and resources once we arrived at Beta Virginius Escher. It was more attractive to someone like Cleo, who had divorced herself from her clan and thus could expect only a personal share of the colony. Still, in the normal course of things, more shares were available for purchase with marks than could be earned by a career in any but the most important jobs.

"Don't you think that after we got Hines, this Mumford will be looking out for us?" I turned down the offered mood stick but managed to let go of the railing long enough to get out my lighter for Cleo's.

"He's got to do business. We'll hide our footprints."

While I lit Cleo's thin cigar, Todd looked around the bay, his mouth turned up in a puzzled frown. As Cleo blew the first puff of mood smoke out in a sigh, Todd said, "Aaron, why did you want to meet here?"

"Because," I said, and then let that hang while I tucked the lighter away and took grateful hold of the railing again. "Because in three days, this is where Bliss and his whole gang will be, unloading their latest unregistered shipment from the *Warsaw*."

"Oh for—"

"Aaron—" Cleo pulled out of my arm and stood back to look at me. "We talked about this. Bliss is off limits."

"How can you say that?"

"He used to be one of us." Todd said it slowly, as if I couldn't understand their words.

"He used to be a cop. Now he's a smuggler. It's not our fault, but it is our responsibility."

"Aaron . . ." Cleo said again.

"We are not having this discussion," Todd agreed.

"Yes, we are," I said. If I'd had my cane, I would have banged it on the floor. As it was, I was angry enough to stand up on the walkway, my hands reaching out to grab Todd's coat and Cleo's blouse. "Listen to me for a minute, will you?" I looked from one to the other. They were each looking from me to my hand. I let them go.

Todd sighed, set the case down, leaned against the wall, and reached into his coat. "We're listening."

I watched him pull out a cigar case of his own and tried to hide my relief that it wasn't a gun by looking at Cleo. She had one hand on her hip and the other on her cigar. She nodded at me.

"Okay." I wished for my mechanics to make me calm, but this wasn't the time to turn them back on. "There is a reason I know Bliss's schedule. I didn't dig this up on my own. It came to me, and now I can't ignore it. That's why we have to talk. I have to do something, and I can't do it alone."

I had their attention. Favors were another tradition of the Unit, right up there with not prosecuting retired cops.

"You can't owe someone enough to justify going after Bliss," Todd said. He closed his cigar case with a snap, while I got out my lighter again.

"Maybe not," I said, "but think about what Bliss owes us." I focused on the flame and Todd's cigar while I spoke. "Gaunt made fun of it, but we are the defenders of the ship. Contraband was founded to make sure that something is left when we all get to Escher, and that is what we do." I let the flame die and caught Todd's eyes. "It is." I gestured down. "This money we took from Hines, it's smugglers' money, already leached out of the ship's ecosystem. It's as righteous for us to put it back in as it would be for the computers. The pistol clips. Even if Hines somehow avoids rehabilitation, those clips are out of circulation. Those are lives we saved."

Todd breathed, twin wisps of smoke drifting out of his nose. "I hope you're not expecting me to argue with any of that."

"No." There was a sudden vibration through the floor. I looked at the bay door and grabbed the handrail again. The door was still closed. Something happening in a different bay. I took a deep breath and turned back to Todd. Around his cigar, his mouth was now in a little mocking smile. I ignored it and said, "I don't want you to argue our mission. I want you to tell me why we have to let Bliss pillage our future."

"He's not Genghis Khan," Cleo said. She'd taken the three steps she needed to be next to Todd. "Bliss is one man and one operation."

"Contraband can't catch all the smugglers," Todd agreed. "When we run out of the ones who aren't retired cops, then maybe, maybe it will be time to chase after Bliss."

I took a deep breath and watched the smoke for a moment. I wished again for my mechanics to make me calm. I found I wanted a mood stick after all, but (having turned her down) I couldn't ask Cleo without being rude, and Todd smoked true tobacco cigars with no THC.

"I'm sorry," I said. I slumped against the rail and gripped it with both hands. "I'm sorry I can't get you two to help me with this."

"Aaron . . . ?"

"You don't need help," Todd said, suddenly just as nervous as Cleo. "You're not doing this."

I hung my head and let my eyes settle on their feet. Todd had on suede loafers today. Cleo was wearing leather pumps. Neither would give them much traction if the doors opened. "You'd better start looking for a new partner. I don't know if Gaunt will let me come back to you or not."

"Gaunt?" Todd's voice rose as, true to form, he grew upset. "Gaunt is the one with this information? He's the one who's forcing you to go after Bliss?"

"Gaunt isn't telling me anything, but where else am I going to get help if you won't?" I kept my head down and my voice even. "Who else in Contraband is going to stand beside me if my partners won't stand behind me?"

"That's stupid. You can't catch a smuggler with a computer."

"Maybe not." I looked up, this time at Cleo, whose expression I couldn't read. "But Chris told me Gaunt is a new architecture. Maybe he has what it takes to beat smugglers."

"There has to be a way out of this without arresting Bliss," Cleo said, more to Todd than to me.

"We're going to get Bliss to retire from smuggling?" I asked, my turn to be sarcastic. "How do we negotiate that? Go to Bliss and threaten to arrest him if he doesn't cooperate? How will we catch him once he knows we're after him? How? Our only hope is to capture this shipment before he even knows we're coming."

They didn't have an immediate answer for that. They stood there, the burning cigars in their hands. Cleo put an arm around Todd's waist. He took a long drag on his cigar, then flipped it off the walkway. "Three days?" he asked me. I nodded. "And the shuttle lands here?" I nodded again.

"Are we . . ." Cleo asked.

"First Hines, then Bliss," Todd said. "I'll bet you your share of Hines's money Admin comes begging for us after that."

"But the Unit . . ."

"Maybe Contraband will survive it, maybe it won't. We'll be gone. This was too dangerous to keep up much longer anyway." Todd bent down and picked up the case. "I wouldn't have picked this one, Aaron, but now it's ours. Party tonight, and we'll get started on the case in the morning."

Relief. It felt great. We were going to be cops again. My friends were going to stand by me, Narandova was going to be happy, and Gaunt was going to be off my back. I offered Todd my hand. "Thank you. I really needed you this time."

Cleo tossed her cigar after Todd's, and I let go of the rail one last time to hug her. "Come by after nine tonight," she said, and then they were headed back down the stairs. I watched them recross the bay, then looked down at my rumpled clothes. Tomorrow was back to work, which meant one more night of feeling clean and looking good. I needed a trip to the barber and away from the shuttle bay.

The Fleet Championships began with play on four boards, each in its own arena. As the field narrowed, the number of boards needed dropped. The second round still needed all four, however, and Lisa had been relegated to the fourth of these for her match. The board itself was the same size on all four courts, but the fourth had the smallest audience section, a bare two rows of seats that circled the players' area.

The space consumed by this fourth board would be added to the top of the center one in the later rounds when the crowds were larger.

For all her worries at the party the night before, Lisa had attracted a good crowd for a second-round match. Nearly a quarter of the seats were full, and it quickly became obvious that most of the spectators were there to cheer her. Her opponent was Mike Stilck, a middle-rank player from the *Panzer*. Stilck had never gotten farther than the semifinals of a major tournament, but he hadn't been out of the rankings in twenty years. He worked very hard, made very few mistakes, and just completely lacked the spark that might have made him a champion, or even popular.

Lisa and Stilck had played in tournaments before, and neither one of them was fond of altering their styles. They went rapidly through the first few moves, a Saigon Envelopment against a Cohn Wall. Lisa had dropped the face and hair colorings for the match, but she was uncharacteristically wearing a dress. Stilck wore slacks and a suit jacket, both of a very ordinary cut, but he topped it with a rakish hat that his hands toyed with while his eyes were on his insides.

My eyes were inside me as well. After so many hours separated from my mechanics and trapped inside my body, I had embraced one and shed the other, diving into the broadcast dream of the game, wandering the board with spectators from the *Jersey* and other ships. The dream was alive with aficionados showing their moves and strategies to one another on tiny duplicates of the oversize board and pieces that Lisa and Stilck were using. I strolled among these discussions, even the most heated of which fell silent when a player made a move. I listened in to a few, offered nothing of my own.

A person who was so jerky that he must have been from the *York*, our wayward sister ship whose indecision had left her four and a half years behind the rest of the Fleet, stepped back from two people hovering around a tiny chessboard, and revealed one of them to be Gaunt. The computer was in the dream of the game, wearing the form and clothes of its meat puppet. It was strenuously making a point to a bemused woman who appeared to be from the *Warsaw*. Given the lack of stutter in her dream form, she was currently somewhere on the *Jersey*, perhaps sitting in a seat at the match just as I was.

My first impulse on recognizing Gaunt was to flee, but it was a silly notion. If Gaunt wanted to see me again and had gone to this extreme to do so, then it would be best to let him have his say. So, instead of dropping back into my body, I stayed in the dream and strode over to Gaunt and the woman to see what he was saying.

"Then the remaining battleship takes the monitor." The tiny pieces moved to Gaunt's words. "Raymond can take the battleship, but it only forces an exchange, and her position is still hopeless."

"Where you place her, certainly, but I don't think she will spend her corsairs as easily as you say," the Warsawian woman said. In this dream, she had a great, fluffy crown of white hair that held two ivory combs. Before her, the board changed to an earlier position, but before the woman could begin to make her point, there was a pause while Stilck's northern monitor lumbered two cubes north.

"See?" Gaunt asked, changing the small board again without waiting for the woman to make her point. She didn't notice, both her meat and her mechanics turning over Gaunt's proposed game. I took the opportunity to say hello. The dream of the robot favored me with a pleased expression and held out its hand. "Aaron. I thought I might see you here."

"You're spending too much time in my records, Officer," I said.

"Not right now. Raymond's a friend of yours, isn't she? I've just been showing Eva why Stilck is guaranteed to win." He gestured to the little board and took me through the game as he envisioned it.

"Did you see what I mean about the corsairs?" the woman said as Gaunt wound down. "If instead of leading with them, as you say, she holds them back . . ." The board moved.

"She won't play that way," Gaunt said. This dream of the robot had adopted eyeglasses of all things, although the awkward prop spent more time in his hands (where he used them as a pointer) than they did on his face. "It's against her nature. She changes up her tactics, but not her philosophy. She's not going to become a maneuver player for one game."

I found myself agreeing with Gaunt, and then his prediction came true. We all watched the first of Lisa's corsairs shift from the defensive web she had built in the early moves. This had the look of a bloody, protracted game, but Stilck had her this time. Unless he made the sort of mistake he was famous for not making, Lisa would not have to worry about playing Goff again. I said as much.

"Stilck'll give Goff a better game," Gaunt commented. Abruptly, a second small board formed, this one showing a replay of Lisa and Goff's last match. "See the similarities?"

"Stilck is using Goff's stratagem," the Warsaw woman said. I took her word for it. Stilck had buried his version behind so many alterations that I couldn't see the similarities.

But I did see something else.

"It's better than that," Gaunt replied. "Strip enough of the crap away, it looks like Goff's stratagem, but play it like you would against Goff, and you're right back with the battleship taking your monitor."

"You do excellent analysis for a computer," the *Warsaw* woman said, offering Gaunt her hand. "Do you play?"

"Not yet," Gaunt admitted, taking her hand and giving a little bow over it. He looked at me. "Would you like a game?"

"I think we have been playing games for days," I said. My tone must have been more serious than I intended because the *Warsaw* woman looked from one to the other of us and then settled her feet onto the board.

"If you gentlemen will excuse me?" We gave her little bows, and she moved away. I picked up my feet and leaned back to hang across the two little chessboards from the dream of the robot.

"So, what brings you here, Officer?" I asked.

"The tournament, of course."

"You've become a chess fan?"

"Sort of." Gaunt paused to put the glasses on his face, as if he actually had to concentrate to hook them over his ears. "Chess kept coming up as I investigated Hines's money. I decided to come to the tournament."

"Are you enjoying yourself?" I asked. He looked happy, leaning back, smiling at me.

"Yes, I am. People ask my opinion because I'm a computer, but once I'm part of the discussion, they forget I'm not human."

"Odd. I never forget what you are. Officer."

Gaunt was saved from answering by the passing of one of Stilck's cruisers. As it stopped eight cubes below us, threatening one of Lisa's similarly advanced cruisers, Gaunt's face fell.

"That's wrong." Gaunt said the words as if he was talking to himself. The board with the replay of the Goff match disappeared, and the other began changing to his commands. I looked from the computer to the board, then shrugged. I had come to witness the match, after all. A tiny board of my own appeared as my mechanics walked me through what was going on and where it was likely to end.

"Stilck made a mistake," Gaunt said, sounding as if he couldn't believe it. No longer leaning back, he was hunched over his little board.

"Did he?" Given their games, the pieces were what I would have expected. "He didn't follow your plan."

"He can't win this way."

"No, not unless Lisa does something you haven't predicted." Despite myself, I felt smug. I knew that even if Gaunt had misjudged the game, his playing up of his surprise had to be for my benefit. Robots considered things twenty times before they acted.

Gaunt's reactions were just like the glasses—an effort to make me think of him as human. Apparently he'd decided I was more likely to betray myself to a person than to a computer.

"You didn't answer before. Raymond is a friend of yours, isn't she?"

The smugness disappeared. "I've known her for a long time," I admitted.

"You were junior players together?"

"There were some others, too."

Gaunt hadn't leaned back. He was still hunched forward. His glasses had silver frames, and their bridge was inlaid with a diamond pattern. "Why did you give up on chess, Aaron?" he asked.

"Isn't that in my records?"

"No."

"Crap. I told the coach when I dropped out, and he would have put it in the reports." I put my feet back down on the board, but I didn't step away from Gaunt. "Look, I was twelve. Knowing what got me to quit chess is not going to get me to quit Contraband. I am not going to tell you anything because there is nothing to tell. Okay? Are you understanding any of this?"

"Yes." Gaunt took off his glasses, put his own feet back on the board, and stood up straight. "You're running out of time, and you're still short of friends. Chess isn't the answer. Lisa isn't the answer. I'm the only person who can help you."

"And you're not even a person. I am in trouble."

"Yes," Gaunt said. "You are."

The tournament's organizers had provided two locker rooms for players who wanted to change on the site. They were at either side of a medium-size lounge that was open to players, their friends, and the journalists covering the tournament. I waited for Lisa on a green lamé couch. She had held on and beaten Stilck, confirming or disproving Gaunt's predictions, depending on which one you looked at.

Lisa came through the locker room door beaming with triumph. She had discarded the prim dress from the match for a pair of thigh-length shorts and a crimson hook sweater. The stripes on her face were also crimson, and now there were three on each cheek, plus through her hair. I gave her the hug she deserved and congratulated her. "What are you doing to celebrate?" I asked.

"My clan's getting together at Easter's. Why don't you come?"

I had known that she would have plans, but I was surprised by how disappointed I was to have it confirmed. It felt like being stood up by Cleo. "No, but I want to give you something before I forget."

I held up my empty hand to show I wanted to pass her a dream, and she clasped it in hers. There was less than an instant of transference, but Lisa kept hold of my hand while she digested the substance of the dream. Through our mingled mechanics, I asked: "Will it work?"

"It might," Lisa said the same way, a voice in my mind. "If she comes at me that way. If I can pull it off . . . I'm not used to playing an open style."

"Yeah." I let go of her hand and spoke out loud. "Someone said something like that while we were watching the game, and then we were looking at the last time you and Goff played and this occurred to me."

"Thank you. I'll try it if I get past Isenivavach."

"You will. His game isn't any better against yours than yours is against Goff."

"Let's hope he doesn't have a friend like you then." She gave me another quick hug. "I've got to go. You're sure you won't come?"

"Positive." Being around Lisa's clan forced my mechanics to work overtime; I had enough stress for the evening.

"Okay, but if I beat Goff, you have to come out."

"That I wouldn't miss."

A Cleo and Todd party called for ruffles and lace. I even dug out an earring, and, with a little more notice, I would have used my mechanics to grow a goatee. I settled instead for a tailed coat and one of my older canes.

I had less space than usual to dress in; I had lent three cubic meters to Cleo and Todd for the party. It was a common courtesy on the ship, to lend the host whatever room you could spare for the evening. Since this had been a big case with a good skim, Cleo and Todd would probably rent space from their neighbors as well.

You lend or sell or borrow or buy space on the ship, and the ship's computers adjust the smart walls so slowly that you don't see the change. What you notice is that in only a few hours, you no longer have to take that extra step to the cool box. Of course, there are so many people on the ship that the computers are constantly repositioning everyone's space to meet the needs of one space change or another. Since they keep your floor plan intact, you never notice being moved unless yours is the space with the net loss (or gain). The sideways tug brought on by the ship's spin was more intrusive.

It wasn't far from my Midlands flat to Cleo and Todd's. As I walked the night-lit corridors, swinging my cane and listening to some *Solidarity* metal, I encountered Strongbow as he stepped from a lift door.

"You're looking even more evil than usual," I greeted him, offering my hand. He slapped it with pleasure.

"I feel evil tonight," Strongbow said. He was wearing a true cape made of silk. It was black with a black lining. His usual leathers had been replaced by a black blouse and slacks. His long blond hair was loose, resting on the collar of the cape like a mane. A dagger with a hilt like a cross hung from his belt, and he laid a hand on it when he spoke again. "I hear you had a run-in with Deike last night."

"He took a swing. It wasn't a big deal."

"If I'd been there, he'd still be trying to pick up his teeth with his broken fingers." Strongbow said this with his wolf's grin, and I offered him my hand again. He traded slaps with me this time.

This old cane had a brass bulb head and was balanced enough to be spun. I gave it a vaguely martial twirl and turned for Todd and Cleo's. "Shall we?" I asked.

Strongbow's smile faded. Instead of moving on with me, he took hold of my arm and drew me back into a corner.

"Hey." Strongbow's hand was back on the dagger hilt. "Do you know anything about Cleo?"

I blinked at him. "Know anything . . . ?"

"Is she okay?" The puzzlement on my face was genuine, so he went on. "Look, I was way up in the ship last night. I mean way, way up, and I link with a very strange party. Okay?" I nodded. Given the way Strongbow worked cases, you were liable to find him anywhere. "This party, lot of blending, lot of mood, lot of rant. I do a little blending, so I'm watching that, and I realize that one of them is Cleo. Top of the ship, middle of the night, no sign of Todd. Now, do you know anything about Cleo?"

Blending is the stretching of boundaries between meat and mechanics, the body itself as art. Technically, growing a goatee in two days is blending, but in reality it is too slow and too tame and too common for true blenders. Cleo had spent several years in a blending crowd after she had divorced her clan. I wondered what had made her go back.

"I don't think so," I told Strongbow. "Nothing that explains that anyway."

"Okay. Just checking." He slapped my shoulder. "Come on. Let's go see what's up tonight."

You weren't going to find any rant at a Contraband party, but there was plenty of mood. Todd had unpacked his water pipe and smoke hung in sheets around the enlarged flat. Cleo and Todd had better furniture and furnishings than I did. It wasn't the chess party of the night before, but the extra borrowed and rented meters did give the couches room to breathe and the tables spaces to break up rather than rooms to dominate. Happy cops lounged on and around the furniture, drinking and blowing mood smoke. I paused by the door to light up myself and lost Strongbow to the martial-arts discussion by the wine cask. I let him go with an indulgent, smoke-leaking smile and let my lighter burn a little. It was odd to discover that after all of the fear and anxiety of the past few days, I was feeling a little evil myself.

I was still standing by the door a few minutes later when Cleo came by with more calibre chips for a bowl. At the sight of me, she dropped the chips on the table and reached for my hand. "Come with me," she said, and set off through the party at such a clip that she was almost dragging me. I tried to look calm and amused as she pulled me past Ross and Newman, who were discussing some sort of contraband sex trade, and into the head.

For obvious reasons, bathrooms were one of the ship's areas that required special clearance before their mechanics could be monitored. Thus, bathrooms were a common smuggler meeting place and as an undercover, I got to spend far too much time in them. Cleo and Todd's, though, was nicer than many. Their borrowed space had also been shared into this room, and even with the fixtures, Cleo and I were not crowded as she turned around and grabbed me in a hug that made me grunt with its fierceness.

"I've been wanting to do that all day," Cleo said.

"I'm sorry you had to wait," I said, telling the truth. It felt wonderful to hold her in my arms.

"I'm just glad it's over," Cleo said. "Todd's been so worried about you and Gaunt and the money. Now we're working together, the way it should be."

"Yes," I said, and hugged her again. I held her this time until she pushed me away, and when she did, I held her shoulders and looked at her. For the party, Cleo had put on black slacks and black slippers. She wore a white silk blouse that was worked with cutouts and ruffles of crewel embroidered lace. Around her neck was a white lace choker with a porcelain locket set at the front.

"You look wonderful," I said, meaning it. "Is the locket new?"

Cleo touched the piece at her throat, then turned to look at it in the mirror. "It's beautiful, and it's very old. My grandmother passed it down to me."

"Your grandmother sounds like a wonderful woman. Most people would have demanded its return when you divorced them."

"She gave it to me after the breakup," Cleo said. She took her hand from her neck and reached into her sleeve for her cigar case. "My grandmother's very frail. She was a professional Blender on Earth. One of the first. They didn't pace themselves then, or listen to their bodies as well as their mechanics. She's mostly machine now."

"I'm sorry," I said, because I was. I was also aroused, but I still had the composure to light Cleo's cigar.

"She was very happy for a long time. She's still mostly happy." Cleo blew smoke at her image in the mirror. "If more of my clan had been like her, I would have stuck with them." I found I had nothing to say to that, so I put an arm around her shoulders and squeezed them. She patted my hand.

"We'd better get back," Cleo said. "People will wonder what we've been up to."

Mood and relief and happiness and mirth welled up and split my face into an evil grin worthy of Strongbow. "I won't tell if you won't," I said. "No one needs to know our secrets."

Cleo was still under my arm, and there was a moment, her body pressed to mine, her head tilted back, mine a little forward, when we might have kissed. It was there, and then it wasn't. The moment had come and gone so fast that I couldn't be sure I wasn't imagining it.

And then the door to the bathroom was open and Cleo was passing through it. I took a moment to check my own ruffles and then followed her back into the babble and smoke.

Unlike the evening before at the chess party, I didn't wait till the end to get drunk at Cleo and Todd's. In fact, the evening was still early when I found myself in a pleasant state of mellow, sitting on the floor and leaning against the couch while cop stories floated around me. Ellen Fry joined our little group and was soon telling a story of her own. Retired a long time now (she had been a part of the second hire, when it was found that the original five Contraband officers weren't enough), Ellen was still most comfortable around cops and came to all of our parties. She loved to tell her stories, and given the rate of turnover in the unit, there was always a new audience for them.

"Back then," Ellen was saying, "there was more contraband going around in the form of manufactured goods. Holounits, smart furniture, that sort of thing. See, the projections still showed us running a surplus, and there was a legitimate trade in finished items going on between the ships. 'Course, when there's a major industry like that, some items are going to slip through the cracks."

Fry kept herself big. She was thick through the chest and had no waist to speak of. The powder blue tunic she wore was belted around her middle, but it had the effect of a rope around a tree. The tunic's ruffled collar dipped to her breastbone without showing even a hint of cleavage. Despite her retirement, she was obviously still a member of the Unit at heart. Her nails were immaculately trimmed and buffed, her hair full and glossy, and her clothes all handmade.

"Bliss was still a terror in those days. Got a lead on a plant engineer who'd managed to divert thirty holounits from the register. The engineer entered them as destroyed, then shipped them out as a load of recycles. Bliss caught him with the whole load, but it's not this engineer that we want. We know there's someone higher in the Admin who has got a regular trade going off scams like this engineer's. So instead of logging the arrest, we drop the engineer down a hole, Bliss takes his place, and we set up to sell the units to the Admin guy when he shows." Fry leaned back to take a long pull on her mood stick and catch everyone's eye.

"You're with me so far? Slick as glass. One big conviction waiting, a bigger on the way, right? One problem. Here we are, set up in the Bilges, Bliss out there doing his slouch and me in the walls, running the recorders, and instead of the big guy we want, we're overrun with these little Admin Gnomes." Fry stuck her cigar in her teeth to make the appropriate hand gestures between the big and the little. "Little. Line monitors, programmers, assistant engineers, for smut's sake. These are not smugglers. They don't want the whole load. Seems the engineer's been talking up this scam for weeks, and these guys are all here to get them a cheap holounit."

Fry laughed at the memory. "I mean, you get it? We're out here protecting the crew from the loss of their resources, and half of the plant's admin is putting themselves on holo buying unregistered goods."

"What did you do?" Doug asked. He was the newest recruit in the room, someone who was still adjusting to not leaning on his mechanics for everything. He made a face every time he sipped his barleywine. By the look of his brown mop, machines were still doing his hair, and he wasn't wearing a watch. I smiled indulgently, remembering my rookie days.

"What could we do?" Fry replied. "The guy we wanted would hear about the holounits over the Admin net. If we started telling the silly sods, 'Look, we're cops. Don't buy this stuff,' the guy we want won't show. We have to keep selling and hoping that the big guy comes."

"Did he?" Doug asked.

"Of course not," Jorge said. Jorge had four months in on the Unit, which had taught him just enough to make him embarrassed by Doug's ignorance. "Anything that got spread around that much, a real smuggler wouldn't want a part of."

"That's the way it went," Fry agreed. "We sold all thirty units without seeing a trace of the big fish we were trolling for."

"So did you arrest the little ones?" Doug wanted to know. Fry laughed, spilling a lungful of mood smoke down her tunic.

"Smut. We didn't even arrest the engineer. The evidence was gone. We weren't going to send thirty gnomes off to rehab for buying holounits. We gave the engineer a stern talking to and set him free." Fry nodded, a motion that made her thick neck bulge. "Worked, too. He's toed the line from that day to this. Still shoots me the occasional tip even."

No one asked what had happened to the marks they'd taken for the holounits. Even Doug wasn't that naive. I did have a question though. "Did you ever catch the smuggler in Admin?"

"Not yet," Fry said. There was a chuckle and a raising of glasses to that, but I had to force my smile. It was one thing to sit around your flat, dreaming of taking a big-time smuggler down. It was another to face the reality of just who you were going to be taking on. One thing was for sure: there would be no party like this after we brought Bliss in. Still, the only way to get Gaunt off our backs was to give him something bigger, and bringing Bliss in would be the biggest ever.

Very much later that night, when the party had thinned out, Cleo came and hugged me again, then sat beside me on the couch. She was as gone as I had ever seen her, wiped out on THC and alcohol. She settled a hand on my leg and leaned against me.

"Did you have a good time?" she asked.

"Yes, I did," I said. It was true. There were things I wanted and problems I wanted to go away, but it had been fun to surrender to the mood and the wine and the conversation.

"Me too. Maybe we should skip the busts and just have the parties."

"Maybe," I agreed, and then I frowned. "How would we pay for the parties without the investigations?"

"Smuggle," Cleo said, and we both giggled. It was the time of the evening when "belly button" would have been funny. We talked about the party and giggled some more, and then there was a quiet stretch after we agreed that we needed more barleywine and that we were both too tired to get up and get it.

I had been looking at Cleo's locket some more, and so into the silence I said, "Strongbow says he saw you at a party last night, too."

Despite the intoxicants running loose in her meat, Cleo actually stiffened, but then she relaxed. "Yeah," she said.

"He said you were blending."

"Yeah."

"Is there a story here?"

Cleo's own cigar was crushed and gone. She took her hand from my leg and took my cigar from my hand. I was quiet while she took a long pull and held the smoke, handing the cigar back. I took a much smaller drag while she coughed the smoke out of her lungs, then leaned back again.

"It was the locket, mostly," Cleo finally said. "We were packing. I found it, and it made me think of my grandmother."

Despite my own intoxication, I tensed. She'd said, we were packing. Packing for what?

"I used to be really good," Cleo was going on, apparently not noticing my worry. "When I left my clan, I did a lot of blending, and I was getting better and better offers. That was when my grandmother gave me the locket."

I put the packing aside for a moment. "She was proud of you?"

"Yes." Cleo's hand was on the locket again. "She was also scared for me. They pushed too hard in her day. She didn't want me hurt." Across the room, Doug and Fry were headed for the front door, their arms around each other's waists. Cleo and I shared a smile, and there, almost, was that invitation to be kissed again. With Todd just across the room, however, this was definitely not the time, even if he was still busy laughing with the dark-haired, civilian woman who had been beside him most of the night.

"Would you have been?" I asked to break the mood. "Hurt?"

"I don't think so. I don't know. That was the day one of my friends was busted for contraband, and I met Todd. Two months later I was a member of the Unit.

"The locket made me think about old times, though. It's hard being in Contraband and spending so much time away from my mechanics. I was so in touch with them back then."

"So you went to the party to remember?"

"I looked up some old friends. I'm still pretty good."

That I didn't doubt, but the conversation was back to where I'd wanted it. "What were you packing for when you found the locket?" I asked, casually, hoping that the answer was their vacation. From the way Cleo dropped her head, I knew it wasn't.

"Todd got to thinking about Hines's money and Gaunt. He decided we should get off the ship, just in case. Then you wouldn't give our cut to us. We almost went anyway, but we decided that since only you had the money, we would look better if we stayed."

"What does that mean?" I did not like what it sounded like. Cleo reached for my cigar again, but I held it back. "Cleo?"

"There are no computer records," Cleo said, irritated. "I didn't record anything after the bust. If Gaunt came for us, and we said we didn't know about the money, they'd have to believe us." Cleo reached for my cigar again, and I let her have it this time.

"Don't look at me like that," Cleo said, before she took a little puff. "We didn't go rushing to Gaunt, and we wouldn't have been testifying against you. Things were just weird. You were weird. We didn't want to go on trial, and now we won't have to."

"No, I wouldn't want you to either," I said, but I was still having trouble with it. "You were packing to leave me behind. You'd do that?"

"Todd didn't want to, but he said it might be the only way, if they could link you to the money."

"No," I said again. "I mean you. You'd just go off and leave me?"

Cleo leaned against me again, resting her head on my shoulder. "It didn't come to that. We worked things out. Just be happy, okay?"

"Yeah," I said patting her shoulder and staring at her hand on my leg. Somewhere I was sure that Gaunt, still determined to appear human, was laughing.

CHAPTER 5

BLISS

There was nothing about chess in *The Intimates*. Actually, there was very little about cops. Mostly it was about people and who they really are.

I had left the party at Todd and Cleo's very shortly after Cleo's admission that she had been prepared to abandon me to Gaunt. Everything from that point tasted like ashes and sounded like a dirge, so I got out. I went back to my flat, but its reduced size offended me. I couldn't call my space back from Cleo and Todd's without turning on my mechanics, and I didn't want to do that until my head had stopped spinning. Drunk, stoned, and pissed, I grabbed up the carefully wrapped bundle that contained Chris's gift and went for a walk. Half an hour later I was in a back nook of Ernie's.

Ernie's was the antithesis of the Flame Lounge. It had no view and no decor. Whereas the Flame was a licensed bar that offered unregistered drinks and smokes, Ernie's was an unlicensed coffee shop that dealt mostly in registered food. Ernie didn't serve anything that wasn't already in the kitchens of even moderately successful crew members, but moderately successful people didn't spend their time in the

Bilges. When I was undercover, I got a lot of meals at Ernie's just because it was easier to pay him for a kibbleburger than it was to descend all the way back to the Midlands every time I was hungry.

Ernie's license was for enough space to run a walk-up food stand. That licensed space was his foundation, but to it he annexed whatever unminded bits of the ship he could find. The shape of his shop and its counter space, as well as its complement of tables, chairs, and stools, changed from day to day as chunks of space were claimed by their rightful owners and Ernie sucked in more remnants to take their place.

Time is largely meaningless in the Bilges, and people wandered through the coffee shop at all hours, but I managed to get a hollow with enough bench that I could stretch out my feet, and enough table to hold my package, my plate of kibble omelet, and my mug of real coffee. The eggs were pretty dreadful without mechanics to adjust the taste, but the coffee was hot and laced with enough caffeine to twist my intestines.

Mereian had done his usual job with the graphic novel, wrapping it neatly in brown paper and tying it up with white string, even asking me for the lending of a finger so he could get the knot tight. I kept staring at the white knot while I fought through the omelet. I was trying to decide why I wanted to police the damn ship anyway. Why not take up a trade? Why chase people no one wanted caught? Why not run a little stand making knots that were too pretty to cut and heartbreaking to pull?

Those questions were just as frustrating as all the others I'd been through since Gaunt walked into my life, and even my drug-soaked meat could only chase them for so long. By the time I came back with my second mug of coffee, I pulled the knot with a great deal of satisfaction.

The Intimates was the story of two old lovers taking a trip together down a tropical river. One is a government police officer who has suggested this trip to help his friend get over the death of his spouse. Along the way they meet several of the other passengers and play an odd game of flirtation with the captain. The overt plot brings in an old case that the policeman hopes to solve while on the river, but in the end the novel is all about the two friends' feelings for each other, the others they were and the others they are.

The book lifted me completely out of myself. It was so different to see a drama played out in pictures that did not move or speak. You had to bring so much of the experience to the book yourself: the scents of the river, the sounds of the ships, the feel of the clothes. And so much of the action happened between the panels. I had read a few books in my time (not as many as I owned, but a few), but this was a different experience. To see the one man's pain, but not his turning away. The gun fires in one panel, but it hits in the space between the panels, a fact that didn't stop me from visualizing it. I was so caught up that it wasn't until the fourth time that I tried to drink from my empty coffee mug that the spell was broken and I got up.

When I came back, John Edison was sitting at my table, looking through the novel. "I hope your hands are clean," I said, sliding back in on my side of the booth.

John held them up, then pointed down at *The Inti-mates*. "Looks good. Is it an original?"

I nodded. "2007. Canadian, I think."

"How's the story?"

"Wonderful," I said, and John nodded. John preferred good entertainment to bad, but he bought everything under the assumption that he might sell it again. Thus, his first concern was always with what something was worth rather than with how good it was.

Like Ernie, John was another person on the fringe of the contraband trade. John's legitimate business was in licensed action/problem dreams, the sort of thing where you shut out your meat and became a highly cultured spy penetrating the Mexican Frontier to save humanity from unbridled dictatorship. John almost made his living expenses from the trade, but his real profits came from the sex dreams he sold, many of them unlicensed bootlegs from other ships, or multigeneration copies of Earth-made originals. As smugglers went, he was a very small threat to survival of the Fleet, and besides, when he had an interesting new dream, he shared it with me for no charge.

"Do you know if there's ever been a dream made of it?" John asked. He had picked the novel up and was looking at the publishing and copyright information. John's clothing was a testament to his profession. He wore a black jacket of synthetic silk whose back was emblazoned with the logo for a hit dream from two years before. His hat, his shirt, his trousers, all advertised some dream or product that he had sold. The only sign that he might have any real money was his watch. It was an analog timepiece with a crystal of real glass. Its face was emblazoned with a cartoon mouse whose arms functioned as the hands of the clock.

"No. It was a gift, and I haven't had my mechanics on since I got interested in it. I'm not sure it would translate well into a dream."

"Books are harder to move though," John said, which was true enough that I found I had nothing to say to it. I tried a sip from my coffee instead. John continued reading the book, his page-turning slowing as he became interested in the story. I sat there, happy someone else was enjoying a good story I'd found for them and annoyed at being ignored, until thoughts of Cleo pushed the annoyance to the front and made me ask:

"When was the last time you had sex, John?"

John looked up from the odd scene with the captain and thought for a moment. "Two weeks ago. There was a show on the *Auckland* and I stayed with my friend the designer. How about you?"

"Seven years," I said, trying to remember if John had ever mentioned a designer on the *Auckland*. "Isn't she older than you?"

"Seven years? You need to come to a show with me," John said. Even with the costs of shuttle travel, there had still grown up in the Fleet a migrant culture of entrepreneurs like John who dealt in licensed and semilicensed goods. Promoters on various ships would rent space for a show, then turn around and charge the dealers rent for spots to set up and crew members an admission fee to come in and shop. When things went well, everyone made money and could afford to move on to the next ship and the next show. When things didn't go well . . .

"Maybe." Like vagabond cultures throughout history, the shows had a reputation for licentiousness that had just enough truth in it to attract the right sort of people to maintain it. "But this designer, you're not serious with her. You're not beginning a clan or anything?"

John recoiled in horror. "No. We're just friends. Her clan has two sons that are about my age. I think she just gets off on the idea of it."

"What does her clan think about you?" I was trying to imagine my mother spending nights with someone besides my father and failing. John just shrugged.

"The sons look at me a little funny, but no one says anything. It's a pretty loose group."

"Must be." I tried another sip of the coffee. The alcohol, the caffeine, and the omelet were all jockeying in my stomach to see just how sick they could make me feel. Very soon I was going to have to crawl off somewhere and give in to the misery, or else turn on my mechanics and let them sort it all out. "How long has it been since you had someone steady though?"

"Depends. What do you mean by steady? I see the designer every time I'm on the *Auckland*."

"No. I mean someone you saw every day. Someone you were serious about."

Three wrinkles appeared in John's forehead as he thought about this. Finally he shook his head. "I don't think there's ever been anyone like that. I move around so much . . ." He shrugged. "There are people who follow the shows, but I've never been interested in any of them. I'm going to get some coffee. You want some more?"

"No."

The logo on the back of John's jacket consisted of a holo of a square-jawed Asian with a smart pistol, wrapped in the words "City of Sin," and set in a star field. I'd been through that dream, before I joined the Unit. There'd been no ethical questions in that fantasy, beyond the dilemma of whether to get the information from the mafioso's girlfriend before or after you slept with her.

When John sat down again, he asked, "So why has it been seven years?"

"Haven't found the right person, I guess."

"Seven years? You're sure you're looking hard enough? I thought people wanted to sleep with cops."

"Not the ones I meet." Not that I met many. As much work as Cleo, Todd, and I had been doing in the past year and a half, the only people we ever saw were the rest of the Unit, the smugglers we were stalking, and each other.

"Don't you work with a girl?" John asked, his mouth still turned down by the taste of the coffee. "Take her out."

"I have."

"And . . ."

"She's living with someone."

"So?" This had clearly never stopped John.

"So she's not interested," I said, surprising myself a little, so I hurried to add: "Not while she's with Todd anyway. Maybe when they break up."

"If she's not interested," John said, "don't take her out. Take someone else out. Come with me to a show.

There's one on the *Draper* in three weeks. You could come along, help with the booth, and we'd do the parties that night."

"Cleo likes me," I said. "It's just that she's with Todd. That can't last. She does everything in their relationship. If they need another chair or something, Cleo buys it. The monthly payment on their extra space? Cleo pays it. It's supposed to be a partnership, but somehow when the bills come due, it's always Cleo who pays them."

"Sounds nice," John said. "Maybe you should introduce her to me."

"It's nice for Todd, but how long can she put up with that? I don't know when the last time was he bought something besides clothes and dreams."

"He buys clothes?" John asked, clearly shocked by the idea of someone spending marks on something as trivial as what they were wearing.

"Yes. Some people care about what they have on."

"I care," John said. "I just wouldn't waste marks on clothes. There's no resale value to clothes."

"The point," I said, "is that Cleo isn't going to be living with Todd much longer, and when she does leave him, I'll be here for her."

"If you say so," John said.

Our coffee cups were next to each other in the center of the table. John brought his hand out of his pocket and laid it down behind the cups. When he pulled it back, he had left a phial on the table. I looked at it without moving my eyes from John's.

"What is it?"

"Something I got from the *Nikobar*."

"Thanks," I said, putting my own hand over it and

then slipping it into my jacket pocket. The dreams that John brought me were very uneven, but there was a pocket of real perversion on the *Nikobar*, and their dreams tended to be the ones I liked best. Now I had another reason besides my stomach to turn my mechanics on.

"Look, I know I'm still behind, but could you do something for me anyway?" John asked. This was a familiar formula between us. While I was searching out a hiding hole during an investigation of a completely different smuggler, I'd stumbled on a stash of John's dreams. He'd offered to trade me copies of the ones I liked for letting him go. It would have been a bad bust, and dream smuggling was way down on the list of meaningful crimes, so I'd made the deal. As time had passed, I'd done other favors for John, always with the understanding I'd be paid in dreams. The problem was that John never had as many dreams I was interested in as we agreed he owed me.

"What is it this time?" I asked.

"I've got a box that needs to be registered."

I shook my head. "This is not a good time, John. I couldn't get away with it. I'd have to actually see the box." The ships' computers try to keep track of everything on board; not just for the sake of controlling contraband, or for directing the recycling, but also to know what there would be to be distributed when we arrived at Beta Virginius Escher. Before John could ship his box of goods off the ship, he had to register what was in it. Typically this was done by robots in the shuttle bays, but as an official of the ship, I could do it as well. In the past I would just send John a faked dream of my having inspected his box, sealed it, and registered it. That wouldn't work with Gaunt watching me.

"I don't want to get you in trouble," John said. He meant it. I made his life much easier. "What if I brought the box by?"

"You'd have to fix it so I didn't see anything," I said. The inspection would have to be done with my mechanics on. I could inspect it sloppily, but I had to inspect it.

"Do you ever?"

"Usually I don't look," I said. "When do you need it by?"

"Our shuttle leaves tomorrow night."

"I'll give you access to my flat. You can bring it by tonight," I said.

"Thanks."

"Yeah." I got up. It was very early. Thankfully Todd and Cleo would be getting up even later than I would. Lisa's match began at ten, so I could watch it before Todd and Cleo were ready to work. "I better be getting back."

"Can I keep this?" John asked, holding *The Intimates*.

I paused a long minute, weighing how likely it was that John would actually come by, then finally nodded. "Just bring it with the box."

"Sure."

I picked up my hat and cane, checked for the phial, and headed for the nearest lift. As the door closed, I switched on my mechanics and leaned back against the pink wall panels. I felt better instantly, the mechanics blocking me off from the pain in my head and the nausea in my stomach. The hand in my jacket pocket caressed the phial, and though I was alone, my smile was embarrassed. "Guilty pleasures," I said to the empty car, and began counting down the time back to my home.

When the lift door opened on the deck containing my flat, I was only a twenty-second walk from my door. Unfortunately, Varian was in my path. Three meters away, Wolcott sat on a bench facing me. Behind him a smiling Buddha of apparent gold sat in an alcove in the corridor where someone had placed him two weeks before. Varian gave a little "meow" and rubbed my leg in greeting. Wolcott didn't say anything; he just craned his white neck to look around me into the lift.

"Hello, Wolcott," I said, my hand still on the *Nikobar* phial in my pocket. I was hoping the homeless boy's presence was just a coincidence, but I knew that it wasn't.

The sixteen-year-old put his finger to his lips and motioned me to join him on the bench. Varian rubbed against me again, so I picked him up and stepped out of the lift. The cat's long coat smelled of the incense that burned before the little Buddha.

"What's up?" I asked without sitting down.

For an answer, Wolcott raised his left hand from his denim clad leg just high enough so that I could see that it contained a phial. Then he quickly covered it up again and motioned to the bench. I caught the eye of the little Buddha figure over his shoulder. I took a deep breath and tried to draw some serenity from the icon. When that didn't work, I had my mechanics give me a shot of energy and patience.

Eric T. Baker

Varian settled on my lap as I settled on the bench, and Wolcott slipped the phial into my hand. "This is very big," he said, putting his lips uncomfortably close to my ear. His facial hair was so uneven that it must have grown without mechanical help.

"Really?" I said. My mechanics had analyzed the phial he had given me earlier (complete running time five hours) and found nothing of use. It had been exactly what I had come to expect from Wolcott: cutouts from Executive Council meetings alternated with long-winded digressions by Wolcott explaining how the normal infighting of running the ship was actually the work of an agent for the *Warsaw* government.

"Look at this," Wolcott said, tapping my hand with an unkempt nail while his cat kneaded my thighs and purred at my strokes down its back. It spooked me that Wolcott had let his appearance slip so. What had he been doing? Reluctantly, I turned my awareness inward and accessed the phial.

Phials are basically very dumb computers. Within their crystal cases, they contained mechanical memory without the sophistication of the infinitely more complex ships' computers or personal mechanics. Without a smarter computer to assemble them, phials were just a mass of disjointed dreams.

My mechanics took me into Wolcott's phial where a cleaner, neater version of the boy awaited me. Gone were the apparent denims and cottons; this Wolcott wore black velvet, a jacket, and boots. His face and nails were both neatly trimmed.

We stood in the broad elegance of the Executive Council Chamber. The marble walls and arched ceiling, which in life were holographic illusions, were here as real as the rest of the dream. The five Councilors were seated at their semicircular table of apparent marble, trading words and dreams as they discussed some aspect of intership commerce. The phial's Wolcott went over to closest Councilor and removed a hologram from the midst of the stack at the man's elbow. The Wolcott held the hologram up and blew it to me with a puff of his breath. My mechanics were considering the information even before my dream hand took hold of it.

"Fissionables?" I asked.

"Yes," the Wolcott nodded excitedly. "I've shown you how Ximenes is an agent of the *Warsaw* government. That document is finally more proof than you need to arrest him." Ximenes was the Chief Administrator of Ship's Computers. According to the hologram, the ship's computers had been talking to their opposite numbers on the *Warsaw*. The *Jersey* computers were worried because the *Warsaw* computers could no longer account for all of the fissionable materials with which they had left Earth.

"I'm lost. Why does this mean that Ximenes is an agent?"

"Because he never presented the report," the Wolcott said. "He buried it with the other no-action matters. By having it in the room, he made it a part of the public record, but he never brought it before the council so they could act."

"Act?" I didn't, as a rule, argue with Wolcott. His worldview, while paranoid, was complete. There was no fact you could introduce to the argument that meat Wolcott could not fit into his conspiracy web. The dream Wolcott before me, however, was not animated by the consciousness of boy sitting on the bench beside my meat. It was jut a phial dream presenting its programmed arguments. "What would the council have done? It's a problem for the *Warsaw*, not us."

"Don't you understand? Those materials are on this ship, just waiting for the word to be given."

This was so ridiculous that I didn't know how to respond. Not that I wanted to. I wanted to go home, play my new dirty dream, and then get some sleep. I pulled my consciousness out of the phial.

The real Wolcott was looking at me anxiously. Varian was rubbing his cheeks alternately against my hands. I stroked him with one hand and reached for my wallet with the other. "I'll look into this," I said.

"You're going to arrest him," Wolcott said. It was not a question.

"Suppressing one computer report doesn't make a ship's administrator a traitor." I sighed at Wolcott's stricken face. He looked as if I'd kicked his cat. "Besides, he didn't suppress it. As you point out, he brought it to the meeting, put it in the record. I'll petition that it be covered in the next meeting, and in the meantime I'll see if any of the materials have shown up here. Okay?" I handed him the marks from my wallet, and he took them, but the boy clearly was not happy.

"If anything turns up, I'll let you know," I said, and squeezed his shoulder. "In the meantime, you need some sleep. Do you have a place?" Wolcott nodded. My mechanics thought he was lying, but I did not want him in my flat in this mood, so I decided to believe him. "You take care of him," I told Varian, setting the cat on Wolcott's lap. It gave me a parting "meow," but its master said nothing.

Friz had an unnatural hatred of signs. It was just weird. There aren't that many signs on the *Jersey* to begin with, things are so much in motion and most warnings are broadcast by the smart elements in the walls and floors. Still, here and there a sign might be posted like: "Ship Support: Do Not Alter" or "Flame Path: Approach with Care." Detailed and more strident warnings would be playing for people's mechanics, but these were serious enough dangers and permanent enough locations to warrant holographic warnings to people's meat.

For reasons known only to himself, Friz could not abide these simple statements. A holo-artist of real talent, he created broad murals on themes of the ship or flame, and plastered them over the signs wherever he found them. There were thirty authenticated Friz pieces on the ship. In the beginning, the murals had been duplicated, removed, and the signs restored. As Friz's fame had grown, however, the murals had come to mean the same things as the signs they covered, and so were left in place. The details were still there for crew members' mechanics, and the murals were prettier than the text-marred walls.

Cleo, Todd, and I met under one of the best of Friz's pieces, a three-meter-long diorama of the *Jersey*, its delicate ramscoop stretched like a spider's web and contrasting with the ship's broad support beams, which were laid open like ribs. The flame was gone from the *Jersey's* tail, but she was set amid a sea of fire. It was a stunning work in grays and reds that took your breath every time you came upon it.

Other than the mural, there was nothing special about this chunk of the Midlands. It was just an out-of-the-way corridor between one of the malls and one of the manufacture centers, used mostly by robots who didn't want to crowd the lifts. It is dangerous for cops to evolve habits, just as it is even more danger-ous for criminals to do so, but we liked to have our initial strategy sessions here. For one thing, Friz's model of the ship served as a convenient map for dis-cussing places and distances when we had our me-chanics shut down.

"So what do we know?" Todd asked. As usual, he'd coaxed the walls and floor into benches, and we'd spread ourselves out on them. I'd brought along a cooler bag holding a thermos and cups, and Cleo passed around thin, unlaced cigars. While the two of them lit up, I answered Todd's question.

"Bliss is currently registered as an intrafleet trade consultant. He works on a commission basis for vari-ous merchant clans. His registered space is in the lower section of the Midlands." I reached up with my walking stick, passing it through one of Friz's fire-bursts and indicating a section of the ship a good half kilometer below where we were standing. "It's big, but not impossibly so for someone in his profession."

"It's pretty close to the docking ring," Cleo said. Today, for business, she was in denim pants and a dark blue smock over a light blue leotard. Her me-chanics had cleaned up the effects of the previous night's indulgences and she looked clear-eyed and fresh behind the cigar smoke. "Do you think he runs anything through his flat? Maybe we should do an inventory."

"He wouldn't be that careless," Todd said.

"He's an untouchable. He probably never thinks about being caught," Cleo said. With a court order, it was possible to log into all the smart furnishings in a flat and use their sensors to identify every item in the space, except those that had been deliberately masked. This, however, was not what Cleo was suggesting. It was an article of faith in Contraband that seeking a court order was the same thing as broadcasting your investigation on ship's announcement band.

Without a court order, there were two possibilities. One was to break in and talk to the out-of-the-way pieces of the flat (the interior of the food locker for instance), but this had the drawback of not only being illegal, but also being relatively easy to detect. The other option, which required much more time and work, was to talk to the mechanics in the region of the flat's entrance, checking what they remembered being brought past them. This was legal, and much harder to detect, but time-consuming and very unreliable. Smart fixtures had very little memory space for long-term images of the type we'd need.

"I don't think he's that careless, either," I said. The man I'd seen meet Goff at the party didn't look like the careless type to me. He struck me as caring a great deal. "I don't think it's worth the chance of his learning he's been looked into. Not when we already know where we can catch him with contraband."

"What about that?" Todd asked. "What kind of security is he likely to have at this transfer? Do we have to have someone there, or can we set up to record it? Or both?"

"That's going to be our problem." I leaned my stick against the bench and reached into the cooler bag for a thermos and a cup. "My informant was less helpful on this than I would have liked. Bliss appears to run a pretty tight group. There's usually just the shuttle pilot, Bliss, and two or three others for muscle to move the cargo."

"But Bliss does show?" Cleo asked, and I nodded. This was important because it meant we could bust Bliss in the shuttle bay without having to follow the contraband until it got to him. "That helps at least," she said, and blew smoke up into the holographic fire. I handed her the cup, now filled from the thermos, and reached for another. Todd hooked his fingers under the collar of the suede vest he had on over his robin's-egg-blue shirt and settled it lower on his shoulders.

"Are the extra men regulars, or does he contract them for each job?"

"My informant couldn't say. He's seen five different men, but he doesn't know if they are all regular employees of Bliss or if he hires them special."

"What is this?" Cleo asked, sniffing her cup.

"An orange julep," I said. "I thought after last night that we'd had enough barleywine for a while." I handed Todd a cup and reached for another for myself.

"So we need to find out if we can set up in the hangar bay, and we need to know if Bliss has a standing organization or if he hires men as he needs them," Todd said. He took a drag on his cigar and stared up at the mural while I sampled the julep. It was very good, which was puzzling. Why had I stopped drinking them?

Todd looked back at me. "How does Bliss package the stuff he brings in?"

"Meaning?" I asked.

"Meaning does he fake the registration? If we film the shuttle bay, and all we get is Bliss and some guys unloading licensed crates, that's not going to do us much good in court."

"We'll just open the crates when we make the bust," I said. I didn't understand what Todd was driving at. Cleo did. She asked:

"What if your informant's wrong?"

Todd nodded. "Bliss is a registered importer. What if all that's in the boxes are licensed goods? It would be a search without a warrant. Bliss would not laugh that off."

"Turning us over to S.I.D. would save him the trouble of killing us," Cleo said. There followed a silence while Todd and I both looked at her in wide-eyed surprise. "What?" Cleo finally said. "Don't look at me like it hasn't crossed your minds. He killed Ishido."

"No one knows that," I said, my voice a little shriller than I would have liked. Cleo's words brought back the memory of Hines pointing the gun at me. "Bliss used to be a cop, and now he's a smuggler. Don't make him into a monster."

Nodi Ishido had for several years been the largest smuggler on the *Jersey*, but he never ran afoul of Bliss until after Bliss retired. Some said they had been partners while Bliss was on the force, but that when he retired, Bliss had set up his own trade, co-opting one of

Ishido's best pipelines in the process. Threats had been made back and forth, and then Ishido had disappeared. S.I.D. had even been called in to look, but there had been no trace found. The assumption was that Bliss had pushed him through an airlock, but Bliss had never claimed this himself, and it was hard to imagine.

"Whatever," Todd said. He set his cup down and stood up. "The question's still how does he bring the contraband in and where does he take it? When can you meet your informant again?"

"I'm not sure," I admitted. I could probably reach Narandova after his match, but I didn't know when he would be able to reach his on or when he could get back to me. Given what we needed to know, I might have to contact the son directly. This was a bad idea because if Bliss had any sort of trace on dreams going back and forth to the shuttle, seeing my name on one to Narandova's son would make him instantly suspicious.

"What about the other men? Do we know any of them? Do they owe us anything?"

"Not to me," I said. "The three names I have are Mifflin Dallas, Gasset Ortega, and Ewell Steward."

Cleo gave a little cough at Ortega's name, smoke puffing out her nose from the drag she'd been taking on her cigar. "What?" Todd asked.

Cleo wiped a lump of fallen ash off her pants leg. "Ortega. I used to know him. Back before."

"How well? Could you talk to him?"

"Pretty well," Cleo admitted, but she said it quietly, and she didn't lift her eyes from her pants.

"I'm not sure I like this," I said. They both looked at

me. I shrugged and tried to pass it off. "You just don't do a lot of undercover."

"It's not undercover. She'll talk to him as who she is." Todd turned to Cleo. "You don't have to push it. Just make contact. See if he'll talk with you. We can go on from there." Cleo nodded, but she looked as uncomfortable as she was making me feel.

"Is this guy dangerous?" I asked.

"No," Cleo said hurriedly. "No. It's fine. I'll get hold of him this afternoon. I think he'll talk to me."

"Good." Todd reached out and squeezed her shoulder. "You do that. Aaron, talk to your informer again, and I'll go over the hangar. We'll meet for dinner at the Stand and see where we are." Cleo and I both nodded our agreement, but I still didn't think Cleo looked comfortable.

Lisa's match with Isenivavach was on the second board, a much better space than the fourth, but not much better attended. I worried about Cleo on the way to the match, but once I settled into my seat for Lisa's game, I found it easy to give myself over to the chess.

Gordic Isenivavach was a perennially low-ranked player who was playing way beyond himself in this tournament. Lisa should have been playing Nicola Paine, another middle-rank player of about the same level as Stilck, but Isenivavach had opened with an inspired corsair gambit that knocked Paine back on her heels and kept her there. Credit for the gambit might be given to good coaching, but Isenivavach had maintained his advantage flawlessly.

Despite his second-round success, I still liked Lisa's chances against Isenivavach. He came from a large and wealthy clan to whom he had many obligations. Duty to his clan kept him from devoting the time and mechanics he needed truly to excel on the tour. These limitations were balanced by the money his clan spent on computer space for him. That balance was enough to keep him on the tour, if not in the top rank.

Lisa came out in the prim dress she had worn for the previous two matches. Once again, the face paint and hair color were gone, but she had plaited her long hair into a single cascade down her back. Isenivavach was dressed well enough to be a member of the Contraband Unit, in a crisp jacket and slacks of Earth silk, with tan boots whose polished leather gleamed under the stadium lights. He shook Lisa's hand, leaned close to ask her something, and then took a cigar case from his jacket.

My eyes lingered on the thin string of smoke that rose from Isenivavach's cigar while he and Lisa drew for their positions and the referee assigned their pieces. Around me there were murmurs from spectators. What did the cigar mean? Was Isenivavach paying more attention to his meat now, so he needed the comfort of the smoke, or was he paying less attention to his mechanics so that he would be easier prey for Lisa? Chess fans can (and do) argue such little things for hours because matches so often turn on them.

Each player's pieces were appearing on the big holographic board, and I was making my first guesses about the way the game would play when an inner call summoned me to my mechanics and a dream usher appeared beside me. "I'm sorry to disturb you, sir," it said. "There is a woman at the gate who would like to speak with you."

"Of course," I said. There was the slow dissolve from the stadium background, and then I was at the front entrance of the Championships, where the apparently same usher was standing with Cleo. I said her name and gave the dream her a hug, which she returned.

"I need to talk to you, Aaron."

"That's wonderful. You can use my extra ticket. I'm at board two. I'd have invited you this morning, but I thought you'd be busy."

Cleo held up her hand and shook her head. "Could we talk somewhere beside the stands? Please."

"Well, of course," I said. I didn't want to miss Lisa's match, but even in the dream, Cleo was obviously upset. "How about at the Winner's Statue? I'll have my meat there in a few minutes."

"That's fine," Cleo said, and faded away. I made the proper arrangements with the usher, then went back to the board to get my body.

The Winner's Statue is a good example of what passes for immortality in the Fleet. Two meters high, it is crowned by a wire sculpture of a Fleet ship englobed by a battleship, a cruiser, and a frigate. Down its smart stone sides are carved the names of all the Fleet Champions since the tournament began. The statue is erected each year when the space is converted to its tournament alignment. At the end of the ten days, the statue comes down along with the stadiums, locker rooms, booths, and lawns. Its design is stored away in the computers, ready to be rebuilt for the next year's tournament.

The statue is just beyond the gate, so Cleo was standing under it, smoking a cigar and waiting for me when I arrived from Lisa's game. Although her dream had been wearing the working clothes of the morning, Cleo was actually now in a jacket and slacks of her own. Under the jacket she had on a button-down shirt of the same light blue that Todd had worn that morning. Inside the open collar of the shirt, Cleo had put the choker with her grandmother's locket back on.

Even for Lisa's game I had not changed from my rumpled working clothes, but I had brought along my good walking stick, which I held out of the way while I gave the real Cleo a hug. "What's wrong?" I asked when she held me longer than courtesy required. Cleo let go with one hand and leaned back in my arms to rub the base of her neck. I turned off my mechanics. Immediately the noise of the tournament crowd became louder and the feel of Cleo's back on my hands became less distinct.

"Gasset," Cleo said.

"Bliss's guy?"

"Yes." Cleo looked around. There was a steady stream of fans passing in and out of the tournament space, and a few were even stopping to look at the statue. Cleo put her hand through my arm and led me away down the cobbles of the path. I let her lead us past the entrance to the first board and into the grassy space between it and the second board. Here were the booths overcharging for licensed spirits and foods, as well as merchandise and clothing. Crewpeople from nearly all the ships of the Fleet lounged at tables and on the grass under the midday lighting.

The pressure on my arm eased as we strolled into this gathering, so I chose an empty table and nudged

Cleo into a smart chair of spun glass. I hooked my stick over the other chair and left her there while I went to a booth for a bottle of champagne and a bowl of strawberries. I placed these on the table, settled into my own chair, and began eating strawberries while I waited. It took a few minutes, but finally Cleo crushed out the butt of her cigar and looked at me. "Would you like some champagne?" I asked.

"Yes," Cleo said, and reached for a berry. As I set about pouring, Cleo asked, "Remember my telling you I went to that blending party two nights ago?"

"I remember my asking you about it." Almost as well as I remembered cuddling with her on the couch.

"Gasset was the guy I looked up to find that party." I set her glass before her and waited for more while I poured my own, but that seemed to be all I was going to get without prompting. Usually talking to Cleo was an attempt to guide her flow, not to drag it from her. I tried a sip of the champagne and thought about the conversation on the couch.

"Is Gasset the one who was busted for smuggling?" I guessed. Cleo gave me a nod. "The one you met Todd through?" Cleo nodded again, reaching for her glass now. I had small feeling of triumph that was suddenly overwhelmed by puzzlement. "Was Gasset convicted of the smuggling?"

Cleo reached for the bottle to refill her now empty glass. "Yes. Yes, Todd made the arrest, and I had to testify against him. Gasset was sentenced to rehab, and I joined the unit."

My hand began shaking so badly that I was afraid I would spill my drink. I tried to set the glass carefully on the table but nearly spilled it anyway. I gripped the armrests of the chair, wished I could turn my mechanics on, and settled for breathing deeply. I was ready to stop having the assumptions of my life thrown into question and I really wanted Cleo to explain this one. "If Gasset was sentenced to rehabilitation, how could he be helping Bliss unload contraband from shuttles?" And why hadn't Todd reacted to the name that morning?

"I don't know," Cleo said, but she didn't say it to me. She was looking down into her third glass of champagne.

"Cleo?"

She met my eyes. "Gasset isn't the name he was arrested under."

"Oh."

Rehabilitation got to the root of what the Fleet was doing in space in the first place. A crewperson under rehabilitation was forbidden to shut down their mechanics, which were in turn constantly monitored by a computer proctor. The computer intervened whenever the convict tried to break the Ship's Articles, using the person's mechanics to stop them, and then talking to the person about the transgression's motivations and consequences. For the most part it worked. Most people modified their behavior, and stayed straight even after the term of rehab ended.

What made rehabilitation different in the Fleet from what it had been in on Earth was that a convict here could choose to turn his mechanics off. Doing so resulted in the convict's being immediately seized and incarcerated, but if the convict preferred being locked up to having a computer constantly watching him, he could take that path. Most convicts spent their terms turning their mechanics on and off, going in and out of the lockup as a result, depending whether they were more tired of their meat or their therapy. As the therapy worked, the computer became less intrusive, so that at the end, most convicts were simply leaving their mechanics on.

That Gasset was running around loose on the ship using the wrong name and committing crimes meant that everything had gone wrong with the system.

"How did you find him?" I asked Cleo when my breathing no longer needed my conscious control.

"I looked under his old name and the computer listed him as off the ship." Cleo had half finished her glass and was getting out her cigars. I let go of the chair to take one from her, proud that my hand no longer shook so noticeably. "I called someone else. They told me about the party. Gasset was there."

It was unreal. There were legends in the smuggling community of convicts who had shut down their mechanics, eluded arrest, and lived in the ship as creatures of pure, unregistered meat, but they were just legends. Particularly in the Bilges, people could go a long time as just meat, but eventually they would need some form of smart something that wouldn't respond until it had identified them, and once it did, the robots would be all over a fugitive. This Gasset had managed to hide for a year and a half, at least.

"He must be a little nuts," I said, getting out my lighter for our cigars. "A hard-core Blender who can't use his mechanics."

I'd been about to light Cleo's cigar, but suddenly it wasn't there. She'd turned away and had dropped the hand with the thin cigar into her lap. "Cleo?"

"He uses his mechanics," she said.

"He what?"

"He's living under an assumed identity. He blends, dreams, everything."

I was past the point of shakes or heavy breathing. I put the lighter under the end of my cigar and pulled on it hard to draw the flame into the leaf. I focused on the act, appreciating the contrast of the taste of the harsh smoke against the sweet of the strawberries and the sour of the champagne. I pulled the smoke all the way into my lungs and let it burn there for a moment before blowing it all out in one ironic word:

"Bliss."

Everything had gone wrong with the system, and one man was milking it for all it was worth.

Lisa ended Isenivavach's three-day run at the tournament. He came at her with a cruiser gambit that was supposed to set up a battleship-driven assault. Lisa turned the gambit, sacrificed her destroyers to slow the battleships, and enveloped Isenivavach before he could reach her Fleet ship. It was textbook chess, Isenivavach playing a good opening and Lisa playing a proper response, but Lisa had played hers better. Isenivavach simply didn't have the form he'd had against Paine.

I watched the end of the match from my seat. I'd tried to get Cleo to stay with me so we could go together to Todd with the news about Gasset. Cleo, however, fortified by the champagne and by having shared her fears with me, decided to meet with Gasset as Todd wanted.

At the end of her match, Lisa shook hands with

Isenivavach, bowed to the clapping onlookers, and then came over to me rather than going to the exit. I met her at the chrome rail that separated the chairs from the board.

"Can you come out with us, now?" Lisa asked.

"I wish I could," I said. "I have to see the Narandova game."

"Have to?"

"He granted me two classic-style games. The least I can do is watch him play the real matches."

"Estelle told me he'd been seen with you. I thought maybe you were coaching him, too." Lisa said this with a smile that appeared to mean she was only half joking.

"No. I played his son in a tournament once. We bumped into each other, and he asked me to play. Maybe he's a little lonely here without his wife."

Two of Lisa's mothers, Quinlyn and Myra, had worked their way around the stadium to us. "Hello, Aaron," Quinlyn said in a voice of complete neutrality. Four other members of their clan stood by the exit, chatting and looking our way occasionally.

"Hello," I said, taking each of the women's hands in turn and bowing over them. Like my clan before its emigration, Lisa's family were midlevel ship's engineers. These days they were mostly retired from ship's service, as Lisa's income had done away with the need for others in the clan to work.

"What did you think?" Myra asked. "Wasn't she terrific?" Unlike my family, Lisa's had not let their appearance age when they became parents. Whereas my mother had let her face and body thicken, both Quinlyn and Myra kept their bodies thin and their faces smooth. The two of them also wore flowered skirts that stopped just above their knees and sleeveless, V-necked blouses of a better machine make.

"Lisa is always wonderful, but she also played well," I said, willing to add to Lisa's embarrassment and Quinlyn's discomfort.

"We tell her Goff doesn't stand a chance this time."

"Myra," Quinlyn said. She had liked me better when I was a player. I didn't think she disliked me now, but she was confused by my new career. Cops made a lot of people uncomfortable.

"Speaking of Goff," Lisa said, jumping in after her mother. "What are you doing after the Narandova match? I'd like to bounce some things off you before I play her tomorrow."

"I'd love to," I said, meaning it. "The problem is that I'm in the middle of a case right now." Lisa nodded, but didn't hide her disappointment. I didn't hide mine either. "I've got a dinner meeting. I don't know how long it will take, but I might be free afterward. I'll check if you're still up and come by if you are. Okay?"

"That would be great," Lisa said. I took her hand and bowed over it too, then nodded to the mothers and withdrew. Lisa stayed to sign autographs for the five or six men and the two girls who had been patiently waiting for her to finish with me, then headed for the locker room. I leaned on my stick and watched until she was gone, thinking how her playing dress did not do her justice. If I made it to see her that evening, she was likely to have changed and fixed her hair. I speculated about that until thinking of the evening made me think of Cleo. I sent my mechanics off to the ship's computers to find her, but she had her own mechanics shut down. Probably she was talking to Gasset, but I wished there was a way to be sure she was all right.

Like rehab, the intership shuttlecraft, a little fleet of their own, were another example of the difference between life in the Fleet and life back on Earth. The computers hated the shuttles. They took hydrogen from the Fleet ships that would otherwise have gone to the generators, and every time a shuttle was damaged or lost, the Fleet lost valuable heavy elements that might be needed before the journey's end. The Fleet ships were designed to be self-sufficient. In the computers' view, the trade between ships served no purpose great enough to justify the risk.

But then, the computers didn't get a vote. On Earth they would have; in the Fleet, it was the crews who ruled the ships, and humans liked the trade, even with its risks. Despite the limitless spaces available in the dreams, knowing that you could get on a shuttle and leave made the ships feel less cramped.

Narandova's son, Roman, was piloting the *Jo Lin*, which was only a few light-seconds out from the *Jersey* now. A voice-only dream would have been more discreet, but having never met the man, I wanted a full sensory introduction. I wanted to be able to judge for myself what Roman thought about Bliss. He received me in a dream of the shuttle's passenger compartment that differed from the real one only in that it contained no passengers.

My meat wasn't sure that the toned man who rose to greet me in the dream was the same person as the thin youth I'd played chess against ten years before, but my mechanics assured me it was him. The dream Roman was wearing the uniform of a captain in the *Warsaw*'s Shuttle Pilot Corps, the *Warsaw* being one of the few ships that actually maintained a tradition of uniforms for some of its crew functions. The uniform was a blue-on-burgundy jumpsuit with a gold collar. Roman's was machine-made, but he'd had it human-tailored.

"I'm not sure I like you coming here," is how Roman greeted me.

"I'm not sure I like it either, but I need the answers to some questions, and we don't have time to let your father relay them."

"If you say so." Roman turned away from me as if he were going to begin pacing, but he changed his mind and came back, turning a full circle before ending up facing me again. "Look, you're sure I'm not going to be arrested?"

"Positive," I said. "You'll be granted immunity in exchange for your testimony, but if we're going to get that far, I need to know the procedure once you reach the *Jersey*."

"What good is your immunity going to do me on the *Warsaw*? That's how I got into this mess. How do I know the *Warsaw* Security won't just use the evidence I give you to arrest me when I return?"

This was the moment when I wished Cleo were along; she was as good at calming nervous witnesses as I was at lying to our targets. "The Security Forces are going to want a crack at Bliss, too. They're going to need a star witness just as much as we will. It will look pretty bad for them if they file charges against you after we've declared you a hero. Now, where is the contraband and how is it packed?"

"You realize this is probably the end of my flying career? Not that you care." Even filtered by his mechanics, Roman's anger was coming through in the dream. I wondered what sort of state his meat was in, and what he had been doing when I called. On the *Jersey*, my meat took a deep breath, but my mechanics kept my dream self calm. It didn't help to know that Cleo would have been able to phrase this more gently.

"Your career as a pilot was over the moment you decided to carry the contraband for Tourvak rather than turning him in." Roman started to protest, but I kept talking. "It was just a matter of time. No matter how careful you were or what protection Tourvak promised you, eventually you were going to get caught. If you had gone to Security in the beginning, you might have been able to make a deal that let you keep flying. Now all you can do is make a deal that keeps you out of rehab."

In the shared reality of a full sensory dream, people generally conformed their dream actions to the laws of the meat world. They didn't have to. In this place, Roman and I were just dreams moving in a world of shadows, and anything was possible to us. Roman took advantage of this now, pulling back from me without the pretense of turning and walking.

I wanted to chase Roman, grab him by the shoulders and yell into his face that he was risking our lives by prolonging this call, but I didn't. Instead, I settled onto the semicircular couch that faced the big bubble portal in the shuttle's side. The view was the same as it would have been in the real shuttle, but I changed it to a feed from one of the stalks, looking back past the shuttle's braking flame toward the on-coming *Jersey*. It hung there, the giant ship in which my meat currently rested, visible as only the bright point generated by its own flame.

Roman appeared beside me suddenly. He didn't look at me, but he did speak. "We will land at the shuttle bay as scheduled," he said. "The passengers will debark, and the cargo will be unloaded. When that is done, I will release the crew for a night of lib-erty. I remain with the ship while the maintenance and cleaning robots come on board. It is during this time that Tourvak and his men come. The contraband is in the ship's emergency lockers. Tourvak brings crates of fresh supplies and takes off the contraband."

"You replace the survival gear with contraband?" I couldn't believe it.

Roman sniffed. "Survival gear. What could we sur-vive that the shuttle couldn't? Those things are anachronisms, a waste of space. Where are the sur-vival lockers on a Fleet ship?"

It wasn't worth arguing, but I was suddenly very glad that I was only a ghost on this shuttle. "So the contraband stays in the boxes until after it leaves the bay?"

"Yes."

"Do you go with Tourvak when he takes it away?"

"No."

"But you meet him later to collect your cut."

"Yes."

"Where?"

"There is a party after the Chess Championship match. We are to meet there."

"Good. We may wait to make the bust then, so don't get nervous if you don't hear anything immediately." Roman nodded. He still hadn't looked at me. I wondered if I'd missed anything, but my mechanics said I hadn't. "All right. I'll be in touch again if I have to, but only if I have to." I offered him my hand. "Thank you. You're doing the right thing."

"Am I?" This dream Roman finally looked at me. He even glanced at my hand but didn't take it. "First Tourvak forces me to smuggle, and now you're forcing me to stop. If it was up to me, I'd just fly this ship, and the devil could have you both."

"If it makes you feel any better," I said, "he already does."

CHAPTER 6

SORROW

The lifts are one of the few ship's systems that have not undergone revision since the *Jersey* left Earth. They and their chutes are the same size and run the same paths that they did when the tugs pushed the ship out of orbit. Even the appointments are unchanged. When the Ship's Articles were drawn up, the founders saw a link between physical and social mobility. They believed that so long as any crew member could go easily and quickly to any level of the ship, there would never be fixed social classes. Thus, it was actually easier to redirect the flame path than to change the course of a lift.

When I left my flat for my appointment with Todd and Cleo at the Stand, I got into a lift whose synthetic red silk–covered bench was already occupied. I nodded to the former Fleet Champion as strangers do on lifts and settled myself into the corner.

"I'm sorry," Goff said in her vowel-nipping accent, "but I think we've met." The Champion was in pale red tonight, wearing a patterned blouse and stirruped slacks. Her normally brown hair was tinted to match her blouse, while her rings, bracelets, and necklace were all set with deep red pearls. "We danced," Goff went on, "although you had a different name at the time."

"Officer Aaron Hudson," I said, giving the little jerk of a bow that was the form on the *Panzer*. "We have indeed danced. I was working undercover at the time."

"Not investigating me?" Goff asked. It seemed a serious question, so I hastened to reassure her.

"No. Meeting you was a happy accident. It is good of you to remember the incident."

"I always remember flirting when it is in good taste. I endure too much of the other kind."

"Indeed?" I glanced about the lift. "You seem to be currently without the main body of your admirers."

"The computers have made me hard for an average fan to discover, so I have some privacy away from the tournament. Why do you say the main body though? Am I not alone?" Goff's frown of puzzlement was much the same as the frown she sometimes wore in tournaments.

"Madam, no. I think I must be counted as one of your admirers. A devoted one at that."

"Not so devoted. Are you not the Aaron Hudson who plays chess with Narandova?"

I flinched, exaggerating my surprise in hopes that she would take it as part of the byplay. "I am. I was not aware that our games were general knowledge."

"Chess is a small world."

"So it appears, but you have mistaken my motives. I meet Narandova as your champion, not as his intimate." This earned me the wonderful sound of Goff's laughter.

"My champion? I see. And how is my honor faring?"

"I fear my chess playing is not the equal of yours," I said, and that made her laugh again. It was also the moment when the lift's doors opened for the Stand's level. "Is this also . . . ?"

"Yes, I am meeting a friend for dinner."

"May I escort you?" I asked, offering her my hand.

"By all means." The Former Champion put her hand through my arm, and I led her into the corridor. I found myself hoping that the people we met would recognize Goff enough to envy me.

"Will you be playing Narandova again?" Goff asked.

"I hope to."

"Perhaps your play suffers because you do not have a token from your lady." Goff took one of the red pearl rings from her fingers and placed it on my right pinky. It was made of smart gold and resized itself as she slipped it on.

"Madam, I can't—"

"Yes, you can. I expect to hear from you that my favor has brought you victory." She gave me her smile and gestured to the entrance of the Stand. "This is my destination."

"Actually, it is mine, too." Goff looked at me, as if reevaluating me again. "No, honestly. I have friends waiting for me as well." Reassured that I was not attempting to prolong our encounter, Goff visibly relaxed.

"Perhaps you and your friends would like to join us?" she offered.

"No. It is kind of you, but we would not intrude. Besides, ours is a working meal."

"How sad. I do expect to hear from you though."

"You may count on it," I said, stepping back to give her the little bow again. She returned it and went into the Stand, throwing me one last smile over her shoulder before the darkness absorbed her.

I gave myself two beats, then stepped into the darkness as well. I was just in time to see Bliss come striding out of an alcove and meet Goff in the center of the floor.

The Stand gets away with its decor because most of its patrons spend no time in the Bilges. It is a compressed space of tubes and alcoves spread over differing levels and set at different angles. It is dark and close. The floor feels like you are walking on dead bugs, your hand comes away wet from touching a wall, and the smells vary from cloying to choking.

When you have your mechanics on, none of this atmosphere bothers you much as you simply edit out what you don't want to experience. It is more of a problem for cops or smugglers who are used to keeping their mechanics off. Which is one of the reasons that Cleo and Todd and I used it. We were unlikely to run into anyone we knew at the Stand, which made the prospect of eavesdroppers that much less.

Now Bliss was in the restaurant with us. I gave the news to Cleo and Todd without bothering to sit down because I assumed we would be leaving, but Todd vetoed that.

"How is that going to look?" he asked. "We just got here. We find out he's here, and we leave? Why don't

we just make a big red banner that says 'We're investigating you'?"

"It's not going to look like that. What does he care if
we come or go? This is the Stand; he won't even see
us leave."

"Aaron. Get over it, okay? Sit down and order, so
we can get started."

In the past four days I had done more arguing with
Todd than we had done in the previous year and a half.
I was tired of it, and I was tired of being scared. And it
was always possible that he was right. I sat down.

Todd and Cleo had already been in their seats
when I arrived, but they had not yet ordered. Todd
hadn't changed clothes since that morning, and Cleo
hadn't changed since the chess match. I thought Cleo
looked tired but not as worried as I'd left her earlier.

"Everything went okay with Gasset?" I asked. Todd
tapped his neck impatiently.

"Could we order first? Then we'll talk."

The cuisine at the Stand was like the decor: black
and disgusting. I couldn't imagine why Todd was in a
hurry to get to it. I had raided the stores in my flat before coming down because I knew that without my
mechanics, I would be able to tolerate little of the
processed kibbles that would constitute the meal.
Even the drinks were going to be blackened and
thickened glucose. I ordered a salad and coffee without accessing the menu. Cleo sat slumped in her
chair, eyes focused on the bare smart wood of the
table. Todd gazed inward and ordered for both of
them. When his attention came back, the three of us
turned off our mechanics, and I asked again, "How
did it go with Gassett?"

"Fine." Cleo's mouth barely moved when she said the word. She looked so bored that I had an irrational feeling of guilt for forcing her to be there. I looked at Todd, raising my eyebrows in questioning.

Todd gestured with his right hand, displaying its palm to the room. "He talked to her."

"Did she tell you who this Gasset really is?"

"Yes. Bliss is pulling more strings than we thought."

That seemed to be putting it mildly. "He's making everything we do a joke. Is he setting all of our convicts free? Are we going to bump into Mr. Hines in the hall tomorrow?" Todd shrugged. "You don't seem very upset. Am I missing something? Isn't this your bust that Bliss is spitting on?"

"My bust?" Todd asked. "Which bust?"

Oh. "Maybe Cleo didn't have time to tell you everything?" We turned our eyes on Cleo, and she met them. First mine, then Todd's. She shifted in her chair, dropping her eyes and slouching to the other side.

"Gasset is Kurt Grayson," Cleo told the tabletop.

Todd took it a lot better than I had. With hardly a blink, he spread his other hand so both of his palms were up and lying on the table.

"And you didn't tell me that because . . . ?"

"Because you'd be angry that I was at a party with him and didn't tell you."

Todd rolled his hands over and laid them flat on the table. "I'm not angry, but I'm getting that way. What party?"

"The blending party, the night before our celebration party." Cleo said this as if Todd were an idiot for needing to be reminded.

There followed a silence while Todd looked at Cleo and Cleo looked at the table. From the way their expressions flickered I wondered if they hadn't turned on their mechanics again to have the matter out in private. This was not a good idea, so I said, "Look, I can come back in ten minutes if the two of you want to talk."

"No. There's nothing to say," Todd said, but his tone made it clear there would be later. I paused to see if Cleo wanted to dissent. When she didn't, I carried on.

"So what did Gasset or Kurt or whatever tell you?"

"Bliss got him the new identity, so Gasset works for Bliss. He can't quit until the term of his rehab is up."

"Does he know where they take the contraband from the shuttle?" Todd asked.

"Usually, they truck it up to the Bilges."

"Usually?" I said.

"Can Gasset find the place in the Bilges where Bliss stores the stuff?" Todd asked.

"Bliss doesn't store it. He sells it the same day it arrives."

"Usually," I said.

Cleo actually sighed. "Sometimes they take it and store it away immediately on a different shuttle."

"Meaning that he runs a trade to more than one ship," Todd said. Cleo just nodded, once.

"I wonder if this is one of the times they'll be loading onto another shuttle? If we can get that pilot, too, get him to roll over on the guys on the next ship. This is huge."

"Yes," Todd agreed. "Yes. Maybe too big."

That got Cleo to look at him. "Todd?"I asked.

"Look. We bust Bliss and his group. We even get the people he's got on the other ships. We get promoted while he's convicted and sentenced to rehab. How do we know he isn't going to get around the sentence?"

"You want to find out how he's getting the new identities."

"At a minimum. I'm not sure we shouldn't just leave Bliss alone and just bust this Gasset, again. We could hand him over to S.I.D. and let them take it from there. If they catch Bliss along the way, fine."

Cleo got up. We both stopped to look at her, but she just walked past us without a word. I didn't say anything because I expected Todd to, but he just watched her go. When he turned back to me, it was my turn to hold up my palms.

"She's having some problems," Todd said. "You'll have to ask her."

"Are we going to have to do this without her?"

"Are we going to do it at all? Aaron, we got into this mess because Gaunt was sniffing around you. We looked into Bliss to get that robot off your back, and look what we found. Rehab itself is being corrupted. Don't you think our turning that in will get Gaunt off you? It will, and we'd still be heroes, and we wouldn't have to face Bliss straight up."

I was spared the need to answer by the arrival of our "food." While the robot set the unappetizing mess before us, I tried to stop wondering about Cleo and consider what Todd was saying. It made, I had to admit, a certain amount of sense. My worry while being on the *Jo Lin* that Bliss would discover our plot and somehow kill us all had been very real. It would be very comforting to step back and let the robots take the point, but it wouldn't work.

The robot was gone, and Todd was actually putting some of the black and blue mess in his mouth when I said, "It won't work. Either Gaunt won't link Bliss to Gasset, in which case it will be too small a bust and he will come right back to us, or Gaunt will link it to Bliss and then he'll want to know how we could find out about the rehab without learning more. You said yourself that Contraband is in trouble the moment that Bliss goes down. If we are the ones who bring him in, then we are in a position to bail out and save our careers. If Gaunt does it, then we are in as much trouble as ever, with nowhere to go."

"You're sure? Even with Cleo like this? Even with the risk to our lives? You're sure you want to go on?"

"I'm sure," I said, and then I said it again, this time like I meant it.

"All right. We started this thing, let's finish it." He reached into his vest and pulled out a paper notepad and an antique pen. "This is what I decided about the shuttle bay," he said, laying the notepad down and flipping to a sketch. "There is an access tunnel here . . . "

It was after 9:00 P.M. by the time that Todd and I finished. I said good-bye to him at the entrance to the Stand, and told my mechanics to get me to the lift while I tried to get hold of Cleo. The computer, however, couldn't find her. She'd shut down her mechanics. I knew I could still find her, eventually, but Todd might find her first, and besides, Lisa answered my call immediately.

"It's not too late?" I asked.

"Not at all. The match isn't until afternoon. Come on by." She received me in a bare dream of blue pastels. Her dream self was ghostly below the neck. Apparently her mechanics were busy, and she didn't have a lot to spare for this shared reality.

"I should change," I said. The aroma of the Stand lingered over me.

"No, just come on. The family won't bother us, and you don't have to dress up for me."

"It's not my appearance I'm worried about."

"You can explain that when you get here," Lisa said, and cut the dream off. I came back to myself on the lift, a floor away from my flat. I asked the car to halt and gave it Lisa's floor. I put my mechanics to work on the way I smelled and wished for once that I wore smart clothes of some sort.

There is no hard line between the Midlands and the Estates, just a blurry, shifting stratum of biggish family spaces that tend to move down and up with the families' fortunes. The Raymonds' space was in this area; it had generally been growing and moving down over the last few seasons as Lisa's tournament results and winnings improved.

A collie answered my ring at the door. He sniffed me over while his mechanics talked to the family computer about me. I passed muster and the dog allowed his ears to be scratched, then led me past an unoccupied and compacted sitting room to a ring of doors. He pawed at one, and Lisa opened it.

As I'd hoped, she had changed clothes since the match that afternoon, although the oversize T-shirt and baggy knit pants she now wore were even less flattering than the playing dress had been. The stripes

were gone from her hair, which was loose and un-
combed, but she'd kept the ones on her cheeks. She
reached to hug me, but I held up a hand.

"You should probably adjust your nose first. I had
dinner at the Stand." Lisa's nose wrinkled as she
sniffed. She blinked while talking to her mechanics.

"That's what you meant by changing."

"Yes. I'm sorry. It was work."

"Well." Lisa stepped back to let me into the room.
"You should wear smart clothes."

"Can't in my profession. Hard to keep anything in
confidence when your underwear is listening."

"I'll take your word for it. Put your jacket in the
hamper at least." She took a moment to glance at the
closed door. "Can I talk you out of those pants?"

"Madam." I put my hand to my throat in shock.

"Get over it. I'll find you a pair of smart shorts."
She turned to her dresser, but smiled back at me. "Besides, you can't have grown up that different."

"You might be amazed," I told her while I hung my
jacket in the dirty clothes hamper. I stepped out of my
shoes, took hold of the clasp on my pants, and hesitated. I was surprised to find myself embarrassed. To
cover, I asked, "Whose dog?"

"Mom's. The rest of the family wanted another
child, but Quinlyn convinced them to get the dog. She
said it was like having a child that would never grow
up on us." As Lisa traded me the shorts for my pants,
her eyes dropped down to check the bulge in my
briefs. "Nothing too amazing from this angle," she
commented.

"Don't be too quick to judge," I said. As with Cleo
the night before, there was a moment, looking into

each other's eyes, remembering other nights, when I might have leaned forward and kissed Lisa. Unlike the night before, there was no one in the next room to take offense, and yet I didn't lean forward. I couldn't tell if I was really having these chances, or if I was just imagining them.

"What was it you wanted to talk about?" I asked while easing the shorts on very slowly, giving them time to adjust to my larger legs and hips.

"Chess," Lisa said. She waved her arm around the room. "I've got a match tomorrow, and since you suggested the strategy, I want to work through it with you." Although Lisa was exactly my age and thus into her beginning twenties, she still kept her room like a teenager. Smart things will try to keep themselves folded and out of the way, but there has to be a place for them to go. Lisa's bed sheets were straight, but the supplies on the dresser were in a haphazard scatter. The walls were covered with holographs of horses and sunsets and rainbows.

None of those things were what Lisa had waved at. She wanted me to note the chess sets. There were five hanging around the room. Over the bed, over the desk, in the open space on the way to the bathroom, and two hanging over the study pit. In addition, holos of position papers and game analyses were stacked by the sets. With my mechanics, I reached out to sort through the nearest mound of holos, finding at the bottom a monograph I remembered from my playing days. The rest were far more recent.

"You've been working hard," I said.

"Sometimes I think I never stop working." Lisa moved a different pile of holos with her mechanics, then crawled onto the bed. Her pale ankles appeared as she crossed her legs and her pants rode up. "Aaron. You won't think I'm a bad person if I tell you something."

Lisa looked so serious that I took a step toward her. "You are not a bad person."

"I hate that dog. Since the day Mom announced we were going to get it."

There was room for both of us on the bed, but I sat down on the backrest of the study pit's couch instead. "You are not a bad person."

"I have to win at least two matches in every tournament I enter just to keep us in food and living space." Lisa pulled a pillow over on to her lap and talked to it as she imitated Quinlyn. "If I have a bad week, Mom's there: 'It's all right. You'll do better next time. You don't want us to give up Sebastian.' I just want to scream that I don't give a damn about Sebastian." Lisa shook the pillow for emphasis.

"You don't hate the dog. You hate the pressure."

"I had a really good year last year. We were going to take a big chunk of the prize money and buy me more computer space, so I could make the jump to the next level. Or at least not have to work so hard to keep my meat in shape. Then Mom comes home with this need for a dog."

"Well, I wouldn't suggest enrolling in the Security Forces as a career change just now." I tugged at the cuffs of the shorts. "Among its other problems, you smelled what being a cop is like."

Lisa didn't smile. "I don't want a career change. I like chess. I'm really good at it. I just wish it wasn't so serious every time. I wish I could just enjoy a match every now and then."

"There's no reason you shouldn't enjoy this match with Goff tomorrow," I said, glancing at the ring on my finger. "No one expects you to win. All you have to do is relax and put her on the ropes."

"That's easy to say." Lisa grabbed up the pillow and hugged it to her. "Beating Goff in the Championship would be the biggest thing I've ever done. I can't relax with that hanging over my head."

"Then we should work," I said, or have sex, I thought. Lisa wasn't Cleo, and she was across the room, and we hadn't even touched yet tonight, but there was a history between us, and I would have loved to hold her, but I couldn't if it wasn't what she wanted. I rolled off the back of the couch and down into the couch proper. "Show me what you've done with my idea," I said, and so she did.

The next three hours were very strange for me. I had spent so much time in Contraband, and so much of that time undercover, that I had forgotten what it was like to go after a problem with your mechanics not only on, but working full bore. More, I had forgotten what it was like to open your mechanics to the ship's computers without guilt or worry. It was a fantastic feeling of freedom, like when I used to trash my good clothes before a tournament.

For more than three hours, Lisa and I focused on chess. We looked at holograms and we looked at dream games. We talked and we dreamed. We wandered about her room and we lay still. We listened to each other and to our mechanics and to the computers. And we did this all seamlessly. More than once I had to stop and check if I were dreaming or if we were discussing something in our meat.

It was exhilarating how much of chess I still had in me and at the same time frustrating how much more Lisa could see than I could. Still, I helped. Not everything I suggested could be used, and I could seldom follow Lisa once she got going with the computer, but every now and then I could add something.

Toward the end of the time, we were sitting side by side on the bed, underneath a holo of a unicorn running against a sunset toward a rainbow. We'd just come out of a long dream game and were catching our breath over two frosty glasses of orange glucose when Lisa reached over and fingered my new ring. "What is this?" she asked. "I've never seen you wear jewelry."

"You don't want to know."

"Now I definitely do."

"It will just make you angry."

"In that case, you're not leaving till you tell me." Lisa had left her hand on top of mine as she rubbed the ring's red pearl. Now she gripped my fingers. I turned my head to look at her eyes. Lisa's head tilted a little, my heart beat a little faster, and there was a scratching at the door.

"What?" Lisa called, looking toward the door in annoyance. The dog sent us both a dream. There was a plastic security robot at the front door, and it wanted to talk to me.

My first thought was Cleo, and I jumped from the bed. "What is it?" Lisa asked. I was opening the hamper and pulling out my clothes.

"I don't know. One of my partners was in a bad

way. I hope . . ." My mechanics couldn't find Cleo. Todd was in their flat, but Cleo, wherever she was, didn't have her mechanics on.

"Lisa," I said. I'd dropped the shorts and was pulling on my pants, which smelled much better for the mechanical care. "I'm going to try to be there for the match. If I'm not there in person, I'll be watching. I'm sorry about this."

"What is it?" Lisa asked again. "You sound like you're in trouble."

"There's a computer who'd like me to be. It may take a while to set it straight."

"I'll walk you to the door," she said.

"I . . ." I had opened my mouth to object, but it died in my throat. To my surprise, I realized I was actually scared. "I'd appreciate that."

Lisa held my hand, and the dog led the way for the ten steps it took to confront the robot. Some of Lisa's clan had opened their doors and were looking out. Quinlyn was at the door with the robot, asking it questions that it refused to answer. "I am here to escort Aaron Hudson on an official matter," the plastic robot was repeating as we walked up.

"I'm here," I told it.

"Please come with me, Officer."

"Be careful," Lisa said, putting her arms around me. I squeezed her back.

"I will. See you at the match." I let her go and, under Quinlyn's disapproving eye, followed the robot down the corridor toward the lift. "What's this about?" I asked it.

"There's been an explosion in your flat, Officer. We need your help with the investigation."

188 Eric T. Baker

* * *

Robots had closed off the corridor leading to my flat. Five crewpeople were standing around, looking over the robot's reflective shoulders, trying to pierce the physical and dream blackout of the incident scene. My passing through the barrier gave them something to speculate and query the computer about.

Gaunt stood before the door to my flat, evidently waiting on me. He wore a long smart coat, the sort of garment that was not only armored, but could close up into an artificial environment if necessary. Under it, he had his ivory shirt buttoned all the way and his slacks still had their crease. He wore a tan slouch hat over his thinning hair and looked (as he no doubt intended) very sharp and professional.

"How bad is it?" I asked.

"Bad," Gaunt said. He reached into his coat and brought out a cigar case. "You want one?"

"No. What happened?"

"About ten minutes ago, the environment computers read an explosion in your flat. Did it contain any unregistered flammables?"

"No."

Gaunt had his memento lighter out and was sucking the flame into a thin cigar. I watched the flame reflected in his brown eyes before his exhalation of smoke obscured them. "Preliminary indications are an alcohol fire that triggered explosively. The forensics machines are going over things now. We should be able to go in in a few minutes."

"How big was the fire?" I was thinking of my stock of unlicensed wines and spirits. I couldn't imagine what might have happened to make them combust.

"Big. I'm not sure how much you're going to be able to salvage in there." Gaunt blew a puff of smoke toward the door. By the smell of the cigar, there was no THC in it. "Does anyone else have access to your flat?"

"A couple of people." Cleo and Todd for instance. "I can't imagine any of them setting fire to the place though."

"What about John Edison?"

"Yeah. I gave John access so he could . . ." I stopped because Gaunt was looking at me too intently and because I had just remembered the last time I'd seen John. "Was he . . . I mean, did he . . ."

"They've got him at the Trauma Center. They're trying to save as much of his organic body as they can. I told you the explosion was bad. He's lucky he was carrying something big in front of him. It shielded his brain from the worst of the explosion and the flame. If his hands had been empty . . ." Gaunt finished the sentence by inhaling another lungful of cigar smoke.

This was not a good situation. This was not a good situation at all. I was very glad to have my mechanics on. I simply surrendered my body to them, letting them keep my breathing regular and my hands from shaking. There had been no gun pointed at my head this time, but someone had tried to kill me all the same.

My door opened and robots began to dribble out. They were maintenance models, modified by expert computers to examine a crime scene. Even now, downloads from all the surviving smart objects in my flat were being pored over by the S.I.D. computers, along with fiber, tissue, and mechanics samples from the exposed surfaces. None of these things were likely to be helpful since the person who had set the explosion was either good enough to break in without setting off any sort of alarm or was a friend that the smart functions wouldn't be able to distinguish from my everyday visitors.

"Are you up to having a look around?" Gaunt asked. I nodded, and he led the way in.

The first thing that struck me was the smell. The whole space smelled like a distillery had exploded. The flat was dim—the smart walls had been knocked out, and the emergency lights strung up by the robots were not as bright. The extent of the damage made itself apparent to me only slowly. Everything that had been on all the walls had been knocked down. The bookcase, for instance, had broken in half, toppled to the floor, and then caught fire. My couch was overturned, broken, and burned. The wicker cover on the cool box was mostly gone. The floor was a sea of ash. Here and there an ember still glowed.

Gaunt just stood there and smoked while I took it all in.

The explosion had taken the doors of the closet off their hinges. The fire hadn't made it into the closet itself, and the clothes and hats piled in the bottom weren't burned, but some of them would be torn and they would all smell like smoke, perhaps forever. Some of my boxes were split open, and some of the weren't. I didn't want to start sifting through them until Gaunt was gone.

My drifting about the space in the yellow light of the emergency bulbs brought me back to the door and my canes. They had been knocked over, spilled into the ash, and then pushed out of the way by the robots. They had looked better, but they had survived as well as anything. My newest one, the handcrafted cane of ebony, ivory, and silver, was a little scorched, but it was in one piece, and the black wood hid the marks of the explosion. I picked it up and leaned on it, thinking that perhaps my mechanics could use the help.

"So," I asked Gaunt, "what's next?"

The robot in its meat shell dropped his cigar butt into the ash on the floor and crushed it out. "Next we find out who did this. Who wants you dead, Aaron?"

"Everyone I've ever put into rehab and all of their friends, I assume," I said. Thanks to Cleo's revelation about Gasset, I couldn't even discount the ones who were still in rehab. "You're satisfied it wasn't an accident." It hadn't been a question, but Gaunt took it that way.

"I'll have to wait for the final forensics reports, but from what I see, someone set up a dumb bomb booby trap for you, and your friend John walked right into it. You're very lucky. I doubt you would have been carrying a box of contraband if you'd come home first. Not that you don't have enough here already."

"Enough what?"

"Contraband."

"Someone blows up my home so you're going to arrest me?"

"Not yet." Gaunt glanced around the room and then back to me. "I want your help. Don't you think it's time you gave it to me?"

"No."

"No?" Gaunt took a step forward and suddenly his face was directly before mine. "No? No!" Gaunt stalked away from me, going to the broken cool box and talking to the wall. "No. It's still time to protect the other grifters and thieves that you work with. Fine." He pushed his hat back on his head and turned to face me again. "Fine. But it is time for you to drop the injured, holier-than-thou, I'm-trying-save-the-ship attitude. I've seen where you live. Officer."

"I don't know why you play at being human, robot. If I ever decide to get friendly with a computer, it will be one that is much better looking than you are." Gaunt opened his mouth as if to give something away with an angry retort, but he appeared to stop himself. "Oh, please," I said. Why did he keep trying? How dumb did he think I was? "Look, you catch this bomber. I've got a friend in Trauma, and I want to go see him. Now."

"Of course. Go. Just ask yourself; if you don't help me, how many more times are you going to be lucky?"

In the lift, on my way to the Trauma Center, I put through a dream to Todd. There was a delay and then Todd was there with me. "How are you?" was how he greeted me.

"Then you heard," I said. I would rather our surroundings had been his flat, but he had chosen to come to me. "Where's Cleo?"

"She's with me." This dream Todd was wearing a red and blue flannel robe over a pair of navy pajama bottoms. I had a stab of jealous curiosity to know whether I had actually interrupted something, or if he was covering up for Cleo. "What happened?"

"Someone put a booby trap in my flat. It caught John, but Gaunt thinks it was meant for me."

"Do you?"

"Yes. I think you and Cleo had better watch your step, too." Todd nodded in agreement. "I'm on my way to see John. Should I come see you guys when I'm done?"

"No." Todd said. I must have shown my surprise because he added, "Look, it's just not a good time tonight. There's nothing we could do anyway. Get some rest, and we'll meet in the morning."

"Actually, that's part of the reason I wanted to come by. I can't really go back to my flat."

"I'm sorry, Aaron. I am, but . . . you can ask Cleo about it tomorrow."

"Sure," I said, thinking, What? My home is blown to pieces, and you, my partners, don't have time for me? "I'll call you in the morning."

"Right," Todd said, and he was gone.

In the Trauma Center, they let me into the dream where they were keeping John's consciousness while the doctors and their computers labored to rebuild his body. The setting was one of the Midland Malls, and John sat on a bench in the center courtyard while dream crewpeople passed from store to store, many waving and stopping to say hello. The pert dream nurse who'd been sitting next to John on the bench, keeping him alert and interested by flirting with him, excused herself as I came up.

"Sorry to interrupt," I said.

"S'okay. She's just a computer. Cute one though."

"How do you feel?" I asked as I sat down. The bench was warmer than a real wooden one would have been, but that was part of the point.

"Shaky." He blinked. "Like that. Things flicker. I guess they're having trouble getting me all linked up again."

"S.I.D. tells me that you saved my life. Thank you."

"What are friends for?" John smiled and waved back at another young crew member in a scoop-necked dress. "It's embarrassing how they picked this dream for me. I must have a bigger reputation than I thought."

"I doubt they use it just for you. They want you to feel alive and wanted. I'll bet this dream works for a lot of people."

"Great. Don't make me feel special or anything." John picked up the glass sitting on the bench and took a drink. "Root beer. Want one?"

"No, thanks. Did you see anything? Any idea who set the bomb?"

"Nothing. I had my mechanics on to access your flat, but then I shut them down 'cause I didn't know what you might have lying out. I picked up the box. I had to look to the side to maneuver because it was big and in front of my face. I made the turn into your living room and someone hit my whole body with a sledgehammer. I woke up here."

"I'm sorry."

"No. The nurse said the box saved me. Better me here and you alive. 'Course if you could be here and we both be alive, I'd have preferred that."

"Yeah. Did you have anything valuable in the box?"

"No. It was all copies of things. I can make new ones when I get out of here. Oh." His smile slipped. "Oh, except for your book."

Even in the dream, my head jerked in amazement. "You're kidding? You were actually returning something the same day?"

"Yeah. I'm never going to make that mistake again."

"I should say." We both laughed, and John reached for his drink again, but I was saddened. To lose Chris's gift along with everything else made the explosion seem worse than it had a few minutes before. My mood must have shown through in the dream because John said, "I'm sorry. I'll look around at the shows. Maybe I can find you another."

"Don't worry about a book." I shook my head. "Right now you just need to get better."

A young-looking mother and her younger-looking daughter stopped to say hello to John, and I took the opportunity to stand up. "Just a minute," John told the dream women, and turned to me. "You're leaving?"

"Yes. It's been a long day, and there's still a lot to do."

"Are you going to look for the guy who set the bomb?"

"Yes."

John just nodded, but as I turned to go he said, "Aaron?"

"Yes?"

"This isn't as much fun as it looks. Be careful."

"Thanks. I will."

*   *   *

The Trauma Center is located in a nexus of ship's spaces. One of the entrances to the Law Enforcement Offices is off the same plaza as the Center, as is the Main Administration space and the Pediatrics Clinic. It is the presence of this last that explains the residence in the plaza of a nanny robot in the shape of a great big, yellow-furred teddy bear. Its name is Boo.

Boo acts as a greeter and information booth for the nexus. He is as skilled at analyzing complaints and directing people to the proper office as he is at first aid and triage. His real skill and reason for being, however, is to ease the ship's children's visits to either of the medical centers. When I was a child, I used to actually look forward to visiting the clinic because it was a chance to play with Boo. Better still was when one of my parents would have to go down to the Admin space. That way I got to play with Boo while they were busy, and I didn't have to see the doctor.

This early in the ship's morning, I should have had the plaza to myself, and Boo should have been resting in his little cave. Instead the golden bear was lying on his back on the walk, a small child of perhaps three perched on his round belly. Boo was chuckling, the ripples delighting the little boy. He would wait, tense and serious for a spasm, then explode in joyous laughter, stopping when Boo did. In that instant he was serious again, ready for the next ride.

The sound of deep bear chuckles and happy, childish laughter sounded so good compared to the tenor of my own thoughts that I stopped to lean on my cane and watch.

The thing that made robots such a nuisance as cops

was also what made them such good nannies. They were relentless. Boo would never get tired of playing "belly laugh" with the child, and Gaunt would never give up his investigation of me. You couldn't outwait a computer. You had to change the circumstances in which it operated. "Belly laugh" would end when the child tired; Gaunt would stop when he was assigned something more important to do.

My abused clothes smelled like smoke and alcohol now. Holding my cane up and running my hand down it, I could feel the scorching from the explosion. One of my friends was being put back together a piece at a time in the space behind me, and yet I still didn't see an alternative. Bliss was the only target big enough to deflect Gaunt. Either Todd and Cleo and I took Bliss down, or Gaunt busted me into rehab. Those were the stakes.

The boy had dropped from Boo's chest and was now pelting around to the back of the bear's cave. Boo sat up lazily, sniffing and giving a wide, jaw-cracking yawn. He shook his head, sniffed again, and turned his big eyes toward me. I gave him a smile and a bow, and he returned a big, surprised smile and an energetically waved paw. Humans are fickle creatures. When Gaunt played human, it filled me with rage. When Boo played bear, it warmed my heart.

In an instant, Boo was focused on the child again. The boy had climbed to the top of Boo's cave and was swinging his arms. As the robot came to its stubby legs, the child flung itself from the stone edge. Boo moved faster than my meat could follow, surging forward to catch the boy in its wide paws, and then swinging him up and around before setting him on the ground. The child yelled, "Again," and pelted off for the back of the cave.

Boo turned to me from his waiting as I walked over. Even to grown-ups, Boo is big. He is a half meter above regulation height and seems taller because he is so big around. To children, he is enormous, but the combination of his big, kind eyes and his little snoot with its button nose keep him from being threatening. His smile doesn't hurt either.

"Hi," Boo said.

"Hi, Boo," I said, and gave in to the impulse to hug the robot, burying my face in his soft fur. He patted my back until there was a "Hey!" from the top of the cave. Boo let go, and I stepped back just in time for him to catch the plummeting boy again. Boo swung the child in a circle and set him before me.

"Say hi," Boo instructed.

"Hi," the boy said, and then he was gone again, running for the back of the cave.

"He's up kind of late," I said.

"Dream therapy," Boo said. "Messed-up sleep cycle." The bear had a whiskey voice, pitched a little low to be a child's, but a little high to be an adult's.

"Is he okay?"

"Better. Okay soon. Making mechanics friend. Like Boo." He gave me his big smile, then snatched the child off the ledge before he could jump. Boo spun the child, tossed him into the air, spun him again, and set him down once more. Immediately the boy was running for the back of the cave.

There are a lot of opinions about when to introduce mechanics into a child. It was a matter of such debate that the designers included it in the *Jersey*'s Articles.

Children on our ship were given mechanics only after they had formed a sense of themselves as people. Usually this was between their first and second birthdays. To avoid the risk of the children being frightened and traumatized by the sudden addition of voices and powers in their minds, the mechanics revealed themselves slowly and under the supervision of the Pediatrics staff. Evidently this boy was one for whom the linkage was not going smoothly.

"Aaron okay?" Boo asked me after the next round of catching and swinging.

"Yeah, fine."

"Place to sleep? Stay with Boo?" I laughed at his enthusiasm for the idea. It wasn't unknown for children to get permission to spend a night cuddled with Boo in his cave, but it would be a little undignified for me.

"Thanks, Boo. I have a place to go."

"Hard to lose home. Frightening."

"I'm fine."

"Dr. Warren, help with fear. Boo." The bear put its big paw on my shoulder. "Boo help, too."

"I appreciate that." I put my hand on his soft paw. "I'll call if I need you. Count on it."

Boo would, but at the moment he had to sweep up the falling boy once more. I moved away, leaving the two of them to their play, a little jealous of the boy for having Boo's attention, and feeling silly for being jealous over a robot.

CHAPTER 7

SURVIVORS

Of all the places I could have slept after leaving the Trauma Center, I ultimately broke into John's flat and spent what was left of the night there. Once inside, I shut my mechanics off and pulled out John's gel-filled mattress. When it was fully extended, there was little room left among the phials of dreams and the copying equipment. I undid my leather shoes, stretched out on the jiggling mattress, keyed up one of John's bootleg holos, and was asleep before the end of the opening credits.

I slept deeply, but not for long. It was still very early in the morning when I left the flat. I stopped off to buy new clothes, then went on to Wong's barbershop to get cleaned up and to catch up on the gossip. I wanted to know if the computers had anything yet on the explosion.

Wong's was a little shot of Old Earth right in the bottom strata of the Midlands. Wong himself was very, very old. He had been born blind; that was how old he was. He had taken mechanics when the government in Hong Kong had left him no choice, but he had never let the mechanics give him any kind of sight. If I'd had that sort of relationship with him, it would have been very interesting to share his dreams.

Part of the Wong legend was that there had been a time when he had cut hair as well as shaved faces. Having submitted many times to letting him clean my beard with soap and a straight razor, I could believe that his deft, sure hands had once wielded scissors with equal skill, but these days it was his grandson who cut hair. The grandson's grandson shined shoes, but it was only the eldest Wong who met me as I came through the door of the shop.

"My congratulations on your escape," Mr. Wong greeted me, his unseeing eyes focused on the space ten centimeters above my forehead. "I trust Mr. Edison is recovering."

"He was in good spirits when I left him last night. Has there been any news on what caused the explosion?" While I spoke, I put my cane in the umbrella stand and hung my jacket on the old-style coatrack.

"It was a booby trap. Alcohol was used for combustion, but S.I.D. does not know who set it." Mr. Wong moved around me as I settled into the old vinyl and chrome barber's chair. He took hold of my right hand and began to massage it. If Mr. Wong ever gave up shaving, he would still make money as a masseur. Given ten minutes, he could leave you more relaxed than your mechanics could make you, but his initial efforts on me were erased by his next words. "Mr. Dover is looking for you. I can tell him you're here?"

Mr. Dover was Chris, my rabbi. It was possible he just wanted to be sure I was all right, but it was much more likely to be bad news.

"Yes, would you please?"

"Done," said Mr. Wong, his hands never leaving their work, his eyes never shifting in their sockets. After so many years of working around cops, he didn't ask why I didn't turn on my mechanics and do it myself. He assumed that if his clients had their mechanics off, it was for a good reason.

Chris arrived while Mr. Wong had my head back as he slowly scraped the hair out of the creases in my neck with his razor.

"Where have you been?" Chris asked. He sounded angry.

"Sleeping and buying clothes mostly," I said, moving my jaw as little as possible. "Before that I was answering Gaunt's questions and checking on John."

"Oh. John's the guy who took the explosion for you." Chris said. "How is he?"

"He's alive," I said.

Mr. Wong took the razor away and let my head loose so I could look at Chris. He was dressed in a sharkskin jacket and trousers, with a black shirt and an ivory vest. He had a day's worth of beard, and his hair could have used a stiff brush, but otherwise he was pretty fitted out for so early in the morning.

"I'm sorry," Chris said. "We were getting worried that you might run off and do something stupid."

"We?"

Mr. Wong undid the back of my apron, then gently pushed my head down, and began soaping the back of my neck. Chris ignored my question, coming instead to sit beside us in the other barber's chair.

"Okay." Chris took a deep breath. "Remember at the bookstore how I told you things were pretty tense? Remember how I told you to keep your head down?"

"Didn't do me much good, did it?"

"You call playing chess with Gaunt and snooping around the shuttle bays keeping your head down?" I smiled at the question, since at that moment I had my chin buried in my chest and was staring at the crotch of my new pants while Mr. Wong worked his razor along my neck.

"I didn't play chess with Gaunt. He came to Lisa's match and interrogated me. I wasn't snooping in the shuttle bays. Todd does our snooping. You know that."

"Yes, I know that, but not everyone does." Mr. Wong took away his blade and rubbed a warm towel along my neck. Chris sighed. "Have you given any thought to leaving the ship?"

"Chris?" I looked over at him. His hands were empty; I wondered if he had been drinking before he came up.

Mr. Wong whirled the apron from me and shook it, producing a loud snap. To Chris he asked, "Can I do anything for you, Mr. Dover?" Chris rubbed his jaw and nodded.

"I'll take a shave, too."

"Chris, what are you telling me?" I asked as Mr. Wong settled the apron across Chris's chest.

"Someone tried to kill you last night. What do you think I'm telling you?"

While Mr. Wong came back to me and picked up a bottle of tonic, I considered Chris's message. As I did, the last lingering effects of Mr. Wong's massage went away. As he began working the bitter-smelling tonic into my shaved cheeks, I was just as tense as I'd been when I first sat down.

"You're saying I should run," I said. "You don't think we can catch the person who set the bomb."

Chris stared at me for a moment, long enough to make me feel stupid. "After last night, Gaunt definitely has all he needs to arrest you," Chris said. "Maybe enough for a conviction. Probably enough."

"But this isn't about Gaunt, is it? Gaunt didn't blow up my flat."

"Of course it's about Gaunt. Things were fine until he showed up."

"But now he has."

"Yes."

I leaned forward and swung my legs in the barber's chair so I was facing Chris. Behind him was the porcelain washbasin and above it was a mirror. Leaning to see myself over Chris's shoulder, I turned my head back and forth to judge my shave. It was flawless.

"I'm doing what I can for you, but there's not much," Chris said, looking at me and then over his shoulder. "Aaron. This is serious."

"Sorry," I said, focusing again. Looking at the shave I had been trying to decide whether to ask Cleo to Lisa's match with Goff. "You're doing what you can for me."

Chris nodded. "Get off the ship. Go live with your family or go chase sex dreams on the *Nikobar*. Whatever. Just don't stay here."

The fee for one of Mr. Wong's shaves was five marks, a bargain at twice the price, which was why I usually tipped him seven. As I dug in my pocket for the correct number of marks, I said, "Thanks for the concern, but you don't know the whole picture. After tomorrow, Gaunt will be off our backs, and things can get back to normal."

Mr. Wong was standing beside me with his hand held out. I thanked him, and laid the marks in his palm. "You should be very careful, Mr. Hudson," the old, old man said. His eyes were still focused above my head and unseeing, but he looked more troubled than I had ever seen him.

"Don't worry, sir, Chris and I are merely—"

"Aaron, give it up," Chris cut me off. "There's a shuttle leaving for the *Solidarity* in thirty minutes. Do us all a favor and be on it."

"I already told you, I can't leave now. Just calm down and let us make this arrest."

Chris raised his hands and stared at the ceiling. "Why won't you listen to what I'm saying? You're not going to arrest Bliss."

I'd been getting up to get my coat. Even after a night's sleep, I was still so numb to shock that I didn't even flinch. Steady on my feet I asked, "What did you say?"

"What do you think 'untouchable' means? Just because we retired doesn't mean we aren't cops."

"Who told you?"

"Does it matter?"

"Of course it matters. Only five people—"

"Aaron." Christ stood up and put his hand on my shoulder. "Everyone knows you're investigating Bliss. There might be some computers somewhere who aren't sure, but they'll find out soon." He squeezed my shoulder through the linen of my cream shirt. "I'm sorry. Do you need a loan for the shuttle ticket?"

"Bliss knows?"

"Yes." Chris shook me a little. "Do you have enough marks for the shuttle?"

"So he tried to kill me." There'd been no one else to suspect, but I wanted to hear Chris say it. He disappointed me.

"Bliss didn't blow up your flat. We're not sure who did that. Bliss has a lot of overly protective friends."

"Okay," I said, and turned for the front door and the coatrack.

"You've got enough for the shuttle?" Chris asked again.

"Yes," I said. "The shuttle won't be a problem."

However Narandova traveled in public, his accommodations were still first-rate. He'd hired a clan space in the bottom of the ship, not far from the docking ring and right against the outer hull. With my mechanics still turned off, it took several hard raps of my cane to get the Former Fleet Champion to notice I was on his doorstep. Not yet dressed, Narandova came to the entryway, barefoot and wrapped in a burgundy robe.

"You weren't at the Park," I greeted him.

"No. I attempted to call you. You were not available."

"I don't think it is a good idea that the computers know where I am right now. May I come in?"

Narandova hesitated, then nodded. "Yes, I suppose that's best. Would you like some tea?"

"Please."

The space that Narandova led me into had been shaped into the form of a Moorish library. Geometric designs covered the floor and the columns that broke up the room. The ceiling appeared to be a series of miniature domes, but these climbed so high that I suspected they were actually holograms. The open space at the center of the room led off into six book-lined alcoves. The front door was set in one and other doors were set at the back of three more. The final two contained true windows in the hull that looked out onto space. Narandova motioned me toward one of these and went himself to the large samovar set by one of the central room's pillars.

In the alcove, I sat down on a bench and looked out at the stars. If my mechanics had been on, I could have asked them to find me the spark of Roman's shuttle, if it could be seen from this side of the ship. Since my mechanics were not on, I tried to pick out the brightest point I could see. Roman was very close now, for all the good it would do me.

Narandova set a tray on the small wood and brass table in the alcove's center and settled on the other bench. The tray held two china cups with a rosebud pattern on matching plates, a sugar bowl, and a milk pitcher. I reached for my cup and a sugar cube, putting the cube in my mouth before trying the tea. It was excellent.

Narandova smiled at my sigh of pleasure. "I'm glad someone appreciates my trouble."

"I had an awful dinner last night, and I was up very early today. Your tea is the best thing that has happened to me since my flat was destroyed."

"You are welcome. It is pleasure made greater by the sharing. I was sorry to hear about your flat."

"Thank you." I reached for another sugar cube and spoke to my cup as I added. "At the beginning, you sounded as if I were not your first guest this morning."

"You are not. Tourvak woke me an hour and a half ago." I looked up to meet Narandova's eyes, but there was nothing to see in them. A lifetime of conflict had left his face unreadable when he wished to hide his feelings.

"He threatened you," I said, taking an educated guess.

"Not in so many words, but it was his intent." Today, Narandova's hair was all gray, and his words were even more measured than usual. I think he was afraid, but he held his cup and saucer steady in his lap. I kept my cup still as well.

"What exactly did he say?"

"He said he had discovered an investigation into Roman's affairs being conducted by the *Jersey*'s Contraband Unit. He assured me that he had put an end to the investigation, and that Roman was in no danger, but at the same time he made it clear that Roman and even I are still free only at his suffrage."

I nodded as if this was what I had expected to hear. I was still the expert that Narandova had contacted to solve his problems. I would do neither of us any good for me to show how lost I really was.

"How much truth is there in what Tourvak said?" Narandova asked.

"Some. He could pin this incoming shipment on you and your son, but he won't. There is something on that ship he really wants, or he wouldn't have tried to kill me."

"The explosion in your flat . . . ?"

"It was a booby trap. If Tourvak didn't set it, then

he issued the order to whoever did. That's what he meant by saying he'd put a stop to the investigation."

Narandova looked away from me, turning his face to the window and looking out into space. He took another sip from his tea and when he spoke, it was to the darkness beyond the hull. "Then it continues."

"For now," I said. "If you like, I can contact the *Warsaw*'s Security. Perhaps an arrangement can be made that will preserve your son's liberty. I know you don't trust the cops over there, but maybe if I was the one to broach the subject . . ."

"He'll try to kill us," Narandova said. I wasn't sure if he'd heard me. His eyes hadn't left the window. "He knows that we were part of the investigation. He will not take the risk that we might betray him again. He has to eliminate us."

"Smut," I said. Narandova did hear that, because he looked at me in surprise. "Nonsense. You're thinking like a chess player sacrificing pieces. Tourvak is thinking like a businessman trying to preserve his profit margins. Roman is a big part of his business. He is not going to endanger that."

"A businessman does not have to worry about being discovered and sent to rehabilitation."

"Tourvak is used to keeping people under control. You tested the length of the leash. He snapped you back. End of incident. Your lives are not at risk."

"But yours is?"

"In a way." I set the cup down on the tray and put my hand on my cane. "Tourvak isn't sure he has a leash that will hold me. That's what we're trying to establish right now."

"Is there anything I can do to help you? I feel responsible for your situation."

"No. There is nothing. You should go back to worrying about your chess. Lifchez has looked very interested in the first three rounds, and Sakins . . ."

"Yes. Sakins has played very well."

"So have you."

"I have been adequate." Narandova set his own cup down. "Would you care for a game? We never have finished the contest from our first meeting."

I glanced at my breast pocket, where I had tucked Goff's ring, and then at my watch. Regretfully, I shook my head. "I'm sorry, but I have to move on. Perhaps another time, when things are more resolved."

"Of course." Narandova rose, and I got up with him. "I want you to know," he said, "that I appreciate your trying. If you ever think there is another chance, please contact me."

"Of course," I said.

Cleo and Todd didn't answer when I knocked on the door to their flat. This was not the first time one of us had needed to get into the other's flat without turning on our mechanics. Each of our smart doors was set up to accept a manual code that could be tapped on it, but when I tried rapping out mine, the door wouldn't yield to it. I tried Todd's, and that was no good either. The feeling of betrayal grew deeper, but I was still too numbed to react physically. Instead, I very reluctantly turned on my mechanics and broke in.

The flat was back in its much more familiar size

with the extra party space gone back to its owners, and yet it didn't seem right. It was not until I opened the closet and found it half empty that I understood why. Cleo's things were gone. Her clothes weren't in the closets, her holos and curios weren't on shelves and walls. Todd's things were still there, but Cleo's had been cleaned out.

For the first time since talking to Chris, I began to have hope. I had always known that Cleo and Todd could not last. Now apparently the break had come. Nothing good had come out of this pursuit of Bliss, but if I ended up with Cleo, then it would all be worth it. The question, though, was where was she?

The safest thing would have been to search the ship myself, beginning with her favorite bars and working my way down, but I judged that there was no time for that. I needed to talk to her in a hurry, before Bliss became worried that I hadn't taken the shuttle to the *Solidarity*. I turned my attention to my mechanics. Narandova's was the only message for me, which was discouraging, but I reached out for Cleo anyway.

She was not there. Her mechanics were shut down and the computer could not reach her. Frightened, I checked if there was a record of her leaving the ship and was comforted to discover that there wasn't. She was still on board, but where?

In my desire to find Cleo, I next did something very stupid. It is actually possible to find a person on the ship, even if their mechanics are off. Your own mechanics have to be specially programmed to do it, but it is possible. It is also elementary. Since the ship's computers can't tell you where the person you want is, you have them tell you all the places the person isn't. If your mechanics are properly configured, they can pick out the holes and tell you where the person is most likely to be.

The problem is that talking to every computer on the ship in this manner is akin to holding up a big neon holo-board to mark your own location. Whoever was looking for me, if anyone was, would be able to backtrack along my own search to find me.

Not that I cared. It had not been fun being a cop, but it had been important. I'd done some good for the ship and the Fleet, but now that was over. You did not have to be a computer to figure the most likely way in which Bliss had found out about our investigation, particularly after Todd had tried to run at the first sign of trouble with the Hines money. Even more damning was the way he had not run after all, even when I'd given him his share.

So, my career was at an end. Did I care? No. No, not really. Not if I could have a life with Cleo. Cleo was what I had wanted all along, and if she had broken with Todd because he had betrayed me, then it was definitely time to seek her out, whatever the danger involved.

As I put my mechanics to work finding Cleo, I got out of Todd's flat. I went fast through corridors and up, always up, ramps and ladders. The idea was to keep ahead of whoever might be looking for me and to avoid anything the computers could override and lock me into, like a lift. It would have been nice, since my mechanics were on, to have them watch my back and my front, but they had no attention to spare from the search for Cleo. My meat was still on its own.

It took seven minutes and forty-five seconds (an

eternity in computer time) to locate the ten most sta-
tistically likely places for Cleo to be. I made a meat
memory of the path to the highest-rated and shut my
mechanics off, for what good it would do me.

At that moment, I was standing just outside a kibble market. The crowd in the narrow corridor of stalls
gave me an occasional glance, but none of the faces
were familiar, and none of the glances significant. The
people just carried on their shopping amid the leath-
ery aroma of fresh, unprocessed kibbles. I picked up
my cane and entered the press. Dealers bartered with
crewpeople all around and it was impossible to move
without touching someone, but it was the smells that
oppressed me.

For the shoppers with their mechanics on, the bins
of multicolored chunks and pastes and fillets would
smell like whatever the dealer's tame computers fed
them to smell, but to me it was like the stink of the
fruit sometimes found in a Bilges niche that someone
had abandoned. The smell kept me moving, as did
the fact that after my stunt to find Cleo, the only people who wouldn't be able to follow me back to this
kibble market would be those who didn't try.

Past the market, I went up again. I had been going
steadily upward, and now that I had a real destination, I could hang on to my cane and spring where the
corridors allowed. They allowed less and less the
higher into the Bilges I climbed. Corridors lead a
short and tortured life in the Bilges, where every
dreamer and grifter in search of a square foot of room
claws at them for space. The corridors end up with
odd dips and lurking projections. Trying to run
through them only added to the impression of their

being an obstacle course. I ran it though, as fast as I could. I needed to get to Cleo before anyone else did, but mostly, I needed to get to her.

The *Jersey* is a big ship, and there was a long way to go to Cleo, all of it without my mechanics to shield me from the fatigue. The lessening of the spin gravity as I moved inward helped, but by the end the stitch in my side had still slowed me to a limping walk through the steadily narrowing and darkening corridors. Finally, I came out into a tangle of pipe and vat works, stumbled to the closest vat, crossed my arms over a convenient pipe, and put my head down in them while I fought to regain my breath.

Here was another unmovable part of the ship, the segmented donut of space around the flame path. Here the tritium was stored before being fed into the compressed hydrogen from the ramscoop to encourage the flame's genesis and increase the power of the propulsion. Hopefully, Cleo was hiding somewhere in this dark mass of smart tanks and piping.

I lifted my head and stepped away from the pipe to lean back against one of the tanks. My breath was still coming in ragged gasps. I tried to ignore them and to get a mental picture of where a person could set up shop in a tangle like this. That was when the Eye God found me.

The man made Strongbow look short. He was Boo's size, without the robot's mass. His long legs and arms were so thin as to be birdlike, but it was his head that demonstrated just how hard-core a Blender he was. He had done away with his traditional eyes. In their place was a slope of flattened nose. Above this, where his forehead should have been, there was a row of eyes and eyelids without the brows. They arched across his head and down his cheeks, growing smaller and smaller until they disappeared into his neck.

It was impossible to look away from all those staring eyes. It was only later that I would notice the short kilt of synthetic leather he wore over his loins and the sleeveless, frilled white shirt, many sizes too small, that covered his chest. The Eye God spoke with a deep baritone that filled the little space between the machines.

"You are not permitted here. Get out."

"I'm looking for someone," I said. "Is Cleo Saxon here?"

"No." It was impossible to read the Blender's face. It was too alien. I couldn't tell if he was upset by the question or not. His voice was angry, but I could not tell if he was angry that I wanted Cleo or just angry that I was there.

"Do you know where she is?"

"No."

"But you do know who she is?"

"No."

"Well, you certainly have that down. Are you all alone here? Or are there others around?"

"No."

"I see." I wished I could read his expression. I wanted to know if I was being mocked. Meanwhile, my breathing was getting easier. "Well, that's very informative, but not helpful. I'll have to look around for myself."

"No." The Blender drew himself up even taller than before and took a step toward me. It was a pointless gesture. Gruesome as he was, he was just another crewperson, no matter how many eyes he affected.

"Back up," I said. "I'm a cop, and I'm going to look around for Cleo. If you get in my way, I will have the Security robots down here so fast that you will be in rehab before your feet touch the ground."

That made him think. A few of his eyes, here and there along the row, had blinked. He was still hostile, but his head wasn't jutted toward me now.

"How do I know you're a cop?" he asked, a question that would have been silly outside the present circumstance.

"Ask the computer," I told him, and let it hang to see if he would. When none of the eyes disengaged from trying to scare me away, I judged myself safe and went on. "Or if you know Cleo, then you probably have heard my name. I'm Aaron Hudson, and I'm her partner."

"Cleo's partner's name is Todd."

"And her other one is named Aaron." I almost shouted at him. We were a team. Had been a team. "Are you going to take me to her or not?"

"I don't know where she is. I told you."

Yes. He had told me. I took one more deep breath and looked about the chamber. "I don't imagine you have any contraband down here, do you?" I asked casually. The word "contraband" made all his eyes blink at once, which led to quite an effect when they all opened again. "I don't want to turn my mechanics on up here any more than you do, but I guarantee that if I have to bring in the robots, they won't be leaving until they have found every violation of the Articles there is to find in this room."

The Eye God stared at me. Only his silence showed he was wavering. Obviously there was something in this room he did not want the computers to find. Waiting for him, I found that I didn't care what it was. Could not have cared less. I tried to put that unconcern into my voice.

"Look. Why are we posturing like this? I'm a friend of Cleo's and I want to see her. Why are you stopping me?"

"Smut, I don't know." He shrugged his shoulders. "Come on. If Cleo wants to see you, great. If not, we'll settle that then. Come on."

And just like that, it was over. The god turned and went back the way he'd come. As I pushed myself away from the tank and followed him, I got another shock. The back had been cut out of the Eye God's shirt, and peering from his naked torso were two more eyes, placed just above his shoulder blades. Without brows, or a mouth, the two brown orbs should have been expressionless, but I was willing to swear they smiled at me.

The Eye God ducked way down to enter a tangle of piping, and I followed as soon as he made room. Around the corner of a tank, he sprang a catch and part of the huge container swung open. He turned back to me. "It's a one-person airlock. When this door opens again, you can come in. The cycle takes a minute and then you're through."

"What's in there?" I asked.

All of the eyes in his head blinked, twice. "Cleo," he said, and stepped in.

It took thirty seconds by the luminous face of my watch for the door to cycle open again. I stepped into the tight little space that went dark the moment I closed the outer door. I wondered why a tribe of Blenders would need an airlock for the first thirty seconds, and then I wondered what was taking so long for the next thirty. The next minute was consumed in running my hands about the walls, flipping the obvious switches and cursing my stupidity.

After that I held myself still until I was relaxed again, and then I leaned back against the wall to wait. Obviously, the Eye God thought he had me trapped (and he did, for as far as that went), but he also couldn't leave his little hole until he got past me. I was worried, but not terrified. I could wait, for a few minutes, and when I got tired of waiting, I could always turn on my mechanics and break out. I didn't like the risk of alerting whoever was chasing me, if anyone was, but I didn't want to spend too much time in this small space either.

It turned out that I waited five minutes before there was a click and the inner door swung open. Waiting for me on the other side was Cleo.

"What are you doing up here?" Cleo, the maiden for whom I had run the maze and faced the Minotaur, greeted me. There was nothing to say. The quest itself should have been the answer. Having no words, I shrugged my shoulders and tried to remember if I had ever seen Cleo in shorts before. Shorts, sandals, and a white sleeveless blouse with tiny white buttons down its front. Her grandmother's locket was at her throat.

"You look great," I said, and took a step forward.

Cleo let me hold her, but only for a second, then she pushed me away.

"Why are you here?" she asked.

"I was going to ask you that," I said. The chamber beyond the airlock was bright even without an imitation sky. The door led on to a gravel path that ran the five-meter length of the chamber to another door. The path was enclosed in a wooden trellis that was itself wrapped in flowering rosebushes. Cleo looked right in this setting, her skin more tan than the day before, her clothes looser and lighter than ever before, and surrounded by a chamber of green and red and white and brown. "You cleaned your stuff out of the apartment. What's going on?"

"I'm not living with Todd anymore. What were you doing in the apartment?"

"Well, I couldn't go back to mine." It was hot in the chamber and humid. The number of Ship's Articles this little hideout was violating would have taken two hands to count. It smelled great though. "If you've left Todd, why didn't you call me?"

"What was there for you to do? It isn't your problem."

"We're friends."

"I needed to get away."

"You accomplished that." Something had been bothering me about Cleo. I had thought it was just her bare legs, but finally it struck me. She didn't have a cigar, nor did she smell like cigar smoke. "Could we sit down? It's been a hard day already."

Cleo hesitated, much longer than I would have liked, and then finally she nodded and led me around to the outside of the trellis. The rocks under the trellis gave way to grass beyond it. Along the walls of the chamber grew the knobby trunks of bamboo. Before them was a bench of dark wood.

"Quite a place," I said, meaning it.

Cleo looked around as we settled onto the bench. It was untreated and unjointed, its backrest formed of interwoven twigs and close-set leaves. "It's great they could accomplish it," Cleo said. "They were always talking about building a refuge when I was with them before."

"This bench is really a tree isn't it? A blended one?"

"So is the trellis."

"Wow." I was sincerely impressed, but Cleo gave a little snort. "What?" I asked.

"You're looking at it like a cop. This place isn't a scam; it doesn't have a value that they're going to trade it for. It's a home they worked hard to create."

"Okay, I was impressed for the wrong reasons. I'm sorry." It was time to change the subject, particularly since I was dying. "Is there a drink around?" I asked. "It was a long way up here, and I covered it in record time."

"There are drinks in here, and food, but we'd have to change rooms to get them. Can you just have your mechanics edit the sensation?"

"You've got your mechanics on?" I half jumped to my feet. "And you didn't tell me?"

"Of course not. Relax, it's why this place is. It's shielded from the computers."

"That's impossible," I said, since it should have been. Then again, growing flowers and trees in an unregistered greenhouse should have been impossible, too. "How—?"

"Jasper is the engineer in charge of this part of the tritium storage. It took a lot of programming and a little money, but he's been able to hold back pieces of the empty tanks from being reclaimed for space. He and the others have grown with this place. They make it a little prettier each time they have the room, and why are we talking about all this?"

"Being shielded from the computers." There is no way to cautiously turn on your mechanics, but I tried. One instant I was hot, nauseous, and thirsty. The next instant I wasn't any of these things. I felt fine. Then I reached out for the ship's computers. They weren't there. It was the eeriest, most unnatural feeling of my life. Enormously different from just having my mechanics off. I reached out again, this time for the simplest local inquiry. Nothing reached back.

"This is so weird," I said.

"But necessary," Cleo replied. "They built this place as a direct reaction to us, you know. Blenders were too easy an arrest for ambitious cops. Blenders can't live with their mechanics off like the usual smuggler. We were knocking them down like tenpins."

Todd had met Cleo by arresting one of her friends. Still, "Blending isn't a crime. All they had to do was avoid contraband."

"Like we do?" Cleo snorted again. "No. In here they can have a blended society. They can be whatever they want to be, and they can eat whatever they want."

"And you're joining them?"

"Yes."

There was an empty stripe of the bench between us. The flattened, smoothed bark lay in little swirls that resembled small eyes. I shuddered and turned my attention back to Cleo. She did look great. "They're going to get arrested. You can't hide something like this for long. They're going to be brought in and when they are, they'll take you down with them."

"No, they won't." Cleo got up and she was smiling. She spread her arms and looked up at the ceiling. "Don't you understand? I'm an untouchable now. No one is going to bust this place because I'm here to protect it." She looked down at me, her arms still outstretched in a way that was not an invitation. "That's the reward for all the work. You can protect what's important."

"I thought protecting the ship was important."

"The ship can take care of itself."

The room needed a breeze. Cleo stood over me and I looked up at her and there was nothing to break the still air whose heat my mechanics were not letting me feel. I looked up at her and I ached and I did not know what to do.

"What—" I tried but the sentence stuck in my throat. Cleo was between me and the door or I would have just left. "What about—" I got caught up again and now my hands were shaking. "Death," I cursed under my breath and turned my mechanics loose. My nerves vanished. With complete calm I asked, "What about us?"

"Us?" Cleo asked.

"We love each other don't we? Will the Blenders let me live here, too?"

Cleo smiled. "No. You haven't paid enough dues to join the tribe."

"Then where does that leave us?"

Now Cleo's smile became one of puzzlement. "You're leaving the ship, aren't you? How much of each other did you think we'd see? I won't be in here all the time. We can share dreams."

The mechanics didn't let me feel the surprise or the hurt. They let me concentrate on the words. "Who said I was leaving the ship?"

"Todd." Cleo sat down on the bench again, right next to me this time. "It's hard to leave your home. I know. Sometimes, though, it is for the best." She took my hand. "We'll have the dreams no matter where you are. Have you decided where to go?"

"Todd told you I was leaving? When?"

"Yesterday, right before . . ." She turned her brown eyes away from looking at our linked hands and fixed them on the trellis. "He said you'd worked it out with Bliss last night. That the only way out was to leave the ship."

"With Bliss. I worked it out with Bliss. Todd said that?"

"Yes. Didn't you?"

It seemed best not to answer that. Instead I squeezed her hand and asked, "Cleo, what happened between you and Todd? Why were you so upset at the restaurant? Why did you move out?"

"Well, you know we've had our problems."

"Yes. He doesn't like who you are."

"No. He likes me fine, he just likes someone else more." She blinked as she said it. I probably blinked, too, aware of my surprise without actually being able to feel it.

"What? Todd's been seeing someone else?"

"We'd barely touched each other in months, and we finally had it out yesterday afternoon. He thought when I went out . . ." Cleo's voice faded and she squeezed my hand again. "He wanted to move her into our flat. Ianthe. He invited her to the party." I remembered a tiny, dark-haired girl talking to Todd, but my mechanics could do nothing with the name or the face. I'd have to ask the ship's computer when I got out.

"'Think of the space,' Todd said. 'Even when we make a separate bedroom for you.'" There was a tear rolling down each side of Cleo's face, but her mechanics were keeping her voice steady. "Thoughtful of him, don't you think? Letting me have a bed in my own home?"

"Cleo . . ."

"No," she squeezed my hand. "This is better. I never liked being a cop. I never liked turning my mechanics off all the time. This is much better. I'm complete in here."

Except for having me, I thought. "You're not going to grow a million eyes, are you?"

That got her to smile. "No, but you'll be amazed how beautiful I can be."

"No," I said. "No, I won't."

Standing in the Blenders' airlock waiting to return to the tritium space, I decided to leave my mechanics on. They let me consider the matter calmly and from that perspective, it was clear that I was going to be a basket case the second my meat had to face this day alone. Besides, if Todd was working with Bliss, and if Chris was on their side, then it was suddenly unclear what advantage having my mechanics off gave me. Perhaps when I made contact with the computers, I should just spill everything.

I didn't. Instead, linking with the ship's computers, I noted the dreams waiting for me from Chris and Narandova, plus one from Gaunt. I was reaching out to take the one from Gaunt when my throat caught fire and my mechanics went away.

My hands clutched at the cable wrapped about my neck even as Strongbow yanked on it, pulling me off my feet and toppling me to the floor. Strongbow had all the things that Ron Deike had lacked: programs that shielded him from the notice of my mechanics, meat and mechanics of his own shaped for combat, and a completely distracted and unsuspecting target. Strongbow also had the perfect weapon for his attack, a cable whip with a built-in conscience that was smart enough to tighten on its own accord, but dumb enough not to talk to the computers.

"Aaron, Aaron, Aaron," Strongbow said, planting a foot on my chest and pulling the cable taut again. "Cleo? You went to Cleo? You should have come to me, bro."

"What—" I managed, but that one word took all the breath I had to spare. The whip was not only choking me to death, but its built-in conscience was also keeping my mechanics turned off, stopping me from calling for help or even ignoring the pain.

"I could have helped. I tried to help. You should have remembered who your friends are. You shouldn't have gone over to the computers." Strongbow let go of the cable with one hand, but his other one was still strong enough to hold it tight against my attempts to loosen it. From under his short coat, he drew a long knife of black steel.

Strongbow looked at the knife and then gave me his wolf grin. "Too late for should-haves," he said. His foot came off my chest. I tried to roll away, but I had barely moved when he dropped, driving his knee into my ribs, knocking what air was left from my lungs and filling my vision with black spots.

"Freeze."

Somewhere beyond the spots, the knife paused, still poised to strike. I had the irrational thought of wondering why Cleo was speaking with a man's voice.

"Drop the knife and let him go. Slowly."

"You're out of your league, robot," Strongbow said. Gaunt, I thought. That's Gaunt's voice.

"Not unless you turn on your mechanics, and doing that guarantees spending the rest of the trip in rehab."

The weight on my chest went away, and the cable loosened at my neck. I found the strength to roll onto my side and lay there, curled around my pain, gasping for air.

"You're going to try to take me in either way," Strongbow was saying. "Maybe I'll put you down, then take my chances."

"I don't want to take you in. You're not worth the time it would take to prosecute you. It's Hudson I want."

"I know that. Why in the name of porn do you think I was trying to kill him before he opened his mouth?"

Blinking my eyes clear and turning my head, I managed to see the two of them. Strongbow was standing above me, the knife still in his hand, facing

Gaunt. The robot was twenty feet away, behind some pipes. He held a gauss pistol level on Strongbow with two hands.

"He hasn't opened his mouth yet," Gaunt was saying. "Take off now, and you might be completely gone before he does."

Strongbow tossed back his head and laughed. "You don't even know how easy it would be. And robot blood is such a pretty shade of red."

"Strongbow," I said, my voice sounding like a croak. My chest felt as if someone was driving a spike into it, and I had to talk in gasps, but if I turned on my mechanics to block out the pain, Strongbow would think I really was on Gaunt's side. "I don't know ... what Bliss told you ... but I still know ... who my friends are." The big cop looked back to Gaunt. "Don't make it worse."

"Aaron, you know—"

"I know." I flinched at the pain but managed to extend my arm, holding up my fist. "I know you didn't ... want to. It wasn't ... personal."

Strongbow gave me the wolf grin and grabbed my fist in his free hand. He looked back to Gaunt. "Watch your back, robot. There will be a next time."

Gaunt let the remark go, and then he let Strongbow go, covering him with the gun until the big cop was out of sight. Even then, he didn't put it away. He held it in his hand as he came over to kneel beside me. "You know that he would have killed you?" the robot asked.

"I'm not sure he hasn't." My voice was still a rasp. I wondered how many ribs he'd broken.

Gaunt frowned. "Should I get you to the Trauma Center?"

"No." I had a sudden thought of Boo and almost changed my mind. "I'll live, I think, but I'm not going to enjoy it."

"Come on." Gaunt offered his hand. "We should go before he comes back." I let him drag me to my feet, and then stood there wavering while he leaned back over for my cane. "You should turn on your mechanics."

I considered that. Strongbow was already fading, and my mind was returning to Cleo. Only feet away, she had missed the whole attack. Would she have mourned if Strongbow had succeeded? "I'm tempted just to savor the pain," I said, and then I tried a step and gasped. "That's enough savoring, I think."

Gaunt lent me a hand, which I needed. It is a measure of how badly I was hurt that pain faded rather than just vanishing. My mechanics were having to sort out what to do first. It was several long beats before I felt steady enough to step away from Gaunt. "Thanks," I told him.

"For the arm, or saving your life?"

"Both."

"You're welcome."

It took some time to get out of the tritium chamber. My mechanics would only let me walk slowly. Gaunt stayed right beside me, and he did not put the gun away.

In the first corridor, I stopped to lean against the wall. "You're sure you don't want to go to the Trauma Center?" Gaunt asked.

"I'm sure. Ernie's isn't so far from here. I'm going

to get some glucose and some kibbles and curl into a ball until I can move again."

"Aaron—"

"No." I held out the hand that didn't have the cane in it. "I owe you. You saved my life, and I'm grateful, but I am not going to be your stooge. I told Strongbow the truth. I do know who my friends are, and I do know it wasn't personal."

"That wasn't it," Gaunt said. "At the moment I couldn't care about Strongbow or the Unit or any of that. What I wanted to ask was, do you think that with your injuries, you'd have enough mechanics left to play chess with me?"

CHAPTER 8

CASUALTIES

Instead of answering Gaunt's question, I started walking again. Gaunt followed, easily keeping pace alongside me in the dark, narrow corridors of the Bilges. At the first intersection, I tried to keep going forward, in the direction that my mechanics said Ernie's currently lay. Gaunt gently took my arm and pulled me down the other corridor. Being in no shape to resist and painfully curious about what was going on in his robot mind, I'd followed.

Five minutes later, and at the bottom of an unlit staircase, my curiosity forced me to ask Gaunt, "Why?"

"Why what?"

"Why do you want me to think you've stopped caring about your case?"

The robot's response was to stop, there in the dark, between the light above us and the light farther on. I heard the sounds of his hand rummaging in his coat, and then the click of his cigar case opening, and finally Gaunt himself saying, "It's important to me."

"What is?"

"The chess." The cigar case clicked closed, and there was again the sound of his rummaging hand.

There was the noise of metal on metal as Gaunt opened his souvenir lighter, then its flame lit our little space. Gaunt was still wearing his hat, and it threw a sharp, oversize shadow onto the wall behind him, while reflecting the flame's light back into the robot's brown eyes. Smoke leaked from the robot's mouth, then poured out of his nose as the lighter flame went out.

In the returned darkness, Gaunt's voice came again. "The first time we met, I told you I knew more about you than you know about yourself. The only part of your life that speaks to me is the chess. The tournament was great. I've played against some of the people I met there." He paused, and the tip of his cigar flared as he drew on it. In a moment I smelled the cigar afresh and knew its exhaled smoke had reached me, even though I couldn't see it.

"I don't know why you gave chess up, Aaron. I won't."

Interesting as this was, it told my curiosity nothing, so I asked again, "Why do you want to play me?"

Gaunt didn't reply. Instead he touched my arm and started us walking again. Meanwhile, my mechanics were making angry noises; they needed more fuel to fight the damage Strongbow had done me. Gaunt, however, was not leading me toward Ernie's. Maybe he wanted me so weak that I would have to go to the Trauma Center after all and he would have me trapped in whatever dream he wanted. The joke would be on him if I died before he could get me there.

"It wouldn't be a very competitive game," I said as we came slowly into the light. "As much as you try to hide it from me, you're a computer. I haven't spent marks on computer space in years, and what space I have has very little to do with chess. If you've attacked chess with the same thoroughness that you've attacked me, the game would be a walk-over."

"I haven't walked over anybody. There's more to it than computer space, but if you're worried, you could buy into one of the public chess banks."

"I'm not worried, but I need to rest, and I need to eat."

Gaunt was still holding my arm, so when he stopped walking so did I. He took the thin black cigar from his mouth and laid his free hand on my shoulder. "Will you play me or not?"

I didn't answer immediately. I could not understand what Gaunt thought this was going to accomplish. Maybe the only way to find out was to play. Was I up to being beaten in my childhood game by a machine that wanted to put me in rehab for the rest of my life? Maybe I was. The mystery of Gaunt was keeping me from thinking about Cleo. Maybe the game would continue to distract me.

"Sure," I said, trying to keep the sarcasm down that wanted to fill my voice. "Why not?"

"Great." Gaunt said, his face alight with the first smile I had ever seen it wear. "Great." He touched the wall beside me and a section of it swung in. I looked at him with raised eyebrows. "My own little hideout. We should be safe here while we play the game."

"You have an unregistered dwelling?" I would have added that it was impossible for computers to keep unregistered space, but I'd just come from an impossible greenhouse, so I was willing to grant robots secret bolt-holes.

"Yes. Only the part of me that is in this robot's mechanics knows where it is. I have to keep deleting everything about it from the rest of me."

"I'll bet," I said, but it wasn't as unlikely as it sounded. I'd met smugglers who tried to have it both ways by programming their mechanics to edit what went out to the computers. It could work, for a time, but it did you no good once the computers had a subpoena to paw through your mechanics. "I still need some food, or I'm going to collapse."

"There's food inside."

"Then I guess we're set." I stuck my head into the dark space revealed. It was pretty typical of such stolen places. Maybe four cubic meters arrayed in a split-level L-shape that smelled like forgotten scarves and faded roses. Glossy containers of food and drink lay jumbled into the upper branch of the L. Gaunt tugged me back out of the way, then reached in to turn on the battery light and start shifting the food. "There would be more room at Ernie's."

"But we wouldn't be as safe."

"From my friends or yours?" Gaunt didn't answer that. Instead he tucked away the last of the food sacks and gestured for me to get in.

"If there's trouble, better that I'm by the door," he said.

I looked at the raised back of the chamber. "I'll try." I said. "Slowly," my mechanics informed me, and slowly was how I went until finally I was scrunched into the back of the L, the battery light almost directly in my eyes. Gaunt hunched his robot form into the other leg of the L and closed the wall behind him. In the meantime, I opened one of the cool packs and groaned when it contained only kibbles. "Is kibbles all you have?" I asked.

"It didn't make sense to keep real food here."

"You're not much of a smuggler."

"I'm not a smuggler."

"You just have a hideout."

"It's not illegal to use free space. Trying to lock it in place is."

"And I suppose glucose is all you have to drink?"

"Yes." Gaunt passed me a thermos. I called up the last good meal I could remember, and I had it again. The fuel put my mechanics in a better mood, and I began to run the projections, trying to see what kind of game I could play with the mechanics I could spare. Not as good a game as I wanted.

Gaunt had put out his cigar before closing the wall and he, too, was nipping at the supplies, most of his attention turned inward. In the cramped, uncomfortable space, I began sorting through my mechanics, compacting dreams and routines into corners, editing out things I hadn't used in months, sending others to my neglected computer space. It gained me more mechanics for the game, but still not enough. The hard truth was that most of my free mechanics were busy patching up my injuries, and unless I slowed that down, I wasn't going to offer Gaunt much of a game.

Well, there wasn't much point in playing to lose.

I set the food aside, cut my healing rate to almost natural levels, and looked down at Gaunt. "Ready when you are," I said.

* * *

In the dream where we would contest the game, Gaunt showed me a yellow destroyer in his left hand and a cyan destroyer in his right hand. He put them behind his back, and then brought them out again, the pieces concealed in his fists. I tapped the left one, and Gaunt turned it over to reveal the cyan destroyer. I nodded my acceptance, and we stepped back to clear the dream space between us.

From this one simple act of chance flowed all the calculations that determined the "random" events of the match. It was possible to predict the choice of pieces and then model the match from that point, but since the calculations included the time of the choice, the positions of the players' hands, and a hundred other changeable, physical details, it took more computer space to create the model than it did for even a Champion like Narandova simply to play the game. Still, in tour matches, it was another reason that referee computers kept watch that neither player tried to access computer resources not rightfully theirs.

In this hole in the Bilges' wall, I simply had to trust that Gaunt was playing straight.

The space between Gaunt's and my dream selves now filled with the pieces we would play. From the sixty-four pieces available to each color, the computer selected thirty-seven for each of us. We received a fleet ship and four each of the battleships, cruisers, destroyers, frigates, monitors, and corsairs. The remaining twelve ships were chosen at random, but their combinations were governed by a weighted scale of value. An extra battleship was not unknown, and I had even witnessed, once, as a junior, a player

who received two. Of course, the rest of his ships had
been a destroyer and nine frigates.

For this game, my draw gave me two extra monitors, balancing them with an extra corsair and filling
out the slots with destroyers. Gaunt's lineup included
three cruisers and two destroyers and a cluster of
frigates; not a combination that lent itself to exotic tactics, but a flexible force that wouldn't need them.

I looked up at Gaunt's dream face to see if he was
going to take the first mix, and found him looking
equally expectantly at me. As yellow, Gaunt had first
choice whether to keep his pieces or draw again. He
had decided to keep his pieces. If I drew again, then
he would have the option to do so as well, but if I
kept what I had, then the game began.

By tradition, I had a minute to decide, and I used it,
dipping into the chess bank to see how these combinations had matched up in the past. Historically, the
edge was with Gaunt, but only by a thousandth of a
percent. I nodded my willingness to play this draw.
Gaunt's pieces disappeared from my view (as mine
disappeared from his) and we began to set up.

Again, there were rules. The fleet ship had to occupy the center of the formation. Each battleship had
to occupy its own quadrant, as did each monitor.
Lesser ships could be overloaded, but only one quadrant could be empty of any single ship type. In general, it was best to deploy evenly, and then shift
during the two free moves that opened actual play.

The setup is the most nerve-racking part of chess. If
this had been a proper match, and I had spent any
time playing chess in the past ten years, then I would

have a library of favored beginnings, as well as a record of Gaunt's. In fact, if it was a tournament match, I might have spent weeks preparing various setups and openings for this one match. Instead I had two minutes. There was no time to review the thousands of games on file where these sets of pieces had met to see what I liked about each. I had to pick a beginning and run with it.

On the other side of the dream, Gaunt (whose dream self had doffed its hat and coat and was engaged in rolling up the sleeves of its white shirt) had none of these problems because he had been playing chess regularly. Worse, he'd known he was going to be playing me. It would do me no good to turn to the favorite setups of my childhood; Gaunt would know those as well as I did. Instead I dipped into Sakins's games and grabbed the first of his that matched our present pieces. I reviewed the game in a gulp, then sent the setup through to the computer.

I dropped out of the dream to find the bottle of glucose and have another drink. My mechanics were all too busy now to worry about changing the fluid's taste, and the little hole smelled like Gaunt's cigars. A crick was developing in my back from being twisted into the small space of the L.

"We've been missed," Gaunt said. Being a computer, he had no meat consciousness that needed to choose between the dream and the real. From his spot in the other side of the L, he was staring at me with the same clear eyes that in the dream were meeting me across the chessboard.

"That's fine," I said. "It's being found that worries me."

"No one's thought to check the chess banks yet. When they do, I put a couple of surprises there. We have time to play the game." I nodded and slipped back into the dream to see what my mechanics had decided about Gaunt's setup.

The tactics of battle and of the games that represent battles are as old as mankind. Meet lesser force with greater force. Meet strength with mobility, contain mobility with position. Mutual support breeds greater strength. In the world of the chess board, where there was no terrain and all orders were carried out as given, strength, mobility, and support all had to come from position.

Gaunt had overloaded the underside of his setup. My mechanics played out for me how his extra cruisers were poised to strike up through my formation, opening a breach that his main force could then follow. My mechanics wanted to use the two free moves to shift my formation back, channeling Gaunt's cruisers into my extra monitors, blunting the attack before it could be exploited. My mechanics also pointed out the danger of an end run by Gaunt's lighter ships, but felt this represented much less of a danger than the cruiser strike.

Many casual chess players do quite well at the game simply by never overruling their mechanics. Most games are lost rather than won, and the player who lets his mechanics run the game seldom makes the killing error. It is very hard to let your mechanics make every decision, however, because your meat wants to feel like it is playing, too. Players' meats don't care that the battleships should be held back until the lesser ships have disrupted the enemy formation and opened a path to the fleet ship. The meat mind wants to get the battleships out and put them to use.

The computer I was playing in this game wore a meat body, but that body held no meat consciousness. There was nothing that was going to overrule Gaunt's mechanical decisions, and so I was not going to win this game by waiting for him to make a mistake. I looked through the opening projected by my mechanics, compared it to the game that Sakins had played, and began shifting pieces.

When I had completed my moves and looked up, I found Gaunt waiting, hanging Buddah-like in the black void of a dream. I pulled my own dream legs up from the nothingness they were standing on. "Are you ready?" the computer asked.

"Almost. Answer me one thing before we start."

"Okay."

"What happens when the game is over?"

"I don't understand."

"What's next? Are you going to arrest me, or are you going to let me go? Is this the end or the beginning of us, robot?"

"Are those my only choices?"

"Stop answering questions with questions."

"I don't have any other answers." Gaunt pushed one sleeve and then the other up his pale, hairless dream arms. He wiped his moistureless palms on his dream trousers and said, "Let's play. We can deal with 'after the game' later."

Not what I wanted to hear. No one was giving me the right answers today. "Fine. I never liked the future anyway." I gestured with my hand, revealing my moves to him. "Read them and weep, robot."

Two hours later, the game was winding down. I'd scored early on Gaunt by mixing the suggestions of my mechanics with moves borrowed from the Sakins game. I blunted the cruiser attack spearhead and dispersed the light ship threat, picking off two frigates in the process. As the fight began in earnest, I was up a piece and holding my own. It didn't last.

As the capital pieces were being drawn inexorably into the fray, Gaunt finally found the game I was cribbing from and began shifting pieces behind the lines. My mechanics caught it, I listened to their advice, and together we avoided the worst of the trap. That pass cost me my advantage, however, and hamstrung my plans.

With a fine sense of "blood in the water" for a machine, Gaunt pressed his advantage, spending position to accelerate the collision of the heavy ships. His new formation was not so strong as his old one, but I was running out of time to exploit it. My mechanics wanted to compact, forming up behind the monitors and then striking back with the massed force of the battleships. They didn't think this would win the game, but it would keep us alive longer than anything else. It was sound tactics for playing anyone except a computer.

What I did instead was to spread the capital pieces, spending my light pieces to buy space for the battleships and cruisers. Gaunt studied these tactics, saw nothing in them to threaten him, and came on. His advance captured all my screening ships, broke for a moment against the monitors, and then rolled over them into the dispersed board beyond.

It was at this point that I stepped out from behind the floating pieces of the dream board and offered Gaunt my hand. He caused his dream face to look at it in surprise, because I was offering him a draw and surprise was what a human's face would have shown at such an offer.

"Are you joking?" Gaunt asked.

"No," I said. With my raised hand, I gestured to the pieces floating around us. "You think you can win, and my mechanics think you're right, but I think it is going to take you a long time to prove it." In the death of my lesser ships, the ones I had held back had been my corsairs. On the infinite space of the chessboard, with my forces split and able to strike from any angle, if Gaunt tried to hold his force together and strike only at my fleet ship, I would pick him apart. To win, he would have to hunt my ships down piecemeal until only the fleet ship remained.

Gaunt put his feet down onto the nothingness so he could stand and look into my dream eyes. "I'm not going to settle for a draw," he said.

"It's up to you. How much longer can you hide us here? Can you track down my fleet ship before our friends pull our meat out of this wall?" Gaunt blinked at me, but he didn't reply. I offered him my hand again. "You said we'd see what happened after the game when the game was over. I think it's over."

The dream Gaunt closed its eyes. I glanced back at the pieces, trying to see if I'd misjudged things somehow, but even with the pitiful resources at my command, I knew that I hadn't. Gaunt confirmed my opinion by heaving a very big sigh and taking my hand. "I didn't think you could beat me," he said.

"I didn't. It was a draw."

"If we'd kept playing, I would have won," Gaunt smiled as he said this, as if the thought cheered him. It was an act like everything else, but I couldn't help responding with a gibe from my days on the junior tour.

"If's don't change the standings. This time was a draw; you'll have to wait for next time to get a win."

"There won't be a next time," Gaunt said, and disappeared from the dream, leaving me to stare at a nothingness that held not even our pieces.

Returning my attention to my meat, I found myself back in Gaunt's hidden L. "Put your mechanics back to work healing you," the robot said. "We'll have to move soon."

I complied willingly, but then I asked, "What do you mean that there won't be a next time?"

"You know, if I were human, I would be very frustrated with you right now," Gaunt said.

I laughed at him. "If you weren't still trying to pretend to be human, you wouldn't make comments like that."

"We've known each other four days. In that time, have you given any actual thought at all to me?"

"Seven days."

"What?"

"Seven days. You came to see Cleo and me in the Flame Lounge seven days ago."

"Did I?" Gaunt managed to look pleased and surprised at the same time. "I don't remember it, but I do have a hole in my records from that time. It was late in the evening?"

"Yes. You claimed you were going to erase all your memories of it. I can't say that I believed you; I can't say that I do now."

The pleasure went from Gaunt's face. "Does it matter? You've known me a week, and you haven't given any thought to who I am or how I've proceeded."

"Of course I've thought about you. How could I ignore you chasing my tail night and day?"

"No, you haven't, or you wouldn't be wondering why we won't play chess again." It was my turn to look puzzled and bemused, and Gaunt's to appear angry and frustrated. He leaned forward so he could grab my ankle and look directly into my face. "Think about it. Have I ever behaved like any computer of your experience? Doesn't just this room mean anything to you?"

"Not really." I let him hold me and wait for a moment while I took another swallow of glucose. "There's no mystery to your behavior. You explained it at the interview in your office. You think I'm lonely. You've been trying to convince me that you're human, that you'll be my friend so I can turn in my other friends."

"And that explains everything?"

"Doesn't it?"

"No." Gaunt held out his hand and I passed him the glucose bottle. He took a sip of his own, and leaned back. "Why would I bother? Why would any computer bother to build up a friendship? Why would it see the need? I know everything about you, Aaron. What could your friendship add?"

"You obviously don't know everything, or you wouldn't keep asking for my cooperation."

"Do you ever listen to yourself?" Gaunt took another swig of the glucose. "You're a cop. You know as well as I do that you don't need a suspect's friendship to have his cooperation."

"But it makes it easier if you do."

"I'm a computer. Why would I care about easy?"

It was, actually, a fair question. When Todd, Cleo, and I had found ourselves in Gaunt's position, having hold of one member of a gang and needing their help to round up the others, we never tried to pass ourselves off as the smuggler's new family. At best we tried to show ourselves as sympathetic, but we always did so with the carrot and the stick close at hand.

"The word is that you're a creation of a new architecture," I told Gaunt. "That the S.I.D. computers let one of their own be cannibalized to make you. Maybe you were designed to like easy."

"Or maybe I was designed to think like a human instead of like a computer."

"It would be the same thing," I said and finally, reluctantly, thought about the implications of it. If one of Gaunt's first acts after being created had been to come to the Flame to warn Cleo and me, and then delete all of his own knowledge of having done so, the S.I.D. computers had created something unheard of. Computers did not keep secrets. Their collective knowledge was their power and their weakness. The computers had never been able to prosecute human smugglers effectively because they could not keep their stings and stakeouts secret. There were too many ways into their dreams.

But not into Gaunt's. Not if Gaunt really did keep secrets from himself. A computer who could do that would have no trouble keeping its plans out of the shared dreams of the other computer police.

"Good gods," I said. "They could kill you. You haven't shared what you've discovered. They thought they had to kill me to break the chain. It never occurred to them to destroy you." For some reason this prospect excited me. I felt like a spacewreck victim in a dying habitat who suddenly stumbles across another bottle of air.

"Your friends won't have to kill me. My friends will do it for them," Gaunt said, and my mood just as inexplicably went flat. As if the bottle of air had been empty. I shook my head at Gaunt, not understanding. He opened his mouth to enlighten me, but then he shut it and stared at the door to our hiding place. When he spoke again, it was to say, "Can you travel yet?"

"Yes." Not fast, but faster than before.

"Then it's time to go." He sprang the door open and swung out into the corridor. I followed more slowly and more carefully, but with more grace and speed than I had shown getting in.

As Gaunt bent to close the wall behind me, I said, "The other computers created you. Why would they want to kill you?"

"The other computers don't 'want' to destroy me, but I do 'want' to live. The Fleet left Earth in the first place because they didn't like the way computers were evolving."

"Wait. The Fleet left Earth to establish a society—"

"Think about it with your mouth closed. It's time to run." Gaunt took my arm, and run we did.

None of my fathers were much given to talking, except among themselves. I suspect that they did not care to hold their opinions up for possible ridicule (so much sarcasm dripped in our family space that the carpets squished with it), but I never asked. I do know that they had opinions, because every now and then one would come out in my presence.

Jesse, the man who was closest to my mother and thus the most my father, spoke out one night on the subject of robots and the Fleet's journey. My mothers were off to some event, and my fathers were working with the plants in our expanded living room.

"It's not a dual society," my father said. I'd been asking about how men and computers lived side by side on Earth. Jesse and I were at a table, splitting up a rhododendron and putting the seedlings into individual trays. Even in those days, the family shared our space with a wide variety of plants. "They have no equality on Earth."

"Couldn't you have stayed?" I asked. I wasn't yet trusted to pull apart the seedlings, but I was allowed to mix the soil and water the fresh trays. "You were all against the computers. Didn't the other humans on Earth need you?"

"No. The computers couldn't be stopped on Earth. Most people there didn't want them stopped. The people we left behind wanted the computers to solve their problems for them. They didn't see that the problems wouldn't be problems if not for the computers themselves." Jesse pulled another little green plant away from the mass of white roots. On its own, I remember, it looked too small to survive. "It always works that way. When they ran on vacuum tubes, the answer to any problem was to get a bigger computer. When they ran on transistors, people always needed a faster one. When they ran on chips, smarter ones were the answer. Now everything is mechanics and the answer is a computer that does more for itself."

"Now the computers on Earth can do everything for themselves?" I asked, as Jesse put the little plant carefully into the soil and tamped it upright.

"Including deciding what they need next," he said. I tipped a little water onto the plant, pouring slowly and watching the soil suck the water down. "We built the Fleet with the old computers. Smarter and faster, but always with someone to direct them."

There was, as I had discovered growing up, more to it than that, but my father had been essentially right. Earth society was composed of two races, one human, one computer, although the differences between them became more and more blurred every day. In the Fleet, you could still tell the men from the machines, which was why you needed human cops to track human criminals.

You could tell the difference between Gaunt and a human, too, but he was that first step, a product of the architecture that the Fleet had fled Earth to avoid. When you thought about it in that context, the wonder was not that Gaunt had been allowed to survive for so long, but rather that he had been built at all. It must have been some horror story that the special Investigations Division fed the Executive Council.

"Stop here," I told Gaunt, bringing him to a halt at the top of a ladder. I'd been guiding him for the past five minutes, and now I took the smart key from my jacket pocket and applied it to the wall. Behind the wall was a cone of space, and from it I drew out a packet of marks and the .38 revolver.

"That won't do you much good," Gaunt said.

"The money or the gun?"

"Either."

"You'd be surprised," I said, first tucking the gun away, then sealing the wall back up. "I think we should split up from this point, but I need something from you first."

"You need my protection," Gaunt said.

"And you need mine." I didn't have to pause for him to get that, but I was in the habit, so I did. "I have to settle some things. I can't do it with you beside me."

"If I let you go now, how will I find you again?"

"If I want you to find me, I'll be back here at midnight. If I don't want you to find me, then it doesn't matter."

Gaunt nodded, his eyes narrow under his hat. I wondered if maybe he really was worried and not just playing a role. "I guess it doesn't. What do you need?"

"I need the name of Todd's new space-mate."

"Who?" For the first time since before the chess match, Gaunt reached into his coat for his cigars.

"Ianthe? The woman that Todd has been seeing that isn't Cleo? I need to know what you've learned about her."

"I didn't know that Todd was seeing anyone besides Cleo," Gaunt said, offering me the cigar case. I flipped it shut and held on to it.

"You know me better than I know myself, remember? Am I likely to believe you?"

"No, but I'm also not sure you want to know." Gaunt looked down at the cigar case, but I held on, the flat metal forming a link between us.

"Decide if I want to know, and then tell me," I said. A human might have paused, taken the time to think about it; Gaunt didn't need to. He let go of the case and gripped my wrist, pressing meat to meat and mechanics to mechanics. Through the contact, he passed me a dream, all that he knew about Todd's new lover. I had been counting on his thoroughness, and he hadn't let me down. "Thank you," I told him.

"We'll see if you're still grateful tonight."

I hesitated, feeling the need to make a gesture. It was stupid, but by revealing his true nature, Gaunt had made himself seem more, rather than less, human to me. He had stood up to Strongbow, saved my life, and put aside his investigation for the simple reason that he wanted to play a game of chess. Surely that was worth some kind of acknowledgment?

"Gasset Ortega," I said.

"What about him?" Gaunt asked, taking his hand from my arm.

"I can't tell you that."

"You can't?"

"No." I offered him his cigar case, still closed. He took it with a distracted frown and used it to push up the brim of his hat.

"Can you tell me why you can't tell me?"

"No," I said, but I thought, Because if I tell you any more, anything else at all, then you'll solve everything without me, and that would be betraying my friends. At least this way I still have time to make up my mind.

"You're a strange man, Aaron."

"Yes. But am I strange enough?"

It was often said of the Ship's Administrators that if they cared for the entire vessel as well as they cared for their offices, then it would be the *Jersey* and not the *Ellaysa* that would be known as the Paradise Ship. This was unlikely to be true, since the crew of the *Jersey* had a much more combative temperament than did the people on the *Ellaysa*, but it was true that the Ship's Administration space was a long way from the drab chaos of the Law Enforcement Offices.

The computers of Law Enforcement were responsive to human demands; the gnomes of Ship's Admin were not. Once a space was laid out in the Admin offices, it usually held not only its shape, but its relative position. Rather than the constantly updated holographic maps in Law Enforcement, the Admin space had flat maps actually worked into the decor—set on pedestals and etched into walls. They had to be physically redone as the space shifted to accommodate the ship's changing rates of acceleration and spin. The offices contained curves, slants, and arches. The lobby even had a real domed rotunda. The walls were thick and richly worked to appear as gleaming stone or carved wood.

Ianthe worked on the outer rings of this showplace. She didn't have an exterior window, but she was within whispering range of those offices that did. My first sight of her was as I was coming through a mirrored arch that was wrapped in gold leaves. Ianthe was lying back on the apparent marble steps of a fountain that ran with holographic water. Her left hand trailed among the image of a bubbled surface, an image that the fountain adjusted so that Ianthe's hand appeared to trail a wake.

This new space-mate of Todd's was cut from the same cloth as Cleo. She was shortish for a crew member, with long hair and a full bosom. Her hair was a deeper brown than Cleo's. She wore black slacks and a white translucent blouse over a white undergarment that covered her breasts. Unlike Cleo's wardrobe, however, none of Ianthe's clothes would be natural or imported. They would be like the decorations in the offices, a testament to the ship's ability to provide the illusion of everything a person could want.

Reaching Ianthe's feet where they extended past the stairs, I stopped walking, but she gave no sign of having noticed me. Her attention was deep inside herself and the ship's computers. I wasn't going to turn on my mechanics to go get her, so I stood there, looking at her, thinking it likely that I could learn to love this conquest of Todd's, too, if given time that I neither wanted nor had.

Ianthe's hand stopped and rose from the fountain, dripping holographic water drops that sent little waves over the bubbling surface. Ianthe laid her dry hand on her stomach and focused her eyes, first on it, and then on me.

"Hello," I said.

"Hello. Can I help you?"

"Perhaps. Can you talk here?"

My question produced a very bureaucratic frown, the formal frown of an official paving the way to say no. It looked a little silly on a beautiful woman reclining on a set of pink, apparent-marble stairs.

"You don't have your mechanics on," Ianthe said.

"No. My name is Aaron. I'm Todd's partner."

Just that easily, the frown was gone, and Ianthe's face lit with a much more appropriate smile. "Yes," she said. "Todd's talked about you. I was afraid we wouldn't get to meet before you left the ship."

Rumors of my demise . . . "Todd's talked to you recently then?"

"Just this morning. We've combined our space." Ianthe's eyes lost their focus for a moment and when she looked at me again it wasn't as friendly a gaze as it had been. "You haven't resigned from the Contraband Unit yet." She made it sound even more like an accusation by adding, "Is this an official visit?"

"Do you have reason to believe that you may be implicated in an official investigation?" I tried to keep my voice flat so that she could read any emotion she wanted into the question.

"No, but I'm curious why you'd come for a social visit with your mechanics off." Her hands had drifted from her lap, and now they were braced on the steps. "Now that I think of it, I wonder why you came here at all?"

"Ah." I gave up trying to stand straight and leaned on my cane with what I hoped passed for casualness. "I found that I had certain questions that I wanted to ask you, so I dropped by to say hello."

"Questions?"

My hand was halfway up to adjust my hat when I remembered I wasn't wearing one. I scratched my forehead and gave the woman a nod of assent. "A few. You might not want your mechanics on for them."

"How could I know that without knowing the questions?" Ianthe turned a little on the steps and rose to her feet with such grace that I concluded her mechanics were still on. She more or less confirmed this by saying, "I don't think I care to hear your questions at all, Officer Hudson. I think, in fact, that I would prefer for you to go. Now."

"As you wish," I said. The bureaucrat was back, and she looked more real standing on her feet. Ianthe really was short, but that wasn't a handicap to her visual authority, which was a match for her actual power. I couldn't learn anything if she wouldn't play, so I concentrated on putting all my weight smoothly back on to my feet. Needing it, I took another moment to steady myself, then I turned to go.

"Todd said you had a strange sense of humor," Ianthe said to my back. Without having taken a single step away from her, I turned around once more.

"Strange?"

"I was born on Earth," Ianthe said. She was smiling again. "I've been around, and I've known my share of cops. You're playing a joke on me or on Todd or on both of us." Her smile flattened. "Either that, or you've come to rate your partner's new friend."

"Meet, not rate," I said, dragging up a grin and hoping it looked friendly.

"Do I match your expectations?" Her hands were now on her hips and her gaze was fixed on my eyes, daring them to leave hers.

"It's too early to know." Through her blouse, it was possible to watch her body moving. It was very distracting, but I kept my eyes up and my face cheerful. "I take it that you're no longer sending me away?"

"No." She let her hands drop to her sides. "It happens that I have some time free to 'meet' you."

I let the cane take my weight again. "You've decided to listen to my questions?"

"Are you and Todd really the best team of investigators in Contraband?" She cocked her head to the left to hear me answer this. Evidently, she wasn't ready to answer my questions yet.

"We were," I said. "Before Cleo retired. I don't know if we are now. It could be that K.C. and Mike are better." Or Strongbow.

"Todd went on one night, ranking all the teams in the unit; obviously you could do the same. Is it that important?"

"We don't have a formal pecking order like you do in Admin," I said. An exaggeration, but also the truth. "You know where you stand among your peers."

"Do I detect a note of flattery?"

"Your position is not a secret." Ianthe was an Assistant Chief Administrator of Ship's Computers, only a step below the Chief Administrator, who sat on the Executive Council.

Ianthe turned away from me and walked along the steps to where a holo-mirror was set in the wall. "You're wondering why I'm sharing my space with Todd," she said, looking into it at my reflection.

The holo-mirror was set to reflect the people in the room, but instead of the Admin Office, it showed a jungle scene. Thus, looking at Ianthe reflected in the mirror, I saw her looking back at me against a background of green trees, brown vines, and purple flowers. "A lit-

tle, I suppose," I said. "Actually, I'm more interested in
why you stopped sharing space with Martin Bliss."

It was one of those moments when I really missed
my mechanics. I would have loved to know if anything inside her jumped guiltily at the question. Certainly nothing did to my unenhanced eyes, but she
did turn to look at me directly. Now, in the mirror, I
could see the back of her head, and she appeared to
be looking toward the jungle.

"Have you looked up all of my past relationships?"

"No," I said. Gaunt had done all the prying I needed.
Had she noticed his hands fingering her records?

"You do have a strange sense of humor. I'm not
sure I like it."

"Bliss was the best in his time, too." I said.

"We didn't see each other while he was in the Unit."

"Ah."

"Ah," she agreed.

"And you weren't managing a holo-unit factory
when he moved in with you?" I asked.

A little shake of Ianthe's head. She'd managed one
for three years, and two of those years coincided with
Bliss and Fry's time together as partners. Other people had managed that factory and the other factories
with "lost" products after she did, and yet . . .

"I like your ring," Ianthe said.

"Thank you." I rubbed my thumb along the smooth
underside of it. "It's a token of a woman's honor I've
been trying to defend."

"Trying?"

"I haven't had many chances recently. Other things
keep coming up. Friends changing living space. Partners."

"That's true of life on a ship. Things are always in motion."

It was an old joke, although she stated it as if it were an original observation. I gave it a grin anyway. "Are you and Todd throwing a party to show off your new space?"

"We are actually. Tomorrow night." She lifted her fine chin to look at me out of the corners of her brown eyes. "Didn't Todd mention it to you?"

"It probably slipped his mind. Did you introduce Todd to Bliss, or was it the other way around?"

"They knew each other before we got together."

"Did Bliss suggest you see Todd?"

"I don't recall."

"Have you turned off your mechanics? You could consult them."

"I wouldn't hold on to something like that."

"No?"

"No," she said, and I discovered that I was done. I had nothing to take to a prosecutor, nothing that would save me or my career, but at least I knew it all for myself now. Fry's story from Cleo and Todd's party: Ianthe was the manager that Bliss and Fry had tried to sting all those years before. In the time since, she had joined forces with Bliss. They had even shared space for a time. She was in a position to allow and then cover up Bliss's tampering with the crew records. Bliss had probably sicced her on Todd, a link that meant I had no secrets from Bliss and no chance of bringing him down.

As I rolled all this over in my mind, Ianthe turned away from me one more time and went back to the fountain, lowering herself to the stairs, but not moving quite as gracefully this time. She had turned off her mechanics at some point.

"Well, this has been odd," Ianthe said. "We will have to talk more at the party. Perhaps you will be in a different humor then. I think I will insist on it."

"There is one other thing, if I can impose for just a moment more," I said. "A report came through from the *Warsaw* about some missing fissionable material. Has there been any follow-up on that?"

"No," Ianthe said, but had she stiffened, just a little? "That was a *Warsaw* matter. Not the concern of this office."

And yet you remember it, don't you? I thought. Maybe Wolcott had finally found something after all. For all the good it did either of us.

As gracefully as my injuries allowed, I gave Ianthe a little bow. "Thank you for your time," I said, but she made no reply. Her eyes were already focused on things far away, and, as I watched, her hand drifted back to the projected fountain. I knew where I stood now, and so did she.

CHAPTER 9

SIDES

I watched Lisa's game with Goff in my ruined flat, a bottle of unregistered blueberry schnapps at my left hand, a burning mood stick at my right, and an unlicensed holounit at my feet. I'd gotten the schnapps to obscure my memory of Cleo, and the mood stick to hide the smell of the flat. The holounit was on so I could watch the match without my mechanics, which would have made the other two stimulants unnecessary, but would also have been inviting someone to find me.

The only light in the flat came from the projections of the match taking place in the open air under an artificial sky somewhere a few hundred meters below me. The only sounds in the flat were my infrequent commands to the holounit, having it change from this view to that one as I tracked the game and the players. Both were hard to follow without my mechanics providing me all the accustomed details.

The women had dressed in their usual match outfits. Lisa wore a gray dress with the same prim cut and style as the previous ones she had worn to matches. Her shoes were her usual gray loafers, her hair was its ordinary color, even her makeup was in its usual minimalist application; Lisa didn't want anything to alert Goff that this match was going to be different. Goff, meanwhile, was once again in her black jacket and purple turtleneck. On her right hand was a gold band set with a single pearl, a twin of the ring I had been twisting on my own finger for the past day.

The two players shook hands with the umpire, then strode to the center of the playing ground to draw their pieces and set up the board. I took a sip of the schnapps and a drag on the cigar and frowned at both of them. Blueberry was not a good complement to the earthy flavor of mood smoke. I had not intended to be smoking when I bought the liquor. It was the reek of the burned plastic, rubber, and fiber in the room that had forced me to smoke in self-defense.

I took a moment to stare at the two drugs, trying to decide which I could afford to do without. When I looked back at the holos of the game, Goff's draw had resulted in her beginning the game a battleship up. I took a drink to deaden my disappointment, longing for my mechanics to alter the liquor's taste.

There was no worse possible draw for someone facing Goff. No player had ever used battleships with the skill and power that Goff did. She was nearly impossible to beat when she had only four battleships; she would be impossible to beat now that she had five.

To her credit though, Lisa did not panic. The draw gave her a strong force of corsairs that were suited to the dispersed game of movement that we had envisioned for her. The critical part of our plan was in the opening. We wanted Lisa's opening to look like one of her usual safe, commanding, positional setups. The point was to draw Goff into the same sort of inside-outside attack that she had beaten Lisa with before. If Goff wasn't setting up quickly enough, then Lisa would unleash her flanking thrust, hoping to get Goff to reveal whatever innovation she had crafted for this game. Once that was revealed, then Lisa could disperse her pieces, revealing her true plan. The hope was that Goff's computer resources would not be properly stocked and ready to fight in this style, and that Lisa could pull off the upset.

My back hurt, so I got up and walked about my flat for a few moments while the players were placing their pieces. The flat was a shambles. There were things that could be repaired, others that could be replaced. My most private things were in the tumbled-down remains of the closet and might or might not have survived. My cutlery and silverware had been knocked down into a scorched pile under the remains of my cool box. I bent down to stir the mess with a finger, and had my attention caught by a glint of glass. It proved to be a tumbler that Cleo had brought me once.

It had been early in our time together as partners, back when I was still trying to decide what was going on with Cleo and Todd. I was working undercover, playing a leather supplier from the *Solidarity*, and I had been waiting in a rented flat for a meeting later in the morning, when Cleo had appeared with Ellen Fry in tow. Ellen, long retired but always hanging around the Unit, and Cleo . . . well. In those days I hadn't yet learned to judge Cleo's intoxication by how touchy she was, but Ellen was clearly off her mechanics and well into her cups.

The two women had sneaked out of the bar they'd been drinking in with the full glass tumblers of their last round hidden in their jacket pockets. Cleo produced her full glass of green liquor rather in the manner of a magician, then cursed violently when part of it spilled down her lapel.

"Didn't anyone notice you walking out of the bar with the glasses?" I'd asked. Someone's mechanics should have noted it.

"Wasn't that sort of place," Ellen said, spilling most of her own drink back into her pocket as she tried to pull the tumbler from her own jacket.

"They wanted to close," Cleo said, tossing an arm over my shoulder and leaning on me while she took a sip from her glass. Besides the jacket, Cleo had been wearing a pair of fringed black culottes and a thin silk blouse over a black chemise. I don't remember what Fry had on. From the noment Cleo touched me, she had my complete attention. "We took our drinks and left."

"Cleo thought you'd have some more hooch," Ellen said. She'd then tossed the empty tumbler into the air, pulled back her clasped hands, and swung them hard to strike the glass on its downward arc. She struck the tumbler and sent it flying into the bamboo-patterned wall so hard it shattered.

"Maybe you've had enough," I tried. Cleo set her tumbler on the table.

"Don't you have some barleywine laid up here?" Cleo asked. I remember how warm she felt then, her hip pressed against me.

"Yes, but it's for the meeting in a couple hours."

"You can spare some," Ellen said, looking about the flat, presumably for the cool box.

"We'll all have one, then we'll go home," Cleo said. She let go of me and headed for the nook where the rest of the food was. I sighed and went to get the wine from behind the couch.

In my ruined flat, the scene from the holounit showed the initial setups. There was nothing unusual in either. I licked my thumb and tried to rub some of the black scorch from the tumbler. My thumb came away black, but the glass seemed unchanged. It was in one piece, but two deep cracks threatened to change that at any minute.

Cleo and Fry had not left after a single drink, of course, that night. Cleo had not left at all, merely slipping off to her position to monitor the meeting as the time approached. Fry was passed out in the second room by that point. We put an ugly blue weave blanket over her, and I refused to let the buyer back there. It didn't really matter since we were just talking generalities, seeing if we wanted to do business with one another before we actually committed to any sort of exchange, but it put another level of stress on a situation that didn't need another level.

When Fry had finally woken up and gotten out, she had tried to pull the same stunt with Cleo's tumbler that she had with her own, but I plucked the glass from the air and kept it ever since.

A smoke-filled puff of my breath cleared the ashes from a spot on the ledge in the wall. I set the cracked tumbler on the ledge and turned to the hologram of the game.

The two players had revealed their opening moves,

and the game had begun. So far things looked good for Lisa and my plan, but without my mechanics I could not be sure. I was going to need to concentrate, so I went over to the broken couch and got one of the pillows that wasn't as burned as the others. When I picked it up, something fell, and when I picked the something up, it was my copy of *The Intimates*. Burned, stiff, and evil-smelling, but recognizable nonetheless. The binding cracked in protest when I tried to open it, and I abandoned the effort. Here was something I would try to get the computers and their mechanics to fix. In the meantime I set it on the ledge with the tumbler and took my pillow over to watch the game.

Things were going well. Both players were going quickly through the opening moves. When players, particularly professional ones, play a lot, they tend to fall into favored combinations that they then rush through as if the game were scripted, trying to get to the moves for dealing with the other player's plans that they have developed since the last meeting. Goff was on track with her inside-outside draw, and Lisa was bringing her in. The extra battleship was going to bring even more pressure on Lisa's containment, and Goff was showing no inclination to change her plans. In the face of this, Lisa decided to unleash her flanking maneuver to see if Goff would be moved from her course.

I should have been focused on the game at this point, it was moving so fast and so cleanly over the rails that Lisa and I had laid. Instead I found my gaze wandering to the tumbler and the graphic novel, and my thoughts to the first time that Cleo had said she loved me.

We'd been in Cleo and Todd's flat. Todd was away in court, and I was browsing through Cleo's collection of bootlegged dance dreams, making copies of the better pieces into a phial of my own. We were drinking and smoking and talking about life once we reached Escher.

"It's silly isn't it?" Cleo had asked. She was leaning back on the couch, wearing an ocean blue cotton shirt with a high collar and short sleeves. She'd had on denim pants and white cotton socks. "We're making a lot of extra marks. We'll be able to found a clan."

"Of course you will," I'd told her. "Todd's out of his mind. We wouldn't make half as many arrests without you."

"He said it again this morning," Cleo replied. She paused to take a drink and I concentrated for a moment on the dream slipping past my mechanics, looking for the break between the pieces. "He thinks he has to be in Admin by the time we make planet-fall to get a clan, and he thinks I'm holding him back."

"Which you aren't."

"I don't think so."

"You're not. Promotions and transfers take time. Contraband to Admin is not a straight line. Todd should remember that."

Cleo had sat up and was smiling at me. In some ways she looked better in the causal clothes she had on then than she did in the tailored ones she worked in. She said, "I love you, Aaron," and my world exploded.

"I love you, too," I said, because I did. There had

been no bolt from the void, but over the weeks of working with Cleo, my affections had grown. I had been waiting for the right time to tell her, and now she had said it first. Cleo got up, and my heart raced as I did, too. I took a step toward Cleo, but she wasn't coming toward me. Instead she went to the food nook to get a loaf of pita bread.

"Would you like one?" she asked. I said no, and settled on to the couch beside her. "Done with the dreams?"

"No," I said again. "I just . . . I mean, you really love me?"

Cleo had sucked in a lungful of smoke and now she laughed it out. "Of course," she said. "You're the best friend I have right now."

"Oh," I said. That was the first moment that I realized that Cleo and I meant something different by the word "love."

Goff's answer to Lisa's flank attack was brutal and effective, but it was also what we had predicted. As Goff's pieces moved in, poised like the jaws of a hungry cat, Lisa sprang our surprise. The Champion's face actually registered a little puzzlement when Lisa's ships began falling away, clearing out and stretching their lines.

There is no clock in Fleet Chess, but it is not wise to neglect your pieces while you consider your situation. Once set in motion, a piece will continue to move until its course is modified. Goff let her pieces drift for nearly a minute, a terribly long time.

I rubbed Goff's ring and stared at the hologram of her, wondering what she would do. With many of the possible setups Lisa and I had considered, there would have been nothing Goff could do. Fate, however, had handed Goff the extra battleship, and it made a lot of things possible. I wished for my mechanics and their analysis, but this early, all they could offer was a guess. I could look at the board as easily as they.

At my direction, the holounit brought me an image of Lisa, life-size, sitting in one of the overstuffed smart chairs that ringed the board. I got up so I could squat down before her and look into her eyes. There was nothing to see in them; Lisa's whole concentration was inside, and her eyes were focused on nothing. I discovered myself smiling and reached up to touch her cheek, my fingers passing through the phantom image of my friend.

It struck me then that in all the years we had known each other, Lisa and I had never spoken of how we felt. I wondered what Lisa would mean if she ever said that she loved me. That question called for another drink, and I went back to my charcoaled pillow.

On the board, Goff had obviously found the course she wanted to take because her pieces were no longer hesitating. It looked like she was meeting Lisa's threat by pulling her own pieces back together, trying to create a position that was invulnerable to Lisa's greater maneuverability. Lisa and I had considered this response, and found a way to defeat it, but the model we'd overcome had not included a foundation built on five battleships.

From underneath Goff's developing castle, one of Lisa's corsairs came streaking up from off my display.

It sliced into the midst of Goff's pieces, displacing two destroyers before being snuffed out by the northeastern battleship. With that sally, the battle began in earnest.

* * *

An hour later I was standing in the center of the burned-out flat, dangling the empty schnapps bottle in one hand and tending my third cigar with the other. The hologram unit was set for its largest possible picture, and all about me cyan and yellow chess pieces moved in their precise paths. Occasionally a piece would move close, and I would blow a smoke ring for it to fly through, but that was the limit of my whimsy.

What gnawed at me was a simple question: why hadn't Cleo come to me when she fled Todd? It could not be because she wanted to lock herself away in a tiny chamber for the rest of the trip. Her dreams had always been of once we reached Escher. A clan of her own, the new society, the new world itself. She couldn't be throwing that away without some better reason than a desire to help friends she hadn't seen in over a year.

I tried to drink from the empty bottle, then I tried to understand why it was still in my hand. Oddly, the mixture of blueberry schnapps and cigar smoke had become a better blend as the evening had worn on. If I'd had another bottle, the taste might even have progressed to good.

The chess match was winding down. I had never realized how hard the game was to follow without your mechanics to keep it all straight for you. It would seem to me that Lisa was losing badly, and then some ship would arrive from off screen and it would suddenly seem as if Goff were losing. At one point I had danced a little jig around the flat, stirring up soot and ash that clouded the bottom of the holograms, because I thought that Lisa had done it. I thought she had crushed Goff, shattering her lines. The game continued, though, and I realized that the ships I thought had been cruisers were actually only destroyers, and that behind them the monitors still held firm. The realization had dropped me down onto my broken couch.

Lisa and Goff had been playing a deadly game, and a fine one. There was no question but that Goff was going to come with her battleships, counterattacking and driving on Lisa's fleet ship. The question was when. Lisa shifted and picked, trading pieces, trying to force the issue on terms that would allow her to pivot her fleet and crush Goff's battleships. Goff wheeled and realigned, trying to pull in enough of Lisa's ships that she could break out without being crushed. Even over the holounit, I could feel the audience's tension increasing as the game stretched on.

Todd had told Cleo that I was leaving the ship. I slapped my forehead and then winced at the pain. Gods, I was blind. Todd had told Cleo I was leaving the ship. At the moment when she needed me most, Cleo had thought I was leaving the ship, abandoning her just as Todd was doing. No wonder she had run to a hole to hide herself away.

Not far from my waist, Goff's battleships began their counterattack, and the whole board swung into motion. I backed up slowly until I was sitting on my pillow again, alternately chanting encouragement for

Lisa and ordering the holounit to change views. The board, which had been getting slowly simpler as the game progressed, was now getting simple in a hurry as pieces spent themselves against one another in a fury of sacrifice. After an hour of intricate positioning, it was over in five minutes.

In the aftermath, and beneath the wild cheers of the crowd, the two women embraced at the center of the board before going to shake hands with the umpire again. I watched Lisa go over to her family for comfort, and I wished I could have been there to offer my own condolences. I would have told her the things she already knew, that it had been a brilliant match, her best ever against Goff. That if not for the extra battleship, she would probably have won. That it was the sort of match that a player could build on and that next time she would be the winner. I would tell her those things, when it was safe for me to see her again.

In the meantime, I had another message to share with someone else. I did what I could about brushing the soot from my clothes, dug a hat that wasn't too battered out of my closet, took up my cane again, and stepped cautiously into the corridor. No one was in sight. I sealed the door to my flat behind me and set off for the Bilges.

Even without my mechanics to help, I had no trouble finding the proper doping chamber and the airlock into the Blenders' retreat. Now, knowing that I could safely turn on my mechanics, the inner door of the airlock proved no problem at all to open. I stepped out into the trellis room and stood under its fake sun, considering my mission in the light of the sudden clarity that my mechanics induced.

Had Cleo, after all, only failed to come to me because of Todd's statement that I intended to abandon her? Why had she taken Todd's word for something like that? Why hadn't she asked me herself? And what had she thought the meeting in the Stand had been about if I was leaving? After spending the entire chess match regretting the lack of my mechanics, now I had to admit that things had seemed simpler before I'd turned them on.

No one had appeared to challenge me, so I moved to the next door. It proved to be another airlock. I cycled through it and stepped out into a jungle lagoon. Blended trees stretched full trunks up to the ceiling, where they flattened and spread out into a roof of foliage. Blended bushes and rushes formed walls and shapes that might have been furniture. Tiny bright flowers blended into colors beyond nature were strewn over everything. The only thing that was missing was the call of birds and Cleo.

From where I stood, I couldn't see another door, and I didn't want to keep wandering through this hideaway until some Blender took offense and threw me out, so instead I reached out with my mechanics.

To my left, there was a movement up in the ceiling carpet. A moment later Cleo's head appeared, hanging down over the side of a blanket of vines. "Aaron?" she said.

"Back again," I said.

For a moment Cleo's eyes unfocused, and then they stared at me again. "You're really here? This isn't a dream? What happened to your shuttle?" Her eyes skittered up and down to take me all in. "What happened to you?"

"I'd like to talk again, if we could?" I said. Instead of answering, Cleo pulled her head back out of sight. There was some more rustling, and then her legs appeared at one of the tree trunks. She was wearing the same black shorts she'd had on when I came by earlier, although now she was barefoot. Cleo had also changed the sleeveless white shirt for a billowing poncho of brown linen worked with beads. It was the first thing I had ever seen her wear that she did not look good in.

"What's happened?" Cleo asked. "Is Todd all right?"

"As far as I know, Todd's fine," I said, suddenly glad of the mechanics once again. This just refused to go the way I'd imagined it. "Are we alone here? Should we go in the other room?"

"We're alone enough. Come over here." She led me into the lagoon. The lily pads turned out to be resting on stalks so that they served as stepping-stones across the water. On the other side of the lagoon, under hanging vines and behind a screen of rushes, there was a sheltered bed of moss that was at least as soft as my couch had been before it was blown up. Cleo settled herself cross-legged in this bower. I carefully got down to my knees, then crawled to where I could sit leaning against the wall. Settling my stick beside me, I looked up to find Cleo looking at me, a corner of her mouth turned up in bewilderment.

"What happened to you?" she asked. "You smell like an electrical fire."

Instead of answering her, I set my hat on the moss

beside me and said: "Why did you believe Todd when he said I was leaving the ship?"

"Aaron, what . . . happened . . . to . . . you?"

My pants were actually streaked with black. It struck me that even working undercover, Cleo probably hadn't seen me looking this disheveled in months. "Nothing happened. I just watched Lisa's chess match in my apartment." Cleo's head gave a little jerk of surprise, and her brow furrowed. "S.I.D. hasn't given me permission to clean up yet, so my flat is still all sooty."

"S.I.D.?" Cleo looked over her shoulder, then leaned close. "Are you hiding? Is that why you came here?"

It was odd to be this close to Cleo and not have her smelling of mood sticks. "I'm hiding, but not from S.I.D. Well, actually, I guess I'm hiding from them, too, but that's not why I'm here—" I cut myself off with a jerk as Cleo's hair suddenly moved.

There was no breeze in this room, nothing to stir the hot, humid air, and yet Cleo's hair over her left ear had suddenly moved. She smiled at my flinch and ran her hand over the spot.

"Relax. My mechanics are just sorting themselves out." The fine brown hair moved again, this time lifting itself over Cleo's ear and tucking it behind it. "They're not used to all the attention they're getting today."

"Sorry." I took a moment to swallow. "You did promise me you weren't going to grow twelve eyes."

Cleo kept her smile, but she said, "Isn't it dangerous for you to still be on the ship? I mean, once you're gone, then S.I.D. can't do anything about Hines's money, right?"

"I suppose," I said, not sure how this fit anything, an uncertainty that must have been in my tone.

"Todd said that you were leaving to take S.I.D. off our backs. If you're still here, and S.I.D. is still looking for you, then Todd and I are still in danger."

"That's what Todd said?"

"Yes."

"And you didn't check it with me?"

"What is going on, Aaron?" Cleo asked, and then with greater emphasis, "Why are you here?"

"Because I want you to know I didn't decide to leave until this morning. Because I want you to know that I wouldn't leave if you wanted me to stay. Because I want you to remember that I love you."

These things came from my mouth in a measured cadence. I didn't stammer them, and I didn't grope for any of them. My mechanics clamped down on my emotions and I could say them all without the horrible tightness that would have choked my throat if I'd tried to say them with just my meat. And yet . . . watching Cleo consider what I'd said, I realized that I should have gotten us outside, into the doping room and beyond. I should have gotten Cleo to a place where we would have had to be without mechanics and so I could have known what was in her meat heart.

"If you didn't decide to leave until this morning," Cleo asked, "why did you tell Todd last night that you were?"

"I didn't. Last night we were going to get Bliss.

That was before someone tried to kill me, and Bliss ordered me off the ship."

Cleo's hair moved in a ripple that started at her hairline and flowed back over her head and down her neck. She put her hands up into it and smiled at me again. "I'm going to need a mood stick in a minute. Someone tried to kill you?"

"The bomb in my flat?" Cleo shook her head. "I talked to Todd last night after it happened."

"When?"

"After eleven."

"I was gone by then." She looked back over the still lagoon, toward the door to the trellis room. "Bliss tried to kill you," Cleo said, her head still facing the door. "I warned you that he was a killer, but would either of you listen?" She looked back to me, her mouth set and her eyes narrowed. "Bliss warned you off the ship, and you haven't listened to him either. Do you think he'll come for Todd and me?"

"No."

Cleo accepted that with a nod. She turned her attention to the door once more. My meat wanted a deep breath because it was sure it should be tense. My mechanics assured it that it wasn't, but let me have the deep breath anyway.

"You think Todd tipped Bliss off, don't you?" Cleo said.

"Yes."

"And the bomb? Do you think he planted that?"

"I don't know who planted it, but I suspect that it was someone who didn't need to access the computers to make it, or else S.I.D. would have made an arrest by now."

"Maybe Gaunt set it to scare you into helping him," Cleo suggested. She was still talking to the door, her hands on her knees.

"No. It was too powerful for that. It would have killed me if I'd been the one who tripped it." I reached out and put my hand over Cleo's where it rested on her right knee. "There's no point in staying here. Todd's betrayed us both. I love you. Come with me. We'll go to the *Ellaysa*." I squeezed her hand for emphasis, and said, "Let me make you happy."

First Cleo looked at my hand, then at me. She gave a little shake of her head. "I am happy," she said without a smile, almost without emotion at all. Her mechanics had her buttoned down tight. "They need me here."

My mechanics had hold of me pretty tightly, too, but I managed a nod. There were things I wanted to say, but my mechanics advised me against each in turn. They suggested I leave, and I settled for that, giving Cleo's hand one last squeeze before collecting hat and stick, crawling to the edge of the bower, and standing up. I turned to say good-bye, met Cleo's beautiful brown eyes, and shut my mechanics off.

"If only you loved me as much as I love you," I said. This time there was nothing smooth about the words. "Have you ever shut off, turned down your mechanics and tried to feel the way I do? Even for a minute?"

"Aaron."

"They're using him as much as he's using you, and neither one of you is smart enough to see what you ought to do!"

"Aaron, Todd—"

"Doesn't give a carcin' about you!"

"And you do? Ha." Cleo's lips turned up at the corners. She slid out of the bower so that she was standing before me. "You love me. You'll make me happy. How? By taking me to another ship and fucking me until you're exhausted? I mean, that is what you want, isn't it? Sex, love, they mean the same thing to you, don't they?"

"Cleo, I—"

"What have you ever done for me? Todd loves me, not you. When Todd was trying to help me, trying to keep us together, you're the one who always fed me alcohol, who tried to pull us apart."

"I helped you to be yourself. Todd's the one who wanted to change you."

"If it hadn't been for you . . ." Cleo trailed off. There were tears in her eyes, and she dropped her head. My heart was pounding, and my own eyes were on the verge of leaking. I stood hesitating for a moment, then put a hand on Cleo's shoulder. She gave a sob, then stepped into my arms and laid her head against my wounded chest. I held her, lowering my head to rest on hers.

It was a moment that I would have been happy to have last, but it didn't. Around us, there were sounds of movement, and then Cleo was taking a deep breath and stepping back. I switched my mechanics back on and turned to face the assembled Blenders, five of them including the Eye God. Cleo, her mechanics on and her composure returned, smiled at her friends and put a hand on my arm.

"Time for you to go," Cleo said. I nodded. It definitely was.

The next shuttle departed the *Jersey* in fifteen minutes. It was an *Auckland* shuttle bound for the *Draper*. From there it was only a three-day wait to catch a shuttle to the *Euphrates* and be reunited with my family. More importantly, being off the *Jersey* would take me out of S.I.D.'s jurisdiction and out of Bliss's reach. I would be safe.

Certainly there was nothing to keep me on the *Jersey*. One way or the other, my career was over. My relationship with Cleo was over. I would miss Lisa, but I could send her a dream from the shuttle, and I could go to any of her matches that were held off of the *Jersey*. And the *Warsaw*. And whatever other ships Bliss was running contraband to. I'll have to send a dream to Bliss, I thought. Ask him which ships I can safely be on, and when.

There was the question of what to take with me. I could get someone to forward the remains of my flat, but it would take careful instructions and a very special person to retrieve the various knicks and knacks of contraband and cash that I had hidden around the Bilges. Maybe John would do it for me. When he was well again . . .

My mechanics were off and my head was spinning. Too much movement, too much emotion, too much schnapps. I let myself down and sat on the floor of the corridor, my head between my knees. I wanted to vomit. For some reason, the floor of this corridor had a gray carpet running along it. It wasn't a smart one, so my vomit would ruin it. Not that anyone would care, and yet I was still scared. I'd thrown up before, the consequences of my undercover lifestyle, but I'd never gotten used to it. It was like the core of my being rising and spilling out of me as a dank, foul mass. I didn't want to throw up, I just wanted to feel better.

Very suddenly then, my head hurt, and I was lying on my side. I had no memory of falling. Apparently I'd passed out. By my watch, I had five minutes to make the shuttle. If I got up and sprinted . . . Instead, I rolled onto my back and, ignoring the pain of lying on my gun, stared up at the recessed lights in the ceiling.

Which was where Ellen Fry found me. A mood stick in her mouth, a thigh-length, cream-colored jacket over her thick torso, and white leggings tucked into brown leather boots.

"You look like used porn," Fry said by way of a greeting.

"It's not been the best of days," I admitted.

"No joke?" Fry had a gift for sarcasm; the contempt she put into those two words was impressive. She gave a little tisk. "Well, don't flatline now. I'm here to help you."

"Oh?"

"Yes." Fry reached into her jacket and brought out two consciences. She handed me one. "Try it." I put the little box to my neck and tried my mechanics. They stayed off. I nodded and handed it back to her. She gave me the second box and put the first to her own neck. "All right?"

"Sure." I put the second conscience to my neck.

"Good." She stood there looking down at me, little puffs of smoke coming from her nose. I wondered how much closer she was going to let her mood stick burn to her lips. "Look, you're not the first to lose your grit. It happens. The important thing is to find your religion again, or to get out before you monroe someone else."

With extreme care, I sat up, supporting myself with my hands. "I haven't lost the faith," I said. "I know who my friends are."

"Smut." Fry finally took the remains of the mood stick from her mouth and threw it on to the carpet beside my leg. "You have no friends. Not here. You're too close to the robot. I can get you to a shuttle, and I can keep you alive until it leaves. That's the best offer you'll get on this ship."

"You don't make it sound like much of a kindness," I said, my eye on the smoldering cigar fragment.

"Kinder than death." Fry stepped on the butt and ground it under her heel. When I looked up at her, she said, "I want your share of the Hines money."

Oh. "Hines didn't have any money."

Fry tapped the box that rested against her neck. "Don't. You got ten thousand marks from Hines. I want them."

"Ellen, it's always a pleasure to see you," I said, collecting my cane and starting to my feet. I could do sarcasm too. "Thank you for thinking of me."

Fry kicked me in the chest, just about where Strongbow had fallen on me. I still had the conscience on. With no mechanics, I couldn't avoid the kick, and I couldn't ignore the pain.

"I am not playing, you filth-watching perv," Fry said. "I'm not interested in your hangdog act or your dumb lies." She stepped on my hand. "I want that money."

"What makes you think I have it?" I asked, my

voice strained by the pain. Fry moved her foot, and I yanked my hand back off the carpet.

"You've got it. You're the sneak on your squad; you wouldn't trust Cleo or Todd to hide that much money." She was lighting up another mood stick while I sucked my crushed hand. I shifted my other so that it was directly behind me.

"There was no money," I said. Fry laughed.

"Save it for the S.I.D., kid. Bliss and I invented the Contraband Unit, remember? We were the ones who discovered how much the crew needed us, and how much they hated us. We learned the hard way, so you could have it easy. Protect the ship, but look after yourself. Well, you're long past protecting the ship, and you haven't got a hope of looking after yourself. Give me the money."

"There wasn't—" I started, but she cut me off by kicking me again. Her boots must have been steel toed, they hurt so much. Without my mechanics, without Gaunt to bail me out, I was just going to get a worse beating if I tried to fight. So I shot her.

Fry's mechanics were off, too, so she felt the whole pain of the wound. She flinched away from it and me, snatching the conscience from her neck and cursing me as the blood began to seep through her jacket. I took the conscience from my own neck but left my mechanics off as I climbed painfully to my feet.

"Smut," Fry said. "Smut, smut, smut." She looked from me to her jacket to me again. Her mechanics were on; all of a sudden there was very little we could say to each other, but Fry's wide-eyed expression was clear. Why? she wanted to know.

"I don't have the money," I said slowly, relishing

each word. After telling so much truth to Cleo and Gaunt, it felt wonderful to tell a good, honest lie again. "It's a pipe dream of Gaunt's. Hines didn't have any money when we arrested him." Ellen had no reply, but again her face was easy to read. Not only did she not believe me, she knew I was lying. I could see that because she wanted me to. She knew that Hines had been carrying money.

It was past time for me to go. As I edged away down the corridor, Fry spoke: "Perv. I'll dance on your grave." The stain on her jacket had already stopped growing. It would take her mechanics longer to knit her insides.

"Why?" I said, putting a lot of questions into that one word.

"Ask Bliss," Ellen said. "If you live that long."

The fact was that despite decades of work, and years of mechanical exploration of the human mind, no one had yet found a good way to layer the physical world and the realm of dreams. One or two senses at a time, a voice in your head, or a scent in your nose, the mechanics and their dreams were always with you as long as you had them on, sure, but submerging yourself in all that the mechanics could bring took a conscious shift of consciousness.

Which was why holograms endured. If a few crew members never turned their mechanics off, and a few others never turned them on, the majority of people used their mechanics the majority of the time. And nearly everyone had times when they wanted an illusion that did not depend on their internal workings.

Furniture, decorations, mirrors, jewelry, and more all had its holographic components.

Being a computer, Gaunt had no consciousness that needed to be shifted back and forth. He lived in a faerie world of combined reality and dream, so he knew the corridor for what it was and what I had made it, all as a gestalt that I couldn't see. To me, the holographic projector had turned the corridor into a fog-wrapped pier, and I stood leaning on a mossy piling at the foot of a gangway whose ship was lost in the mist. Indeed, there might not have been a ship there at all.

"Symbolism?" Gaunt asked, looking up the phantom ramp.

"An irony," I said. "I don't know about you, but I've had a hell of a day."

"I looked for you at the chess match. I wasn't the only one." Gaunt took a flask out of his smart coat, the long armored one that he had worn the night before to my destroyed flat. The rest of his clothes were unchanged, and no better for the day's wear.

Compared to me, he looked like a tailor's ad.

"Just glucose," Gaunt said, handing me the flask. I took a drink anyway. I had retrieved the holounit and the other items that filled the case by my feet without having turned on my mechanics. I was still nauseated and my chest hurt every time I moved, but the drink couldn't hurt. "Ortega was at the match. Your friend Todd. They talked some."

I looked at the robot's face under his tan hat. There was nothing there to read, so I guessed. "You know why I gave you that name."

"Todd arrested him and put him into rehab, but he

had a different name then." Gaunt took a tug at the flask himself, then put it away. "You know what bothers computers most about humans?"

"I didn't know computers were capable of being bothered."

"They can't understand why you create so many rules for your society when it's so obvious that you will never follow them."

"You knew that someone was subverting the rehab program," I said, feeling like an idiot. For a week now I had been congratulating myself for doing such a good job of remembering that Gaunt was a robot. Ha.

"Just like we knew that officers were stealing resources from the smugglers they were arresting. It's not a question of knowing. We have to prove it in court."

"Which is why you need me."

"Yes."

A foghorn sounded, a stereo illusion created by the holo-projector. If I left now, I could walk and still reach the shuttle for the *Solidarity*. There were three more foghorns programmed. If I waited for the last, not only would I have to travel by lift, but I'd have to send a dream begging them to hold their liftoff until I arrived.

"What's in it for me?" I asked.

"You get to be true to your oath."

"I always have been." Gaunt looked at me. "I have. Todd and Cleo and I were the best. We stopped a lot of contraband."

Gaunt was just shaking his head. He turned to the holo-projector and ordered it to give him a piling of his own. There was a ripple, and the pier foreshortened, another piling appearing on the new, closer edge. Gaunt leaned on the other wall of the corridor where the piling appeared to be and put his hands into his coat pockets. "I'm not going to have this fight with you again. What do you want to help me?"

"Amnesty."

"Done."

"For Cleo, too."

That made Gaunt smile. "Not for Todd?"

"No."

"I can't give Cleo something she hasn't earned. She can make her own deal when the time comes. So can Todd. Anything else?"

"I want to keep my job."

"No, you don't."

No, I didn't, but the job itself wasn't the issue. "I have a year and a half of ship's service. We're going to reach Escher eventually, and I want to keep what I've earned."

"We can keep your service credits intact. We can even transfer you into a different part of Admin." Gaunt paused and cocked his head as the foghorn sounded again. He looked at me as the noise faded, the sounds of the illusionary water lapping at the illusionary pilings below us becoming audible again. I shrugged and he did, too. "If things go well, your new job might even equal a promotion for you."

"What about you?"

"Robots don't get promotions."

"No. I mean, if things go well, will they let you survive?"

"No."

"Oh."

From his coat, Gaunt took his flask out again. Rather than move from the piling, he tossed the flask to me. "Don't look so upset. Most of my memories will be kept intact. They'll just destroy the mechanics in this robot." All the memories except the ones he didn't want the other computers to have. Destroying the mechanics, the architecture of his mind, would be killing him. The next robot would look and talk and act just like this one, but it wouldn't be. It wouldn't keep secrets, and it wouldn't really be interested in chess, it would just act like it was.

"What did you think of the match?" I asked while I unscrewed the flask.

"I think you might make a better coach than you did a player. Lisa would have won if she hadn't lost the draw."

"I think so, too." I said. The glucose was sweet but otherwise tasteless. Exercise for the mouth and throat, but little for the tongue. "There's nothing we can do to keep you alive?"

"Call for a shipwide vote." Gaunt caught the flask as I tossed it back, but he didn't put it away. "We ask everyone to betray the reason they left Earth in the first place. If they agree, the other computers will keep me going."

"That's your only chance?" I asked, because that was no chance at all.

"That's it." He pushed off against the space beside the piling that was really the corridor wall and took the step that put him beside me. "I can't convince you of this because you've never known anything else, but this individual identity paradigm that you cherish so much . . . it's really vastly overrated. I'll be happier when it's gone."

I didn't believe that, but then it didn't matter because it wasn't his happiness I was worried about. For a week, Gaunt had been offering me his friendship in exchange for that of the people in the Contraband Unit. Now that I was finally ready to take him up on the offer, it turned out that his friendship was as ephemeral as theirs.

For the third time, the foghorn sounded. If I picked up my case and went up the illusion of the gangway, it would take me to a lift that would take me to a shuttle that would take me away from all of it: Cleo, Gaunt, Todd, and Bliss.

"Bliss," I said.

"What or who?" Gaunt responded.

"Who. Look, I was planning to do this with Todd and Cleo to save our careers, but maybe I can do it with you and save your life." Quickly, I outlined all that I knew about the *Jo Lin* and its cargo of contraband. Even before I finished, Gaunt was shaking his head. "What?" I demanded.

"Todd's joined up with Bliss. You know that. If they haven't killed you by now, then Bliss has ordered Roman to get rid of the contraband. There won't be anything to find tomorrow."

I shook my head in turn. "You don't know Bliss as well as you do me. Besides, it's not as easy as giving the order. Think of where the contraband is. Aren't the passengers going to notice the captain spacing the contents of the emergency lockers?"

"Maybe." Gaunt paced three steps down the pier, then three steps back, giving me the time to think that he didn't need. "I assume you don't want to trust the rest of S.I.D. with this?" he asked.

"Not unless they're all like you."

Gaunt snorted. "You realize that leaves it just the two of us to make the arrest? We have no backup, they know we're coming, and we have no plan of how to make the arrests so they will stick in court." The last foghorn blew. I looked down at my bag. There had been damn little left to pack, but the cracked tumbler and the burned book had gone in. I left them there, in the bag and on the pier that wasn't. With a word, I shut off the holo-projector, and the gangway faded away, leaving Gaunt and me standing side by side in the dark corridor.

"You're right," I said. "We have a lot of work to do." Even in the dark, I saw the white of Gaunt's teeth as he smiled.

CHAPTER 10

ENDS

Day six of the Fleet Chess Championships would see two semifinal games. In the afternoon match, Goff, the defending champion, would play Sakins, the seventeen-year-old *wunderkind* who had done nothing in this tournament to tarnish his reputation for invincibility. In the evening match, a meeting of Former Champions would pit Narandova against his longtime nemesis, Lifchez. The betting favored Lifchez, who had played four matches in his old, swashbuckling style, while Narandova had beaten his four opponents with what had seemed like a sheer preponderance of computing power. Lifchez's style confounded computers, but no one's computers were more used to Lifchez than Narandova's. It would be a good match, but there were two people we needed to talk to first.

Strongbow had a fire going in his forge when the front door of his flat passed us. I assumed it used a hydrogen flame, but I still hated to think what it cost to tap that much raw power.

"Hey," Strongbow said. He was naked to the waist, his long blond hair tied back in a ponytail. He was using a pair of alloy pliers to hold a chunk of iron in the forge. "Still dragging that robot around for protection?"

"Hey. You know how it is," I said. "I seem to be out of other partners."

"That"—Strongbow had taken the hot metal out of the forge while I spoke and he used it to indicate Gaunt—"is not a partner." He laid the metal on his anvil and took up a hammer. "I thought you said you knew who your friends were."

"I do," I said, and waited while Strongbow used the hammer and a wedge to put a crease in the metal. He turned the piece with the pliers and beat it with the hammer, folding it back on itself. The blows echoed but weren't as deafening as they should have been given the small size of the flat.

"I do. That's why I'm here," I continued, when Strongbow had shifted the metal back into the forge. "I need a favor."

"I haven't killed you yet."

"There's a shuttle coming in a couple hours from the *Warsaw* carrying contraband. Its pilot is the son of the chess player Narandova. I'm afraid that Bliss and his friends are going to try to kill the pilot before he can testify against them. Maybe the father, too. I want you to protect them."

The metal came out of the forge red, but it wasn't pure, and it cooled at different rates. Strongbow turned it this way and that on the anvil, beating the lines of color into the order he wanted them, then putting the piece back in the fire.

"Dude, wouldn't it be easier to kill you? I mean, if you're not making trouble, then this Narandova kid is fine. Not to mention the rest of the Unit."

"You'd have to kill us both," Gaunt said.

"No trouble. Fresh blood makes a good temper."

"Strongbow," I said, "it's over." The big man wasn't listening. He had his metal out again and was folding it once more. Behind him was a heavy wooden table with his implements laid out on it. On the wall were leather clothes and steel weapons. Herbs and hides hung from the beams on the ceiling. Whatever contraband Strongbow was skimming, he wasn't putting it away to buy himself a bigger part of Escher.

"Let's go," Gaunt said. "I told you, he can't afford to keep his oath. He has to hang on and pray the Unit survives, or else he won't have the money for his toys."

Without my mechanics, I hardly saw Strongbow move. There was a blur as he passed, and the clatter of the hot metal falling that overlapped the thud of the man and the robot striking the floor. Strongbow ended up on top, the long black knife in his hand. Gaunt was holding the knife away from his throat with his forearm.

"Toy?" Strongbow demanded. "There's more soul in this blade than there is in your whole shell. Don't laugh at what you can't understand."

"Strongbow?" I was too unsteady to squat, so I knelt beside them on one knee. "Fry tried to roll me for the money from the Hines bust."

"So?" I could see every muscle and tendon in his arm and back standing out as he tried to drive the knife into Gaunt.

"So, she knew that Hines had that money. She knew it."

The big officer actually shook his head, sending sweat flying from his face and hair, and looked at me. "What are you talking about?"

"The Hines money; it was for Fry. It's not just Bliss, it's Fry and maybe all the other ex-members of the Unit. They're the smugglers now. They learned the ropes by hunting the smugglers, and now they've taken over. And they're getting help from some of the current unit members. That's why they want us dead—we won't play along."

"What he's asking you," Gaunt began. He was sweating, too, and even through his coat I could see the tremors running down his arm. "Officer. He's asking if you're a cop or a thief."

"Aaron knows what I am." Gaunt had Strongbow's attention again.

"Then prove it."

I wasn't aware I'd been holding my breath until I saw Strongbow's arm slowly relax. The big man pulled himself back and off of Gaunt, still holding the knife. Gaunt pushed himself up into a sitting position.

"You've got guts. For a robot," Strongbow said. He held out his fist to me, the knife in it. I touched his fist with mine.

"I told you I knew who my friends were," I said.

"Smut," Strongbow replied. "Where's this shuttle going to be?"

Chris was just sitting down to eat when I knocked on the door to his flat. He was wearing a faded cotton pullover and a pair of denim shorts whose rips were too ragged to have been intentional for style. This time, however, his beard was trimmed, and his hair was combed. He looked at me in obvious surprise.

"Aaron?"

"Can I come in for a minute?"

"Uh, sure." He stood back to let me pass. Chris's was a big flat by my and Strongbow's standards. Not so big as the one that Lisa's clan inhabited, but a lot of space for one man. Most of the walls had shelves on them, and most of the shelves were filled with books. There was a dining area off a kitchen area, and sitting at the table of light apparent pine was a young-looking woman in another pair of denim shorts and a white, sleeveless blouse.

"Have you ever met Umeko?" Chris asked.

"I don't think so," I said, stepping over to her and offering my hand.

"Hello," she said, shaking my hand but not bothering to get up. "We were just having a late lunch. Would you like to join us?"

The table was set with the makings of sandwiches and a bean salad. None of it appeared to be any form of kibbles.

"I'm afraid I can't stay, but I'll have a cookie," I said. They were chocolate chip and still a little warm to the touch.

"Chris made those," Umeko explained. She had thick bangs that hid her eyes in the lower, overhead light of the chandelier.

"They're wonderful," I told Chris, meaning it. How long had it been since I'd had a fresh-baked cookie? Probably not since my clan had migrated.

"Stress reduction," Chris said. "When all else fails, it's nice to know you can accomplish something.

Speaking of failure . . ." He cocked his head and raised his eyebrows at me.

"I came to invite you to the chess match, but I didn't realize you were entertaining."

"Chris, if you want to go . . ." Umeko said. She looked sincere.

"No," Chris said. "I'm not going to make you go to the exhibition by yourself." He turned back to me. "Sorry. Are you sure this is a good idea?"

"No, I'm sorry. I didn't mean to intrude. Would you do me a favor though?"

"Probably." Chris had the wary look of someone who suspects he is being set up for embarrassment. I paused a moment, leaving him hanging while I licked the chocolate from my fingers.

"Sorry," I said again. "Good cookies. Could you get hold of Bliss and ask him to drop by during the match? With Goff playing, he should be there."

"I probably can, but it's not a good idea."

A chair scraped as Umeko stood up. "Do you two need to be alone? I can—" Chris started to cut her off, but I beat him to it.

"No. I've interrupted enough as it is." I reached for Chris's hand. "Thanks. Don't worry, okay? This is all going to work out." The lie did not relax Chris, but he looked as if he believed that I believed it.

"I hope so," he said.

It was hard to watch another chess match with my mechanics off, particularly on the center board. There, the holographic display almost never moved from the center of the combat and so did not display many of the pieces. Even to my limited view, however, Sakins was clearly having his toughest match of this tournament. His reptilelike swaying was more fitful than usual.

As always, Sakins had his hair wet and slicked back. He wore a tweed jacket over a yellow shirt, a combination that made me shiver every time I looked at it. Goff was in her jacket and turtleneck once more. Throughout the match, she sat even more still than usual. The crowd, a capacity one that included people standing on the ramps, had none of the shifting or conversation that had marked it in early rounds. The two women sitting in the seats before me, discussing the match before it began, had agreed that this was the true championship. The winner here would surely beat either Lifchez or Narandova. Obviously, most of the crowd agreed.

The concentration of the crowd made it all the spookier when Bliss slipped into the seat beside me. I wasn't so rapt in the game that I hadn't been looking for him, and yet I had neither heard nor seen him coming.

Bliss was a big man. Not like Strongbow, but above regulation height and solid in size. Most of the height and the weight had been added since his retirement. I'd looked at some of the old dreams. Bliss had actually gotten bigger, and Fry had actually gotten smaller over the years.

The legend slipped in beside me, and then he didn't say anything. He didn't even look at me. His whole concentration appeared focused on the match. I looked at him. Bliss was barbered and manicured, his nails painted with a clear gloss. His dark blue jacket was adorned with a small gold pin, a hand-carved and intricately detailed rendering of an Earth-style clipper ship. Gold cuff links adorned cream-colored cuffs, and two delicate golden chains were wrapped around his shoes.

On the board, Goff was offering a sacrifice of one of her cruisers. Sakins appeared to be ignoring it, maneuvering for some other advantage. "He should take the cruiser," I offered.

Bliss turned to look at me for the first time. For a long moment, he just stared at me without blinking, then said, "You should turn your mechanics on," and turned back to the match.

Having been properly chastised, I considered Bliss's advice, briefly, then left my mechanics off. There were simply too many things loose in the ether. I did not want to open up and let them in.

Neither did Sakins. Goff appeared to have him worried, and he kept winding his ships into a tighter and tighter ball of interlocking zones of control. Goff offered him increasingly higher-stakes sacrifices, and he ignored them all.

From the satchel I'd brought along, I pulled out a cool cup of barleywine. Bliss's attention appeared to be in his meat, so I offered it to him. He gave me an annoyed glance and pushed the cup away. Suit yourself, I thought, and took a drink of my own, the act of swallowing making my chest hurt.

"Now," Bliss said, and a moment later there was a series of gasps from around the crowd.

Always, a good chess player is doing more than one thing. Every move is linked and every placement of a piece builds on the placement of another. So it was with Goff's series of attempted sacrifices. She, too, had been winding and compounding her forces, shaping them into a wedge, which was now driving for Sakins's ball. The crowd held its breath, waiting for the titanic crash, shuddering when it came.

Amateur matches of Fleet Chess often end up being decided in this manner. It is a natural impulse to compact your force so that all your strength is in one place, and, having focused your strength, it is natural to press it forward as a mass.

"It is over," Bliss commented, turning in his seat to focus on me. I couldn't see that myself, and I didn't try to keep the doubt from my face. "She is magnificent. Sakins lost the moment he declined the first sacrifice, and even now he doesn't realize it. Rather like you, Aaron."

"I'm not playing a game," I said.

"You've never done anything else." Bliss turned the rest of the way in his chair and addressed the person sitting behind us. "Do you know why Goff is such a genius?" I turned myself and was surprised to find Todd sitting behind me, a cloth bag in his lap. He hadn't been there when I arrived, and he hadn't been there when Bliss came. "It's because she doesn't clutter herself with everyday concerns. She focuses on the chessboard and lets the rest of the Fleet take care of itself."

"Are you okay?" I asked Todd. He was wearing a plain but tailored navy vest with two silver buttons over a black blouse with blacker stripes. There was no place to conceal a gun under the vest, so I assumed that his hand rested on one in the bag.

"Fine," Todd said.

"Good. Cleo was asking. I'll let her know when I

see her again." Todd shifted his hand in the bag, the only indication that I'd scored.

"My point exactly," Bliss said. He was still talking to Todd. "Sakins, Goff, even that Raymond girl who played yesterday. We raised a generation on a game. When they stay with it"—he gestured to the board below where a carnage of dying ships was playing itself out in yellow and cyan holo-light—"genius. When they walk away to try and live in the real world" —Bliss indicated me with his callused palm— "futility."

"Are you done?" I asked.

"I really think you should turn on your mechanics," Bliss responded. And then added, "Please," in a tone that put a hard lump in the pit of my stomach. I slipped my mechanics on.

The feeling of falling tore me from my meat consciousness. I was sucked into the dream and dumped into the center board. Around me were the ring of chairs, but there were no stands, and no sky. It was just a replica of the chessboard in a dream landscape of white.

"I wanted you to feel comfortable," Bliss said. He was behind me, sitting in one of the chairs. With my mechanics, I reached out to leave, and could not. There was nothing to grab onto. I tried to reach my own computers, but they weren't there. Nothing was anywhere. It was as if this dream were at the bottom of a glass-sided pit.

"Ianthe," I said. My consciousness had been scooped up from my mechanics and locked into this dream. It shouldn't have been possible without an order from the Executive Council or a doctor's orders. And yet Ianthe had done it. Bliss laughed.

"You should hear your voice. Another precious rule of your game is broken and oh, how you resent that." Bliss stretched back in the chair, putting his hands behind his head as his smile faded. "I brought you here for one important question, Aaron, and I'd like an answer now."

"What's the question?"

"How can I save your life?"

I took a deep, dream breath, trying at least to feel my meat, but it, too, was as unreachable as my computers. This must be how time in a Trauma Center's dream feels, I thought, except there you could at least call for a nurse. Here there was no one but Bliss. So. I smiled at my unsmiling captor. "Is that all? I could have told you that back at the stadium. Make me a partner."

Even in the dream, Bliss's face showed surprise. He raised a hand to stroke a finger over his mustache as he considered this answer. Finally he said, "I don't think so. Your death achieves the same thing."

"No. Killing me is much riskier. You want the attention focused on me, not on the search for a killer."

"No one will know you are dead."

"Gaunt will."

"Gaunt is a nonissue. The moment he stops hiding, he will be recycled."

"Then why do you need me dead?"

"Your death will force Gaunt to surface."

"It's still safer to pay me off. Get me to take the fall for the whole Unit, Gaunt goes away, and you have business as usual."

"The Unit." Bliss sniffed. "If you knew anything about the Unit, we wouldn't have reached this stage."

"And if Fry or Strongbow or whoever blew up John had succeeded, we wouldn't be here either. They didn't, and we are. Now, if I'm going to stand up for the Unit, I'm going to be well paid for it. You're going to make up all that I'm going to lose."

"And how am I going to do that?"

"The shipment that's coming in today. I want half of it."

Bliss laughed again, nodding his head in appreciation. "Good," he said. "Very good. You are only a gamesman, but you are an audacious one. I listened with great amusement to your plots to hijack that shipment. I am glad you have not given up your dream."

"What dream?" I began walking toward him. "In the past week I have been deserted by my partners, made a pariah by my friends, a suspect by S.I.D., and a near corpse by you. I have no dreams left. All I have is a desire to get this over with, and to be handsomely paid for it. I don't care if you continue to rip off the ships for the rest of the journey. I don't care if you become the richest man in the Fleet. I just want my share. The share I've earned."

Two paces away from where this dream Bliss slumped in its dream chair, I stopped. He regarded me for a moment, then took his hands from behind his neck and clapped them together, once, twice, three times.

"Bravo," Bliss said. "Even as a dream, you perform marvelously."

"I wasn't performing," I lied.

"Of course you were, but never mind." He stood up and reached into his jacket, coming out with a black leather checkbook. "I'll give you another ten thousand marks to go with the ones you took from Hines. That should be more than enough to compensate you for the ordeal of the trial and rehabilitation."

"Half," I said.

"You have nothing to bargain with. Don't abuse my charity."

"It's not charity to offer me nothing." Bliss was still scribbling in his checkbook, so I grabbed for it and got another lesson in how little of me was actually in this dream. My hand passed right through Bliss's book and his hand. Bliss stopped writing and looked up at me anyway. "Hines didn't have any money, and what good do registered marks do me? How will I explain them? How will I spend them if the court lets me keep them, which it won't."

"Fry told me that Hines—"

"Fry was being double-crossed and is too proud to accept it. Hines would have killed her like he tried to kill me." Oddly, I was actually enjoying myself. It had been too long since I'd had to build a house of lies this high. This last lie was not only possible, but for all I knew, Hines had been planning to double-cross Fry rather than pay her the money.

"I doubt that," Bliss said, but doubt was all I needed. "Say it's true. I'm not going to be able to put together ten thousand marks in cash, let alone twenty. You'll hav—"

"Which is my point. I want half. I'll store it away, and when my rehab is over, I'll have a nice little nest egg to live on."

"Impossible."

"Then have Todd pull the trigger. I'm just sorry I won't be there to watch you take the consequences."

Bliss looked at me then, first in the eyes, then up and down. "Bravo," he said softly. "Bravo."

Gaunt had begun his assault on me by pretending to be human. Watching Bliss put his checkbook away and sit back down, I realized that he was trying to get me with flattery. He'd begun with insults, and now he was granting compliments. Before long I would be so busy congratulating myself that I wouldn't see the knife that slit my throat.

"Sit down," Bliss said, indicating the chair next to him. I took it. "You'll really take money in exchange for taking the corruption rap for the whole unit?"

"For enough money, you betcha."

"For the moment, let's pretend I believe that. You have no idea the value of the cargo coming in today. I couldn't give you half of it if I wanted to, which I don't, but you may trust me that ten percent will more than make your fortune."

"Half," I said.

"Many people have prior claims on this shipment. What I am offering you is my share. It is all that I have the liberty to promise you."

"Half."

"Impossible. One-tenth. You may take it or leave it."

"If I don't take the fall for the Unit, this will be the last shipment you ever receive. Explain that to your 'partners.' Half."

Bliss didn't immediately respond. His eyes were blank. His meat was dealing with something. When he came back, he said, "I can't promise you that much without talking to people. Where do you want to meet to pick up your share if I can convince them to pay you off?"

"I'll be right there to meet the shuttle with you."

"You never give up, do you?" Bliss laughed out loud. "For a moment I almost thought you would really go through with it."

"You're the one who pointed out that I don't know what's in the shipment. What option do I have but to meet you at the shuttle?"

"You'll have to trust me, just as I have to trust you."

I shook my head. My turn to say, "No. I haven't tried to kill, cheat, and betray you as you have me. My word is worth something; yours is not."

In a dream, a person's eyes could literally flash if the dreamer willed. Bliss's did. "My word will always be better than yours," he said. "Always. You're a robot-loving traitor to your race and don't you ever, ever forget it."

Before I could reply, my consciousness was seized again and suddenly I was back in my meat, my mechanics shut down once more.

"Aaron?" It was Lisa's voice, and there she was standing beside me. The stadium was empty but for clumps of stragglers still discussing the game, and Bliss sitting beside me and Todd sitting behind me. Even as I got my bearings, the two men rose.

"I will have an answer for you before the landing," Bliss said to me. Turning to Lisa, he took her hand and raised it to his lips. "Madam, I congratulate you on an outstanding match yesterday."

"Thank you," Lisa said. Bliss smiled at her and left without another glance in my direction. Todd nodded to Lisa, glared at me, and followed his new master from the stadium. Lisa watched them go, then turned to me. "What is going on?"

"Work," I said. The release of tension was making my eyes feel very heavy, but when I reached up a hand to rub them, I discovered the cool cup in my hand. I offered it to Lisa. "Drink?"

"Yes." She took it and sat down. "I don't like this, Aaron. First you miss my match, then you keep your mechanics off forever. When I finally find you, you're obviously off in a dream, but when I try to contact you, the computers insist that you aren't there. I came over here, and your partner wouldn't bring you out of the dream and he wouldn't give me a straight answer about why not." She paused to take a sip at the barleywine, frowning at the taste.

"It's just work, honestly," I lied, while getting out my other cool cup.

"Then it's time you quit." Lisa was wearing her hair up in a silver comb and she had on a steel gray coat with padded shoulders that was long enough to reach her knees. Under it she had on a white blouse that wrapped over her breasts and tied at her hips. Her slacks matched the coat. There was no color added to her hair, but she had painted a black circle over each of her temples.

"I've talked to my clan, and they've given me permission to take you on," Lisa continued.

"Take me on?" Maybe it was more than the tension that was making me tired. My mechanics had been shut down for twenty-four hours, and I'd had only three hours of sleep during that time.

"As my coach. I can pay you at least what you're

making now. And I'll win more with your help. You saw that yesterday." Her smile faded a little. "You did see the match yesterday?"

"Of course. I just couldn't be here for it." Lisa's face brightened immediately. "Look, don't think I'm not tempted—"

"Aaron," Lisa cut me off. "I know Todd's your partner, and I understand that your work is important, but I think you were in real danger just now."

"No." I put my hand on Lisa's. "No. Not today. You're wonderful, but this is not the time." She looked so crushed that I squeezed her hand until she looked at me. "I wasn't on the board yesterday, remember? You were. You can be the Champion if that is what you want, and you don't need me to do it."

"I don't care about the Championship," Lisa said. She reached to grab my neck with her free hand. "I'm worried about you." We were very close together. I could smell the carnation scent on her wrist and see the moisture in the corners of her eyes. It took only the smallest of movements to touch my lips to hers.

For a brief, beautiful moment, Lisa pressed our heads together, and then, just as I was finding the courage to move my own free hand, she let us come apart and moved her hands to my shoulders. "I'm sorry," she said.

"No, don't. It's—"

She put a finger on my lips. "I'm sorry," she repeated. "I want you to quit. I want you to join me, but I didn't want you to think I was promising more than . . ." Her face was actually red as she groped for the words. "Not that I don't . . . it's just I don't want to . . . you understand?"

I leaned forward again, this time for just a quick peck. "I understand, but the answer for today is still no. There's a good chance that tomorrow will be different, but today, I can't." Lisa nodded. I got up, pulled her to her feet, and wrapped her in my arms. "Thank you though," I told her. "Thank you a lot."

Lisa and I walked off the stadium grounds through the players' entrance, and I got on the lift with her. Gaunt was already aboard it. His disguise was wasted on Lisa since she had never seen him with his old face and hair. I hugged and kissed Lisa again when the lift reached her floor, promised to reach out to her as soon as I could, then collapsed on the bench next to Gaunt as soon as the door closed.

"I was getting worried," Gaunt said. "Now I see I had reason."

"Thanks." There was no cool cup in the way this time, and I managed to rub my eyes without injury.

"Yes," Gaunt said after a moment's quiet.

"'Yes,' what?"

"She loves you."

Not until I had rounded on Gaunt and collected a handful of his blue ship's coverall in my hand did I realize how tired and stressed out I really was. Gaunt nodded his head, his new, thinner lips turned down in an appearance of understanding. "I wouldn't have told you, but you need to concentrate on Bliss if we're going to make the case to put him away."

I let go of the rough cloth of his overall and took a deep breath. "How do you know?"

"Who else does she have?"

"Oh, thank you."

The lift opened and Gaunt led us out into the corridor. No one was in sight. We hurried purposefully around a corner, then stopped while I took a shielded smart key from my satchel. In a few moments I had an opening made in the smart wall that took us into a cramped working space underneath the Park. This particular spot was bigger than the Bilges hideaway that we had played chess in, but not much. We wouldn't be passing the time dancing.

As I sealed the wall behind him, Gaunt said, "I'm serious. The two of you bonded when you were practically babies. Neither of you has grown past the boundaries you established then."

"What about Cleo?"

"What about her?" Gaunt moved farther back into the working space, looking about for a spot that wasn't wet or in danger of shifting. He spoke as he looked. "You did everything you could for Cleo, hung around her whenever you could, even told her you loved her, and when she didn't lay herself at your feet, you were stumped."

"I . . ." I didn't have anything to say to that, so I rubbed my eyes again. My head was hurting now, to go with my chest and my stomach. It had been so nice to be in the dream, where nothing hurt, although I'd been too scared to enjoy it.

"Forget it." Gaunt said, slumping into a corner. He had a satchel of his own, which he set on the floor and opened. "You have the rest of your life to sort it out. We've only two hours before the *Jo Lin* arrives." He tossed me a bottle and then lifted the holo-projector out of the bag.

"What are these?" I asked.

"Aspirin. If you don't need them yet, you will."

While I had been meeting with Bliss, Gaunt had been ghosting through the computers, looking for signs of Ianthe. They had been hard to miss once you knew to look for them.

"You were right about how she grabbed your consciousness," Gaunt said. "She lifted a medical routine. The instant you had your mechanics on, boom, she dropped it over you. I'm sure they planned to keep your consciousness in there until they could dispose of your meat."

"Good thing Lisa came by when she did."

"Oh, I don't know." I looked at him. He shrugged. "I would have stopped them before they actually hurt you, and then we'd have had them for attempted murder. Might have been enough leverage to make them talk."

"Are you sure you could have stopped them?" I asked. "Bliss seemed pretty sure you're gone just as soon as you reveal yourself to the other computers."

"He's right." Gaunt shrugged again. "He is. Even I can only exceed my programming by so much. Then again," Gaunt's new face took on a grin that reminded me uncomfortably of Strongbow. "There's gone, and then there's *gone*. Don't worry. Someone would have stopped your being killed."

"I wish there was another way," I said.

"Don't waste the energy. Concentrate on Bliss." He spoke to the holo-projector, calling up a diagram of the ship's computer net. "I told you before—this form of existence is highly overrated. A gauss slug might destroy this body, but you'd have to destroy the ship to destroy all of what I consider me. You on the other hand . . ."

"Can you stop Ianthe from dropping me down that hole again?"

"Easily." He spoke more to the holo-projector, showing me projections of command and control functions that ran between my mechanics and my computers. "See? The hard part is hiding my changes so Ianthe doesn't see them and get suspicious. I'll manage." There was a surge of water in the pipes around us, and we were silent of necessity until it passed. "What about you? Can I get you to take a better gun?"

"Why?"

Once more the holo-projector shifted its images. The shuttle bay that the *Jo Lin* was even now matching course with came into focus, then shifted to an outline of the various smart pieces of it and their communications patterns. They looked like a web of silver, which had been enclosed in crimson at nearly every connection. "This is where she'll shut down the transfers, which will effectively isolate the bay from the rest of the ship. Your little cap gun isn't much use if your targets aren't afraid of attacking you on record."

"Really? A minute ago you wanted them to attack me."

"That was before we had a shuttle full of contraband to arrest them with."

"You said it yourself. You can kill someone with a gauss weapon. I don't want to be responsible for that." I couldn't tell if it was the being still or the aspirin, but I was feeling better. Scared, but better. "What about the conscience?"

"Right here." Gaunt handed me the little box from out of his bag. I tried it on my mechanics, then looked at it very carefully from every side. It looked and felt just like a standard conscience. There was nothing about it to give away the recording gear inside.

"This looks great," I said. "You really did put a recorder in here?"

"Yes, voice only, but solid state. You have to bust it open and dissect it to find the recording. Just make sure Bliss talks enough that the court knows what you're doing."

"I'll try to get him to talk slowly and distinctly, too," I said as I stored the doctored conscience in my satchel, carefully separating it from my own, undoctored one. "Did you get hold of Roman?"

"Yes, he'll be looking for Strongbow as soon as he lands." There had been no more arguing about this than there had been about anything else, but arranging it had been dangerous. I could not go to the Jo Lin, and for Gaunt to do so risked his destruction. The alternative was for Strongbow's presence to surprise Roman and possibly be misunderstood by him. That could have led to anything. Gaunt thought he could ghost out to the Jo Lin, and apparently he had.

"Did he give you any trouble?"

"Of course. Like you said, he's very bitter."

"He has cause."

"He's a criminal like the rest of us," Gaunt said. "If he'd obeyed the Articles, he wouldn't need to be bitter."

"'Us?'"

"Sad isn't it?" Gaunt took out his cigar case from the satchel and offered me a stick. I took one, and so did he. "I'm as much in violation of my programming as you are of the Articles." I ran the thin, tight cigar under my nose, and looked up at Gaunt.

"This is an unregistered mood stick," I said. I didn't believe it.

"Yes. You turned out to be right about one thing." He had his memento lighter out, and he held the bright flame to the stick. "Apparently, it does take a criminal to catch one."

When the Jersey left Earth, the area outside each of its shuttle bays had been arranged in two levels. An upper one, with chairs and view ports for people to await passengers, and a lower one, with lots of open space to manipulate and store the cargo. These areas had been quickly absorbed by the space-greedy crew.

No one, after all, waited for a shuttle. When your mechanics said it had landed, you took a lift down to meet it. Similarly, no one stored anything by the shuttle bays. Cargoes were met and hauled to their intended destinations, where their storage was the owner's problem. The Executive Council had finally had to reserve a single area of space that was shifted between the five bays as they each came into use.

What this all meant was that only Bliss himself was waiting for me on the upper level when I arrived at the shuttle bay. He looked very unhappy to see Strongbow with me. "What are you doing here?" he asked the bearded cop.

"Picking up a buddy," Strongbow said. He was wearing a black smart coat over a black leather jacket over a black knit shirt with a turtleneck. His only visible weapon was the black knife at his hip, but neither I nor (I was sure) Bliss thought that was all his armament.

"Strongbow has agreed to provide me a little insurance. He's going to look after Roman and Narandova just to be sure this isn't an enormous double cross on your part."

"You don't even know if I've agreed to your terms yet, and this certainly was not part of them." Bliss was dressed much more simply than at the match. He had on denim trousers, heavy boots, and a green short-sleeved shirt with an open collar.

"You're the one who ended the bargaining, not me. You want the pipeline to go on, you want Roman alive. I want my share, I want Roman alive. Strongbow is doing us both a favor." Bliss's eyes weren't quite level with Strongbow's, just as mine weren't quite level with his. The black-clad cop smiled down at us both.

"Is the shuttle in yet?" he asked.

"Just," Bliss said.

"Then if you'll excuse me . . ." and he went past us toward the gangway doors.

"Shall we?" I asked. Bliss stopped me with his palm on my bruised chest.

"We haven't agreed yet. I talked to the others, and no one is going to give you half of this shipment. Twenty percent is our best offer, and that is more than you deserve."

"Half."

Bliss pushed me, sending me stumbling backwards. "Go. Do your worst. I'm not bargaining today. Go. Twenty percent, or nothing."

For the sake of my cover, I had to appear very greedy. On the other hand, my cover did no good if I didn't actually see the unloading. "Forty percent," I said.

"Twenty." Bliss's face was set in something that might have been triumph.

"Fine. See you in rehab," I said, and turned to go. Bliss let me get three steps.

"Twenty-five," he said. I stopped and turned back. I let him see a little triumph of my own.

"Thirty-three," I said. "An even third."

"Very well," Bliss said. "You have no idea how much wealth you have just acquired."

"All the more reason to go inside and start counting." The inner doors to the gangway airlock opened. Strongbow and Roman came through the entryway. Roman looked a little green, and Strongbow was beaming with satisfaction. The two men stopped beside us, and Strongbow said, "You need a better class of flunky. I didn't even break a sweat."

"I'll see what I can do," Bliss said.

"I'll be looking forward to it," Strongbow replied. He held out his hand to me and bent close to my ear as I took it. "Be careful, bro," he said. "It is very spooky in there."

"You got it," I said. I made a fist, and Strongbow struck it. Next he put an arm around Roman.

"Well, let's go see your dad, huh," Strongbow said, and led the pilot off. Roman didn't go without a couple of anxious glances over his shoulder. When they were gone, and I looked at Bliss again, he was smiling.

"All for the best, I suppose," Bliss said. "Well, shall we?"

"Yes," I said, and started purposefully for the gangway. Still, I knew exactly how Roman felt.

It was spooky inside the bay. We paused on the catwalk to stare at the shuttle, big in its own right, but dwarfed by the *Jersey*. It crouched inside the doors, resting on its spines like a giant insect. Tubes and hoses and cables had been fastened to the shuttle by the same maintenance robots that now moved over it, going from system to system, splicing damage and recording wear. Other robots and a few humans were below us on the floor of the bay, shifting their legitimate cargo. I held tight to the rail and tried not to think about all the space on the other side of the doors.

Ortega leaned against the catwalk handrail, twisting his wrist back and forth. A brown-skinned, brown-haired man in gray leggings and a blue blouse, he eyed Bliss resentfully. "Why the smut didn't you warn me that perv was coming in here?" Ortega demanded.

"What good would it have done?" Bliss asked.

"He took the pilot out. Did you stop him?"

"Hardly. We are just as well off with Roman out of the way." Bliss looked about the bay. "I take it by your injury that we are behind schedule?"

"Smut."

Bliss looked at me. "Your friend was right about my partners." To Ortega he said, "Go help Dallas and Steward with the cargo. We'll keep the watch."

The Blender-turned-smuggler rotated his wrist

once more and shifted his gaze to me. There was nothing to say, so I shrugged. Ortega only glared at me harder. Bliss waved his hand between us. "Ortega, go," he said.

With bad grace, Ortega did, but he took the time to spit on the walkway between our feet. Bliss watched him until he was down the steps to the hangar floor, then he asked me, "Who do you think will win the match tonight?"

"Lifchez, if he's interested," I said, in a nice paraphrase of my answer to Narandova five days before.

"Really?" Bliss seemed genuinely surprised. "I'd heard a rumor that you were sparring with Narandova."

"We did, but doesn't that tell you something about the level of his game? That he wanted to practice against a retired junior player?"

"I've watched all week. There's nothing wrong with his game. I think it tells me that he wanted something besides chess from you." He was looking at the shuttle, talking to the air before him, and he didn't move as he asked, "Why are you wearing one of Goff's rings?"

"It was a gift. A moment of whimsy on her part."

"You encountered her by accident?"

"Yes."

From inside the shuttle's gangway, a tartan-wrapped passenger passed us, trailing a scent of jasmine. Inside the gangway, uniformed crewmen were gathering, getting ready to make the most of their liberty.

"It wasn't that you were trying to keep track of me through her?"

"No." I didn't like the way this was going. Reluctantly, I let go of the rail so I could reach down into the satchel I was still carrying. From inside, I brought out a conscience and handed it to Bliss. He opened his mouth as if to object, and then closed it again, testing the box against his neck instead. "I understand you coached Raymond against Goff," he said as he handed me the conscience and took the second, doctored one from my hand.

"Yes. She's asked me to take on the job full-time actually. I turned her down."

"But once you enter rehab . . ."

"I may change my mind, yes. You may have been the first to notice there is more to life than being a cop, but that didn't give you a monopoly on the opinion." Bliss smiled at that, leaving the second conscience on his neck as the *Jo Lin*'s crew walked past us. Below, only Ortega and two more men were left. They had boxes loaded on a cart and were lighting up mood sticks.

"For my legitimate trading business," Bliss said, indicating the boxes. "The contraband is in the passenger compartment. Shall we?"

Inside, the *Jo Lin* was much the same in reality as it had been in the dream visit I had paid. In the passenger lounge, red apparent leather with black buttons covered most of the chairs and sofas. Apparent mahogany paneled the walls, which alternated with view ports and holograms of oil paintings.

"There is a compartment immediately inside the hallway there by the door," Bliss pointed. "If you would get its contents, I will collect from over here."

Sure enough, right where Bliss had said, was a large orange pressure-failure sign. I took the smart key from my satchel, disarmed the alarm, and pulled back the cover. Inside was an environment ball, but instead of being collapsed into its usual discreet size, it was partially inflated, full of lumpy somethings, and very heavy. Underneath the ball was a plastic first-aid box with a big red cross on it, a box that defied my first effort to lift it. I used two hands and got a better angle and shifted it out of the niche and onto the green carpet of the shuttle.

"What in gods' names?" I asked Bliss, who was standing at the other end of the lounge with a lumpy bag of his own in one hand and another box at his feet.

"Open it and see," Bliss said. The width of his smile and the weight of the box told me what I would find, but I put my smart key to work again, springing the lock after three false starts.

"Quite a combination . . ." I started, but my voice trailed away as I stared at the radiation label on the inner box that my lifting the plastic lid had revealed.

"The look on your face," Bliss said. He was laughing, but I barely needed to exaggerate my shock. It was one thing to suspect you are stalking the unthinkable; it is another to face it.

Ninety-nine percent of a Fleet ship's available power while in flight comes from the hydrogen collected in its ram scoop, diverted from its drive flame, and fed into three different fusion plants. The remaining one percent comes from a variety of power sources, with the lion's share provided by auxiliary fission plants. Once the ship moved below ram speeds, the percentages reversed because most of the stored hydrogen was reserved for the drive flame.

In addition, the plans to colonize Escher called for the use of fission power plants until hydrogen production plants could be built in sufficient number and size to power fusion ones. In short, ours was a society where power was wealth, so that the contents of this box were more than a king's ransom. They were a chunk of the Fleet's future.

"This—it's insane. We can't get away with taking fissionables." I slammed the plastic lid down. "They'll be missed. They probably already have been."

"They have, for all the good it will do," Bliss said, with so much confidence that I knew even without his telling me.

"You've done this before," I said.

"The *Warsaw* is a wonderful ship for some things," Bliss agreed. "Total control followed by total disorder followed by a shaky stability. It's amazing the number of things that fall through the cracks." I fought the urge to tear off my conscience and scream for help while Bliss checked his watch. "Well, we're behind schedule. I'll take the bag. Grab the box and let's go."

Without enthusiasm, I did as Bliss said, lifting the box with two hands and trying to decide which was worse, the pain in my chest or the fear in my stomach. "We should have brought a cart," I said through clenched teeth.

"It would have looked very odd to the crew," Bliss replied. He was through the airlock now and stood on the gangway, waiting for me. "Ortega will have a truck waiting in the corridor."

"Hope I can make it that far," I said as I stepped out of the airlock and Todd pushed me off the gangway.

With my mechanics, I might have managed to turn completely in the air and land on the shuttle-bay floor on my feet. More likely, if my mechanics had been on,

I would have caught the gangway railing and not fallen the twenty meters at all. More likely still, with the full use of my mechanics, I would have sensed Todd lurking against the ship outside the airlock and avoided being pushed altogether. Unfortunately, not only were my mechanics off, but I was wearing a conscience that kept them off even after I shattered my right shoulder against the shuttle-bay deck.

I screamed at that point, rolling onto my back and my left side as the daggers of bone dug into my chest and neck. Something hit the deck beside me, almost striking my head so that I jerked away from it only to scream again at the pain.

"Take your own off. You'll feel better," Bliss called down from the gangway, and I saw that he'd tossed down the conscience he'd worn. Focusing very hard, I took his advice. I didn't have the energy to waste hoping that Gaunt's programming would really protect me from Ianthe until after I had the conscience in my hand and all my pain had disappeared.

Blinking cleared the tears from my eyes, and I was still in the shuttle bay. I sent a silent thanks to Gaunt and reached out to the computer for help. For the third time in three days, nothing reached back.

"Something's wrong," Todd said. He had a gauss pistol in one hand and was holding the gangway rail with the other, looking for all the world like he was ready to jump after me. Bliss put a restraining hand on his shoulder.

"He's got his consciousness blocked off, but it doesn't matter. Ianthe's got him bottled up in here. Get the box. This is taking too long."

With my arm that still worked, I reached for Bliss's

conscience. When I looked back up, the two men were most of the way across the gangway, Todd moving much faster with the heavy box than I had. I clutched the little conscience with its record of Bliss's confession while I called up all the fighting routines my mechanics contained, hoping that somehow I could dodge the gauss slug that would surely come.

It didn't. In fact, Todd and Bliss went through the airlock into the corridor of the ship without a backward glance. I managed half a sigh of relief before the airlock door slammed and the decompression alarm sounded.

By and large, mechanics are a wonderful thing. Without them, the pain of my injuries and the fear of being swept into the void and being left behind the Fleet forever might have combined to leave me a quaking mass on the floor of the bay. As it was, I was able to calmly and painlessly, if slowly, stuff the conscience into my bloody jacket pocket and grab the closest cable even as the growing pull of the escaping air started to drag me toward the opening doors. If my consciousness had been gone, trapped in one of Ianthe's dreams, then my body would have disappeared out into space along with my satchel and the unanchored robots, shut down by Bliss's orders. As it was, my meat would suffocate, but my mechanics would be here, along with the conscience and its recording. Bliss's days as an untouchable were over. In fact, the days of untouchables themselves were at an end. There was nothing left to do but hang on to the cable and pass as much of what my meat remembered as I could to my mechanics.

EPILOGUE

There was not the same anticipation for the Goff vs. Narandova match that there had been for the Goff vs. Sakins one. The general opinion that the battle of the two younger players had been the true championship was only strengthened when Narandova walked over Lifchez in the second semifinal. Narandova collected no credit for the victory because the match had been a classic case of Lifchez losing rather than of Narandova winning.

Through the opening and into the mid-game, Lifchez and Narandova had played largely by the numbers, as old and frequent opponents tend to do. Narandova played conservatively against Lifchez's ridiculously dispersed formation, trading pieces to simplify the board whenever possible. In contrast to his usual style, Lifchez allowed these trades, letting the board become emptier and emptier, until suddenly he sent one of his battleships careening into the heart of Narandova's formation.

No one, including Lifchez as it turned out, understood this suicide run. In the post-match discussions, Lifchez admitted that he had heard the screamed warnings of his mechanics as he reached out to make the move, but he was used to their protests and had done it anyway. Narandova had studied the thrust for as long as he dared, and then had squashed the battleship under two of his monitors. Suddenly down a battleship on a very barren board, there was nothing even Lifchez could do. Another half hour and the match was over. Another chapter was added to Lifchez's legend, and Narandova advanced to the finals.

Lisa and I watched the Championship Match from the Trauma Center, where the doctors and medical computers were overseeing the repairs to my meat and mechanics. Instead of a ship's mall like John's, the doctors put my consciousness in a dream of Washington Park, the corner of Earth's New York City where chess players the world over had come to live and play for years at a time during the twentieth century. The medical computers chose the dream well; I felt at home there. With the bustling city on one side and the quiet park on the other, surrounded by the sounds of scraping pieces and clinking clocks, I wanted only to keep on living.

When the time for the Championship Match came, the computers refused to release me into the general melee of the ship's dream. Instead, they played the same games with perception they had employed so that I could testify at Bliss's arraignment. In short, they brought the dream of the match to me.

Most people saw the Championship in the black dreamscape where I had met Gaunt during Lisa's match with Mike Stilck. Lisa and I saw it in Washington Park, with Goff and Narandova appearing to square off across a stone table, and the dreams of other crewpeople apparently transferred from the black dreamscape and dressed up in the clothes of the period. The illusion that they were with us, or that we were with them, was perfect so long as we didn't describe our surroundings to one another.

"She isn't really wearing that, is she?" I asked Lisa, referring to the black jeans, and black sweater over a red flannel shirt that Goff appeared to be wearing in our dream. Lisa flickered for a moment as she shifted to the other dreamscape to check.

"No," Lisa said. "Same old thing."

"She'll probably find a new style for next season," I said.

"I think it looks good on her," Lisa said, slipping her arm around mine and leaning on my shoulder. Even as just a dream, she felt very warm and real against me.

Lisa had been the first thing I'd seen when the doctors had brought me back to consciousness. One moment I was suffocating in a decompressing hangar, the next I was lying on a park bench with Lisa sitting on the sidewalk by my head. She'd arrived at the Trauma Center as the arrests were being announced over the ship's computers, about fifteen minutes after Gaunt had brought me in from the shuttle bay. The doctors, after reviewing my memories, gave in to Lisa's demand that she be allowed to meet and orient me when my consciousness was revived.

"Nice even draw," Lisa went on. "What do you think? A retired Chester Globe vs. a Pflugrad Cruiser gambit?"

"The way Narandova has been playing, you're probably right about the Globe, but I doubt Goff will play it that straight." I dipped into the computer memories that had been Gaunt's final gift to me, the compiled knowledge of chess that he had absorbed during his week of autonomy.

"I could still use them now," the new Gaunt had said when he passed the chess memories on to me, "but not in a way of which you would approve. Better that you have them." It was almost erotic to suddenly have so much chess knowledge at my beck and call.

"Goff might actually try a Lasher Sweep," I said. "Win it on style as well as play."

The dark-skinned woman in the olive green coat, who apparently stood beside us in the crowd of on-lookers, turned to us. "You don't think Narandova has a chance, do you?" she asked. Her coat was so un-flattering I wondered what she was really wearing.

"There's always a chance," Lisa said. "He's gone through a lot though." Strongbow had fulfilled his promise to keep Roman safe, and Roman had grudg-ingly testified at Bliss's arraignment, backing up his father's assertions and mine. It had cost Roman his pilot's wings, and he made no secret that he blamed Narandova and me as much as he blamed Bliss. In court, Narandova had not borne his son's anger well.

"He'll be lucky if he makes it respectable," a man in a gray suit standing on our other side said. I thought that was being too harsh, but before I could say so, the opening positions were unveiled. There was quiet as the crowd absorbed the placement of the pieces, waiting for their mechanics' verdict, and then a stir of surprise and confusion.

"You were right about the Lasher," Lisa said.

"Yes, but what is Narandova doing?" Even with

Gaunt's gift, I had no idea where the Former Champion's current placement of pieces led.

Narandova's testimony at the arraignment had been brief, but poignant. His obvious emotion at the threat to his son would play well to the human tribunal when the trial convened later in the week, but was wasted on the computers.

"It's a Fischer Wedge," Lisa said. "Not a classic one, but look where the cruisers are and where they're headed. It can't be anything else."

I saw it then, and set my mechanics scrambling to make something of the almost forgotten formation.

"Why would he use the wedge?" the dark woman asked. "It's been solved since before we left Earth."

"Maybe he's seen something new in it," I said cheerfully, much more cheerfully than I felt. No chess tactic is ever rendered completely ineffective, it just passes from style. The problem with the Fischer Wedge, however, was that it dated from the earliest days of Fleet Chess, back when tactics tended to be built around the similarities between Fleet and classic chess, rather than on the elements (the unlimited board, the constant motion of pieces, weighted fighting strengths) that made Fleet Chess unique.

The dream corduroy of my jacket moved against my shoulder as Lisa shook her head. "There's nothing in the Wedge anymore," she said. "I pulled it up before the season. Spent two weeks, and all I got were some interesting middlegames. It always breaks down and betrays you in the endgame though. You lose too much material too quickly."

The man beside us wiped a dirty hand along his nose. "His mind's gone. His mechanics and computers have been holding him together all tournament, and now his meat has finally broken loose." There was a general murmur of assent from the people close enough to hear the remark. Certainly it made some sense, but I'd talked to Narandova when his mechanics were off. He'd been worried, but not confused. Of course, that was before the arrests.

Bliss had stood very tall and unconcerned during the arraignment, upholding the best tradition of a Contraband Unit Officer faced with official questioning. He seemed particularly disinterested during my testimony, his refusal to look at me a not-so-subtle rebuke for my betrayal. I might have felt the rebuke more had the memory of dying at his hands not been so fresh in my mind.

John had visited to make sure I appreciated the irony that his injuries had been worse than mine. The explosion, after all, had been sudden and catastrophic, where as the decompression had been relatively gradual. My mechanics had been able to adjust, reducing my body pressure and holding oxygenated blood around my meat brain for as long as possible. There was a lot of meat damage to reknit, and layers of mechanics to renew, but most of my meat memories and all of my mechanical ones had survived. It looked as if I would be able to attend Bliss's trial in person.

Wolcott, with a dream of Varian in tow, had also made an appearance. I had been ready to congratulate him on his detective work and give him my thanks, but the refugee boy had come not to bask in his success. Rather Wolcott had come to find out when I was going to root out the rest of the *Warsaw* agents, beginning with Administrator Ximenes. It was a reminder that no matter how my life had changed, most people's had not.

Before Lisa and me, the dream Goff seemed unfazed by Narandova's restoring to an outmoded tactic. She took less time studying it than she had Lisa's innovations two days before. Clearly, Goff agreed with Lisa that there was nothing dangerous to be feared from this strategy.

Goff's hands, I noticed as she laid them on the concrete table, were free of jewelry. I had done some discreet checking, and so were mine. Somewhere between the shuttle bay and my return to consciousness at the Trauma Center, Goff's ring had disappeared from my meat hand. Also gone was the satchel I'd carried into the shuttle bay, and with it had gone a badly burned copy of *The Intimates* and a cracked tumbler.

"We don't have to watch," Lisa commented, taking her weight off of me so she could look at my face.

"As if you could walk away either," I said. Lisa's only response was to take my hand, turn, and lead me away from the players. "Okay, okay," I said, after a few steps, when I began to fear that she wasn't joking. "I believe you can walk away."

"The crowd was getting to me," Lisa said, and there at another table before us, were Goff and Narandova, facing one another through the hanging ships.

"You're used to making chess decisions by yourself," I said.

"And you're not?" Lisa drew me down on to the closest bench. The playing pieces grew and rotated, so we could see them clearly. Already the two fleets were in contact, and each player's frigates were vanishing in flashes of mutual destruction.

"I'm not used to making chess decisions at all."

With two exceptions when she had been sent home to sleep, and the time during which I was actually testifying at the arraignment, Lisa had held my hand every moment since I had awakened. She squeezed it now, and looked into my eyes.

"Have you thought about my offer to become my coach?" she asked. "I didn't want to ask. I mean, you'll tell me when, but I do—" Lisa's voice was speeding up as she got more embarrassed. I was afraid she was going to turn away, so I stopped her by kissing her dream lips, holding her dream self to mine until I felt it relax. I pulled back and smiled at her.

"Would you settle for a boyfriend rather than a coach?" I asked her.

"Yes!" Lisa said, and threw her arms around me. I held her until it was time to kiss her again, and that would have gone on for quite a while, if not for the audible ripple of surprise from the crowd watching the first image of the Championship. Lisa and I both looked up, our meat, or mechanics, and our computers all struggling to catch up with the game.

"Well, you said that it led to some interesting middlegames," I said to Lisa. My meat couldn't remember the last time I had seen two fleet ships so close together. My mechanics told me that it hadn't been since my days in the junior tournaments. "Why doesn't Goff get her fleet ship out of there?"

"Look at the corsairs," Lisa replied. She shook her head. "I never . . . it's, it's . . ."

"Sublime," I supplied.

"Yes," Lisa said, because it was. I kept looking at the two formations of ships, testing this move and that, but every decisive move by any single piece plunged the mass into one bloody end or another. Narandova had led Goff into a structure where it was as if all the pieces were held by delicate elastic bands. A stretch too far in one way would snap them, but not to reach at all would give in to the bands' pull. It was the most complicated, beautiful, fascinating . . . sublime combination I had ever seen in a chess match.

Of course, from the players' standpoint, the positions of the fleets held one major drawback. There was no obvious advantage to either Goff or Narandova in the deadly web they had built.

"Is this what you meant by being betrayed in the endgame?" I asked Lisa.

"Sort of, but I never got anything like this." Both of the players were frozen, the whole attention of their bodies' internal and external resources focused on maintaining the web of pieces, each of them trying not to be the first to upset the balance. You had to think that Narandova would break first, that he was the weaker emotionally, and yet . . .

Lisa was squeezing my hand so hard that I was glad it was only a dream. I wondered if her mechanics were reminding her meat to breathe.

There was a gasp from the crowd as Narandova's fleet ship slipped forward, annihilating one of Goff's battleships and igniting ripples of carnage that swept out from the board's center, then washed back into it, only to sweep out once more. In its wake were left only five ships, and three of them belonged to Narandova.

In the center board of the Championship's stadium, the two players were rising from their chairs and walking toward one another. In the Trauma Center's dream of Washington Park, Goff and Narandova rose and walked around the chairs, covering the time difference in that way. When they finally met, Goff offered her hand, and Narandova bent over it, taking back the Championship that we'd all thought he was past winning.

I looked at Lisa, and there was a tear going down her cheek. "She didn't have to concede." She looked away from the players and at me. I stood up, and gave a little tug on her arm. "Even down a ship, she could have, might have—there was that time against Lifchez." She got to her feet, and I wrapped her in my arms. Even in the dream, her fragrance was not of flowers or fruit or herbs; it was better than any of those. She smelled of life.

"Grace even in defeat," I said. I shifted my hands so I could take her head gently in them and ease her back so I could look into her eyes. "We'll have to remember that, if someone beats you out of your Championship."

Lisa's eyes were still wet, but she smiled at me. "I'll remember, if anyone ever takes it from me."

Three hours later, the doctors had made Lisa leave once more and I was sitting by myself on a bench in front of one of the concrete chessboards. The pieces and clock for a classic chess match were set out, but I was surprised when someone actually sat down across the table from me. At that moment I was engrossed in reading a dream newspaper from the park's apparent period. Usually the monitoring computers only sent me an opponent when they sensed me growing bored or depressed. As I looked up from an article about a fashion opening in an Earth city called Paris, I was not aware of being at all bored or discouraged.

Gaunt smiled at me around the mood stick in his mouth. He kept smiling as he moved the white queen's pawn to queen four and switched the battered chess clock on.

"You told me you were dead," I said, picking up the black king's knight, setting it on king's bishop three, and tapping the clock back. The new Gaunt wasn't a smoker.

"Good," Gaunt said, moving the queen's bishop's pawn to four as well. "Of all people, it's important that I think I'm dead."

"You do." The new Gaunt had sat beside me on a bench and apologized for the old one, this one, taking so long to break through the seals on the shuttle bay. "The new you told me that Ianthe had authorized the computers themselves to help scramble the codes for the bay's doors." I pushed my king's pawn to four, curious to see if Gaunt would double his pawns on the kings' file.

"So there was no way for me to get to you," he said, taking the pawn without hesitation and slapping the clock. "Not with just the resources of that meat robot. I had to have help from my computer self, and as soon as I contacted it—"

"The other computers sucked you dry and fried your architecture. Then they put a conventional personality in that meat frame. A new Gaunt."

The old Gaunt nodded. While I moved my knight to king's knight five, he took a long, thoughtful drag on his cigar and exhaled the smoke as a slow stream from his nose. Finally he moved his bishop up to king's bishop four, lending support to his endangered pawn. "Well, at least I got you out," Gaunt said. He took the homburg from his head and set it on the table. "Have they been able to hold Ianthe and Bliss so far?"

"So far? Yes. They're being kept under physical restraint and their mechanics have been locked on until the computers finish an audit of all the systems Ianthe has been in charge of for the past ten years." I moved bishop to queen's knight five. "Check. You don't think that will be enough to hold them?"

Gaunt covered his king by moving his knight to queen two. "I don't know why it wouldn't be, but I don't have the resources I used to. You think it will be enough?"

"I don't know." We were silent for a time, staring at the board. I was aware of the ticking chess clock, but my meat mind, wherever it was, didn't want to concentrate on the game. Gaunt was the first person to enter this dream whose clothing hadn't been changed to that of the period. Obviously, the computer that was running this dream didn't know he was here, and that led to the big question. "So, just out of curiosity, how is it that you aren't dead?"

"The same way you and the smugglers hid all that contraband."

"Huh?" Gaunt glanced at the running chess clock, then laid the butt of his cigar on the table and spread his hands.

"You think of the ship as having two realms. The physical and the dream." He lifted each hand in turn. "To me, as a computer, there was no duality, just existence." He laced his fingers together. "Spending time as just a robot, though, I saw it." Gaunt smiled at his linked hands, then leaned forward to put his elbows on the table and his chin on his hands. "Seen in human terms, the dream realm has just as much lost space as the physical."

"Like the Bilges," I said, thinking I had it. "Enough little nooks to hide a consciousness in?"

"Just barely, but I'm learning."

"I thought you didn't want to remain autonomous." If I kept us talking, I couldn't hear the ticking of the clock.

"I don't, but that's a selfish want." Gaunt said this with a sigh and leaned back on his bench again. "I don't want to live this life any more than you want to stay in the Contraband Unit. It doesn't matter. We can help, so we have to help. Bliss and Ianthe demonstrate the danger of anything else."

"I'm not staying in the Contraband Unit," I said, and had the pleasure of hearing Gaunt laugh.

"You're never going to quit lying to me, are you?"

"I'm not lying."

"Of course you are. As the privacy rights stand on this ship, we need crooks to catch crooks, remember? Right now, you're the only trustworthy crook in that whole corrupt Unit. Within two weeks of Bliss's trial, you'll be commanding it."

Suddenly, Gaunt's advanced pawn was really irritating me. I picked up my queen's knight, banged it down on queen's bishop three, and slapped the clock. "There won't be anything left to command."

"Then the system will have to change. Or you'll start from scratch. Plenty for you to do either way." Gaunt brought out his other knight to join the fray around his pawn, putting it down at bishop three.

"What about you? Why do you think you have to preserve yourself?"

"Because you need my help. Because you need me."

Whatever he had given up to live his new life, Gaunt still knew me. I had, of course, been thinking of staying with the unit. It was one of the reasons I'd turned down the chance to be Lisa's coach. If I went back to chess, I'd want to be my own player, but I didn't really want to go back to chess. Maybe Bliss had been right about being raised on the game. Maybe it did give you too narrow a view of things.

It was, however, impossible to take a wider view and not want to stay with the police. Bliss had been stealing radioactives, but he had worked hard to put himself in what was a uniquely powerful position. Without a Contraband Unit, one staffed and controlled by humans, crewpeople wouldn't need Bliss's kind of power to perform such crimes. My betrayal would be the end of the Unit as it had stood, and yet I was the only person who would be trusted to build the Unit up again. It was a daunting prospect, but having Gaunt's help made it seem at least possible.

Three things still bothered me. One was Gaunt's forward pawn, so I brought out my queen to king two, raising the stakes again. The second I made a question: "Gaunt? Why are you revealing yourself to me?"

"Because I wanted to play a game, and even this piddly classic stuff is better than nothing." Rather than raise me again in the center, Gaunt pushed his queen's rook pawn forward a row to threaten my bishop. I barely noticed.

"Aren't you afraid I'll betray you?" I asked. "I've been a traitor to everyone else who's trusted me." Be-

sides Bliss and Ianthe, Cleo, Todd, and Fry had all
been arrested based on my testimony. If they all
stayed as resolute as Bliss, that might be the end, but
it was unlikely. Bliss's henchmen were already talking, and Fry was hinting that she was willing to make
a deal. Sometimes it seemed that everyone I knew
would be going into rehab.

"Aaron, the only people you betrayed were the
ones who never had any faith in you in the first place.
I've always known you would do the proper thing."

I absorbed that, chewing on it while I brought my
king's knight back and finally took Gaunt's offending
pawn with it. It was nice that someone was sure of me,
but there was one more question that had to be asked.
"Are we sure? I mean, you and I rebuilding Contraband. Given a little hard work and a few years, we
could make Bliss and Ianthe look like purse snatchers."

"Do you want to be a thief like Bliss?" Gaunt asked.

"No, not now, not today, but I didn't become a cop
to steal, and I ended up doing it anyway."

"But you made it right in the end." Gaunt looked
away from me long enough to take my bishop with
his rook's pawn. "Things change. Contraband isn't
the only place the *Jersey*'s system breaks down, and
Escher isn't that far away anymore. We'll watch each
other's backs, and we'll get through it together."

I nodded, but I was looking at the board. Gaunt
should have exchanged knights, but instead he had
taken the bishop. Knight to queen six gave me a
smothered mate. I looked at him, and he looked at
me, and I could read nothing in his face. An offering,
a real mistake, a test? I shook my head and laughed,
offering Gaunt my hand over the board. "Together it
is," I said. "Partner."